A KILLER S

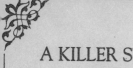

AUGUS

Persuaded by manager Robert Archibald to desert Kent for a position at the London Galaxy Theatre, the Duke's former chef satisfies his culinary creativity amid the glitter of the chorus line and the glamour of a society playground.

ROBERT ARCHIBALD

The manager of the Galaxy treats his famed Galaxy girls with the devotion of an overprotective father, but it's a testament to his marketing genius that they have become an institution off stage as well as on.

OBADIS BATES

He's been guarding the stage door to the Galaxy for fifteen years and prides himself on protecting the girls from any stage door Johnnies courting trouble.

EDWARD HARGREAVES

The composer and leader of the band is hiding his own bit of scandal and he's deadly sure it must remain secret.

THOMAS MANLEY

The Greek-god good-looking actor is married to Florence, the star of the show, but he has an eye for the ladies and is jealous of his wife's admirers.

FLORENCE LYTTON

The darling of the Galaxy gods, she's adored by audiences and cast members alike. Everyone loves Florence. Why then, is someone sending her ghastly little gifts . . . bearing messages of murder?

MURDER
—IN THE—
LIMELIGHT

AMY MYERS

AVON BOOKS ◆ NEW YORK

AVON BOOKS
A division of
The Hearst Corporation
1350 Avenue of the Americas
New York, New York 10019

Copyright © 1987 by Amy Myers
Published by arrangement with Headline Book Publishing, PLC
Library of Congress Catalog Card Number: 92-93058
ISBN: 0-380-76585-3

First Avon Books Printing: September 1992

AVON TRADEMARK REG. U.S. PAT. OFF. AND IN OTHER COUNTRIES, MARCA REGISTRADA, HECHO EN U.S.A.

Printed in the U.S.A.

RA   10 9 8 7 6 5 4 3 2 1

For our mother – our loving supercook

Author's Note

The Galaxy resembles in many respects the old Gaiety theatre in the Strand which was closed in 1903 for the construction of the Aldwych. However, whereas the Gaiety was always in the forefront of technical progress, the Galaxy lagged, and by 1894 had not yet installed electrical lighting.

The Gaiety restaurant was over the front Strand entrance of the theatre, extending along to Catherine Street, but Auguste Didier's domain occupies a ground-floor position on the corner of the Strand and Wellington Street, with its entrance on the corner. The stage door of the Gaiety was in Wellington Street, but the building of the restaurant of the Galaxy necessitated the moving of its stage door to Catherine Street.

The characters of those that work within the Galaxy, in no way correspond to their Gaiety counterparts, except for Robert Archibald whose professional life and approach to it to some extent necessarily overlap those of the redoubtable George Edwardes of the Gaiety, and his predecessor John Hollingshead.

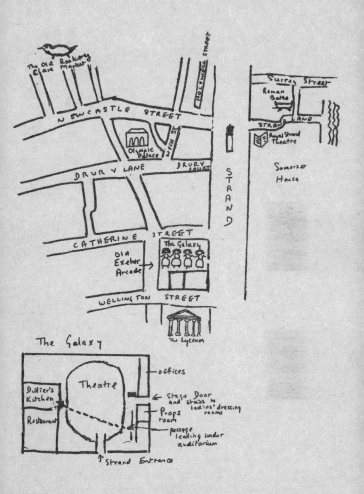

Inspector Egbert Rose's rough sketch of the Galaxy Theatre
and its neighbourhood

Prologue

It was cold on the Wapping reaches, nor did the task of the two bowler-hatted men, muffled against the enveloping fog, contribute to the raising of their spirits. In the murky gloom of the strand, lit only by the glimmer of the gaslights from the distant roadway, two constables blended into the background, stalwart sentinels, as their confrères from the detective branch went about their grim business.

'Execution Dock, they called this,' remarked Rose, rubbing his hands against the cold, which was unseasonal even for late November. Their examination over, they were waiting for the police van, straining their ears for the sound of approaching hooves.

'Someone's bin keeping the old tradition going, then,' commented his companion jovially.

Inspector Egbert Rose of the Criminal Investigation Department of Scotland Yard regarded his subordinate with some dislike. His name was Stitch, but Twitch was more like it, in Rose's opinion. There was a touch of the bloodhound about him; he'd trample over everything and everyone if it would bring promotion closer. He was nice enough in his way, keen, certainly – and clever, sharp as an organ grinder's monkey. But give Rose a good honest villain any day!

'Hung 'em down by the water's edge. Pirates, you see, and traitors. Them that got above themselves, got in their superiors' way,' added Rose evilly. 'You can still feel 'em around on a night like this, can't you?'

1

Sergeant Stitch couldn't, not being the imaginative type. But he believed in humouring inspectors, particularly those as idiosyncratic as Egbert Rose. He was not blind to Rose's gifts. He was too sharp for that. Rose might not be orthodox, but somehow he'd got the ear of the Commissioner. He'd been one of Williamson's blue-eyed boys, and even though Williamson was gone that still counted for something. He got results; luck, Stitch thought. But you couldn't discount luck.

'You will have your little joke, Inspector,' he said uneasily.

'No joke, lad,' Rose retorted instantly. 'No joke that threw this poor lass in the water, tied a brick round her, and doubtless went back to his home well satisfied with his night's work.'

Stitch stared at the bloated, decomposing mass of flesh at their feet. How the inspector could refer to it as a poor lass was beyond him.

'Three weeks, I'd say, sir.'

'Longer, lad, longer. Six weeks at least. Probably more.'

The yellow fog was thickening now as the steady clip-clop of hooves at last signified the approach of the van. Out climbed the figure of the police doctor, none too happy at being brought out into the East End yet again. There was always the chance of another Ripper – or even the return of the old one. It had never been proved he was dead, after all.

'Evening, Inspector. Another suicide?'

'No,' said Rose, not taking his eyes from the bundle at his feet. 'Not suicide. Take a look.'

Dr Crispin stared down with distaste. There was no mistaking this death for suicide. The victim's hands were bound crosswise and deliberately across the chest in a travesty of a mediaeval effigy.

Chapter One

'It is disaster! It is tragedy!' Robert Archibald's voice boomed out in despair. 'We shall be ruined. Does no one *care*?' he moaned.

Up in the flies, the gasman shivered; underneath the stage, the cellar-men paused; high up on the gridiron, the carpenter dropped a hammer. The stage manager shrank back in the wings, and Props disappeared. In her dressing room, Florence Lytton smiled to herself. She had heard it before. They had all heard it before. Robert Archibald was well known for his pre-performance nerves. He had been the same at the run-through on Saturday; tomorrow, for the first night of *Miss Penelope's Proposal*, he would be worse. No one took it seriously. The play would be a success simply because plays at the Galaxy were always a success, even if *Miss Penelope* were only the second in this new genre of musical comedy.

Only Auguste Didier answered the summons. Not because he truly believed that disaster had struck, but because as a maître chef, he alone could sympathise. Only he could feel the agony that Robert Archibald was enduring. Was not the dress rehearsal of a new play somewhat like the preparation of a huge banquet, where all was laid ready, only awaiting the guests? Was everything perfect? Had something, however apparently trivial, been overlooked? The eye of the master chef, as that of a theatre manager, must be everywhere; it only took the merest detail to go awry and the banquet could be ruined.

So, pausing only for a moment to add a touch of tarragon to perfect a dressing of which the Chevalier d'Albignac himself would not have been ashamed, he left his kitchen in the theatre restaurant to hasten to the auditorium of the Galaxy. Robert Archibald stood in the middle of the pit, his eyes riveted on the set on the dimly-lit stage with an intensity that Auguste recognised – that of the master engrossed in his art.

'There's something wrong with that set, Didier,' he pronounced as the chef approached. 'Something very, very wrong.' He paused and tugged worriedly at his long walrus moustache. 'Only I don't know what it is,' he added querulously.

Framed by the ornate blue and gold proscenium arch was the main set for *Miss Penelope's Proposal* – a toy shop. Auguste studied the array of puppets, train sets, dolls, toy theatres (each carefully made by Props to resemble the Galaxy), hoops and kites – the trained eye must move to a system.

'Check from left to right, monsieur. Remember what you envisaged in your grand conception.'

There was a short silence as Robert Archibald hopelessly surveyed the stage. 'It's no good, Didier. Can't see it. I just know there's something wrong. There's doom hanging over this production – doom!'

'It is clearly luncheon you need, monsieur,' said Auguste practically.

'Luncheon?' Robert Archibald yelped. 'You talk of luncheon when my livelihood, the theatre's livelihood, the players' livelihood, depend on –' A hand mopped a brow.

'Food, monsieur, as Brillat-Savarin maintained, provides the answer to many problems.' Auguste was undeterred.

'Nothing too rich, I hope,' said Archibald, momentarily diverted from his study of the stage.

'Fillets of turbot with Dutch sauce, though I maintain, monsieur, that Francatelli errs when he –'

'Turbot?' yelped Archibald. 'For all the company? Sprats

4

were good enough for me at their age.' He was fond of referring to his Hoxton youth when it suited his pocket, yet the slightest hint that one of his beloved company was in trouble and, miraculously, money was no object.

'Sprats, pah! Good enough to feed the roses, monsieur, but not the palate.'

'Let me tell you, Didier –' Robert Archibald began animatedly, paused, then whirled round surprisingly speedily for such a portly man. A gleam came into his eye. 'Props!' he yelled. 'Props.' Distantly a door banged.

'I knew it, Didier,' he said triumphantly. 'Something *is* wrong. Two of those damned dolls are missing.'

The Galaxy was a testament to the theatrical genius of Robert Archibald. Now fifty-nine, he had been running it for twenty-six years, ever since it opened in 1868. Burlesque had been the order of the day then, with its parodies of well-known stories, everyday tunes adapted to new words; Daisie Wilton in her tights as principal boy, captivating male and female alike. Ah, those were the days. But times change.

A year or two ago he had been taking the air with Mrs Archibald on a spring day in Hyde Park. It was warm, and bright colours were fashionable. He watched three young ladies feeding the ducks. His eyes lingered and Mrs Archibald's followed them. 'What pretty girls,' she had observed. 'Such lovely dresses.' The result had been the Galaxy Girls. There was something magical about the word 'girl' in the theatre. His Girls didn't have to act, and only some of them had to sing. The rest had simply to adorn the stage, looking desirable, rich, and unattainable – as they were sternly advised to be in their private lives also. As a result several of them had already married into the aristocracy, and few of them would want for a penny in their old age.

Then Daisie left the stage to marry and an entirely new

5

idea had occurred to him. How about *new* music, *new* stories and girls with even prettier frocks? The days of burlesque were over. *Lady Bertha's Betrothal* had been the first musical comedy, as he'd termed his new concept. There was little to the book, a story of titled ladies, disguises, lords and loves. But the clothes were by Worth, it all ended happily, and the audience departed delighted. *Playgoers' World* had devoted three pages to Miss Florence Lytton's Paris gowns, Robert Archibald noticed. Those for *Miss Penelope* were even prettier. Everyone in the company must have the best, that was his rule. No dressing the chorus in last year's Grecian tunics. The crowds round the stage door had doubled for *Lady Bertha*. It was even more of an honour to take out a Galaxy Girl to supper.

Two years ago, in 1892, Archibald had observed that the Galaxy Girls were an institution off stage as well as on. Across the Strand, the fashionable, flamboyant Romano's was always crowded with theatre folk, where they rubbed shoulders with royalty, society and any lesser mortals fortunate enough to find a table. His principals as well as his Girls lent their lustre to the lure of Romano's. That seemed a pity, mused Archibald, when the Galaxy had a restaurant of its own . . . And so he enticed Auguste Didier, the thirty-three-year-old French maître chef to the Duke of Stockbery, to desert Kent for the lights of London. It had not been easy for there was little about the Galaxy restaurant to tempt a former apprentice to Auguste Escoffier. Robert Archibald was, however, a diplomatist. He made mention of the lovely girls of the chorus – a momentary gleam had been replaced in Auguste's eyes by the remembrance of his attachment to a Russian princess. But then Archibald persuaded the chef of the reputation he could make by establishing a superb restaurant at the Galaxy. At last Auguste had succumbed.

Auguste flattered himself he knew how to handle Archibald. He hadn't, naturally, wished to seem too eager to accept the offer, but he was ready for London. He could no longer bury his art in the country. Many people had sought his services but this offer had strongly appealed. There were, after all, those lovely Galaxy ladies . . .

He had been at the restaurant two years now. Previously it had been a place into which pit-goers and gods would scuttle to save seeking further in the rain. Now it was a mecca to which those in the boxes and stalls would eagerly repair. Romano's viewed this development with dismay, and insidiously planted the idea in the minds of the Galaxy Girls that guaranteed privacy in the booths and private rooms of Romano's would further their matrimonial prospects more than sampling Didier's *cuisses des nymphes d'Aurore*.

Auguste did not mind. He had plenty of Galaxy Girls all day – and one at night. His darling Maisie. He had explained to her he must always be true to Tatiana, though Fate had meant they could never be united, but Paris was a long way away . . .

'I don't like it, Auguste, that's straight.'

'What, *ma petite*?' he replied guardedly, momentarily distracted from the sight of Albert stirring the hollandaise far too rigorously.

'Things aren't the same. I know they seem to be, but they're not. Not for a couple of months now. Not since the beginning of *Lady Bertha*. Not since –' Maisie broke off.

'Not since *la belle* Christine left, perhaps?' said Auguste quietly.

Maisie shot a sharp look at him. With her sturdy East End commonsense, she was inclined to discount Auguste's Gallic perceptiveness.

'Tell you what, Auguste, you're not so bad, for a Frenchman.'

'You do me too much honour, *chérie*,' he murmured. 'But do not forget, I had an English mother.'

7

'Yes, that's true,' said Maisie prosaically, and Auguste laughed to himself. Lovely Maisie. Lovely, cuddly, dependable, oh so English Maisie, with her full breasts, ample figure and generous loving heart. 'You don't think she went to France then, to the Folies Bergères? That's what she was always boasting she would do.'

'No, I think not, *ma chérie*. She was not the type, that Christine, to go to a foreign land on her own.'

'With someone then? And anyway, Auguste, why should that have any effect on us here now?'

'I do not know. But something, just something, is making this lovely mayonnaise of a theatre curdle.'

Another custom instituted by Robert Archibald for the good of his company – and his plays – was the company luncheon. For, so his straightforward thinking went, if the company and stage hands were together for this meal, the resultant unity would weld them together for afternoon and evening – and however long it took to get the dress rehearsal perfect.

The restaurant, all that Monday morning a silent empty cave, was suddenly full of life as chorus girls, show girls and principals erupted into it, filling the air with scents that vied fiercely with the aromas emanating from Auguste's kitchen. If they were on edge for the rehearsal that afternoon – or for any other reason – they gave no hint of it as they settled at the long tables set out thus to unify the company. Yet it was noticeable that however democratic the theory, in practice principals sat in due order of precedence, the chorus and show girls and musicians well below the salt, the stage staff at another table by unspoken agreement.

'Mr Brian.' Florence Lytton paused behind the chair occupied by the young pianist. 'Do you think my marionette song at the end of the second act – just a little slower, perhaps? Like this – *pa, pa, pa, pa*, pa pom!'

This had been a controversial issue throughout rehearsal.

8

But who could resist an appeal from Florence Lytton? No one. Not even Percy Brian, though his preferences lay in another direction altogether from the pretty flaxen-haired blue-eyed heroine of the play. So – even though it would annoy Edward – Percy wavered. His eyes went momentarily to Edward Hargreaves, the composer and leader of the band, listening stonily to a show girl's chatter. He would placate Edward at home tonight. He could talk Edward into anything.

'I do dislike asking,' Florence added disarmingly.

She did indeed, for she liked to be liked. Not that there was any difficulty about that. She was the darling of the Galaxy gods and had only to trip on to a stage, pause delightfully for that moment of applause and breathless anticipation, then sing in her beguiling, tremulous voice – and the house was at her feet. Everybody loved Florence, even the manager, an unusual state of affairs for the London theatre and one of which Archibald, recipient of the tantrums of Florence's predecessors, was devoutly glad. Her husband too loved Florence.

Yet Auguste, superintending the arrival of *le turbot*, noticed that for once Thomas Manley's eyes were not on his wife. Seated several places away, he was talking with unusual animation to one of the show girls.

'I think your best moment's in the third act,' said Edna Purvis with practised artless charm. 'When you come on like that, singing "Take my heart, little bird" – oh, it's wonderful. You look so – so –'

'Do you really think so?' Thomas's good-looking face, reminiscent of a Greek god ranking rather junior in the Olympian hierarchy, flushed with gratification.

'I do. Why, if you were my husband I'd –'

She broke off in maidenly confusion, leaving Thomas to reflect that, wonderful though Florence was, all too often he found himself telling her how beautiful she looked without receiving any reciprocal assurances, and that

9

her – quite understandable – exhaustion after a performance contrasted rather sharply with Edna's playful exuberance. Momentarily he imagined himself in bed with the handsome Miss Purvis, then hastily dismissed the idea, shocked at his thoughts. Florence was his sweetheart, his wife, his only love. All the same, Edna's obvious admiration was very pleasant. He edged his chair very slightly closer so that in adjusting his napkin his hands might accidentally brush her satin-clad thigh.

He hastily restored his hand to a more proper position when he noticed Herbert Sykes' watchful eye on him. Herbert's total devotion to Florence was well known. Her bull-dog, Florence called him, giggling about her admirer. Poor Herbert; he always looked so sad, so deadly serious, yet he had only to walk on stage and make the slightest gesture for the house to collapse with laughter. Like the great Grimaldi, he did not need words for his art. He was one of nature's natural clowns. Thomas didn't resent his paying attention to Florence. There could, after all, be no danger from Herbert. At only five foot two inches, and aged around forty, his roly poly figure typecast him for the role of unrequited lover. All the same, there was something in Herbert's eyes that made Thomas uneasy. What, after all, did they know about him? Was he married? Where did he live? He said nothing about himself – and somehow Thomas had never liked to ask.

'Mr Sykes,' Florence appealed to Herbert and he was instantly all watchful attention. 'Do you not agree with me? The dance in the last act –'

'A trifle heavy, Miss Lytton. Like Mr Didier's puddings.'

Everybody laughed – except Auguste, who frowned. Not so much at the slur on his puddings, perhaps not quite his forte, but because it was not like Herbert to make a joke that might hurt, that smacked of impoliteness. The Galaxy was a united company.

Wasn't it?

10

* * *

'For you, miss.'

Props pressed his daily floral tribute into Florence's hand and, as was usual, darted away.

'Props!'

This time Robert Archibald's roar stopped him.

He turned slowly in his tracks, apparently unwilling to face his master, or perhaps Miss Lytton. A rather weaselly-featured, tall, thin young man, William Ferndale gawped helplessly in the presence of his idol, tongue-tied at being forced from the shadows.

Robert Archibald came panting up the corridor. 'Dolls, Props.'

Props blinked.

'Two missing.'

Still Props said nothing.

'There are two dolls missing,' repeated Archibald patiently.

Props stood, twisting his hands nervously together.

'I'm not blaming you, Props. Just find them,' said Archibald firmly.

'A-a-all there this m-morning, Mr Archibald,' Props managed to stutter, with an air of finality. Props was as perfectionist in his way as Mr Archibald in his.

'I don't doubt it. But they're not now. Find them.' It was a command. Props, interpreting the tone aright, hastened through the wings to the stage to check the set, muttering to himself in bewilderment.

He had checked only the left-hand shelves when a scream pierced the air, silencing the chatter in the chorus girls' and show girls' dressing rooms, and percolating to the far side of the theatre where the men's dressing rooms were situated.

Identifying the shriek through experience, Thomas rushed down the stairs and, ignoring protocol, up the steps towards his wife's dressing room. Props too identified the source and stood gazing up the staircase. Even Obadiah

11

Bates came out of the stage door keeper's cubbyhole, though without abandoning his post totally. A female scream was not worth that dereliction of duty.

Auguste Didier, interrupted in the midst of a *boudin de volaille*, followed Thomas up the steps, his curiosity for once overcoming the exigencies of his art.

Florence was standing at the door of her room, her dresser in mild hysterics by her side. She was staring at the mantelshelf, where a goodwill offering had been placed ready to greet her as she came into the room.

One of the missing dolls was found. But Props would have his work cut out before she could adorn the set of Mr Hoggis's toyshop once more. For the doll had been neatly strangled, its china head split open and half twisted from its torso. Its arms had been torn out of the flimsy muslin dress in order that they might be neatly crossed and tied across its breast.

'It's just a nasty practical joke, my dear,' said Robert Archibald comfortingly to a distraught Florence, who was sitting with Thomas' arm around her shoulders and taking calming sips of Auguste's camomile tea.

'Yes,' he repeated, as if convincing himself, 'that's what it was, a practical joke.'

'But why me?' wailed Florence afresh. 'Why me?' She looked piteously at Thomas, then at Archibald, then at Auguste.

None of them could supply the answer.

A thoughtful Auguste made his way downstairs, leaving Robert Archibald surreptitiously regarding the pocket watch he held in one hand, and patting Florence ineffectually on the back with the other. Seeing Obadiah still standing at the doorway of his cubbyhole, Auguste instinctively paused, the detective in him coming to the fore. Then he reconsidered. He was a chef, a maître, not a detective, good though he was at solving mysteries. On the other hand, just one or two questions perhaps . . .

'Could anyone have come in from outside, Obadiah?' he asked, having explained the reason for the commotion.

'No one gets in past that door without my seeing. You know that, Mr Didier. And you, Miss Maisie,' he added, seeing her come up behind Auguste. Maisie was a particular favourite of his, hence this sign of favour in addressing her by her Christian name. Invalided out of Roberts' army in the Khyber Pass, he was now, at sixty, a veteran of the Galaxy, having manned the stage door with a fierce pride for the last fifteen years.

He was as much an institution as the Galaxy Girls themselves. No stage door Johnnie escaped his gimlet eye. No trick they might invent for entering the forbidden precincts escaped him. He would sort out the good 'uns from the bad 'uns, give the girls invaluable advice about their escorts, rid them of unwanted admirers, and tactfully deal with broken hearts both sides of the stage door.

'But are you sure, Obadiah? No errand boys, no outside people at all since this morning?'

'No, Mr Didier. No one at all.'

'So this – joke – must have been played by one of us. One of the company.'

'No one would play a wicked trick like that,' said Obadiah reprovingly. 'Not at the Galaxy. And at a dress rehearsal?'

'I thought we only held second place in your heart, Obadiah,' laughed Maisie. It was an established theatre joke that Obadiah's heart belonged principally over the road at the Lyceum, and that he had been broken-hearted when the opening of the restaurant had necessitated the moving of the Galaxy's stage door to Catherine Street which meant he could no longer hope to see his idol, Henry Irving, walk along Wellington Street by the sacred portals of his theatre.

13

'I'm part of the Galaxy, miss,' said Obadiah with dignity.

'But you don't like the plays.'

'I saw this new one on Saturday, miss. Saw Miss Lytton singing away: "If only you could hear . . . " I remember that. Then I had to get back – can't trust these youngsters on the door for long.'

'Did you enjoy it, though, Obadiah?'

'You all looked very nice, Miss Maisie,' he said carefully. 'But give me something classical. *King Lear* now. "Howl, howl, howl, howl, howl".' His eyes strayed longingly in the direction of the Lyceum.

Auguste laughed. 'Half the doorkeepers in London would exchange places with you for no wages at all, just to be amongst the lovely ladies of the Galaxy.'

Obadiah eyed him gloomily, then said kindly, 'Of course, you're French, Mr Didier,' as though that explained it. 'We're like a family here, Mr Didier.'

'Of which one member has a perverted sense of humour,' observed Auguste thoughtfully.

'Five minutes, Miss Lytton. Five minutes, ladies.'

A concerted shriek went up from the dressing rooms, followed by: 'My hare's foot, where's my hare's foot?'

'My osprey!'

'My button hook!'

The dovecote heaved under the turmoil as the Galaxy Girls fluttered into position.

Florence, fingers still slightly trembling, adjusted a strand of hair and rose to her feet purposefully. The play depended on her. She must not give way.

On the gentlemen's side, Herbert Sykes averted his gaze from the mirror that told him remorselessly how unattractive he was, and that he could be of no interest whatsoever to Florence Lytton. But he made her laugh, he reminded himself stoutly. Manley never made her laugh.

And, somewhat cheered, he left for the stage.

In the orchestra pit Edward Hargreaves smoothed his sleeves nervously over his impeccable cuffs. He wished he didn't have this horrible feeling that everything was going to go wrong. He enjoyed dress rehearsals normally as he enjoyed everything at the Galaxy – that is, when he could forget his awful fear that their secret might be discovered. It was all very well for Percy. He liked living dangerously.

Robert Archibald had taken his seat in the stalls. He gave the signal to Hargreaves. The baton came down, the orchestra struck up and, at the piano, Percy Brian moistened his lips excitedly. Soon his fingers would be on the keys again, swept away in the wonder of his music – or rather Edward's music. But it would be interpreted as only he, Percy Brian, could interpret it.

Another dress rehearsal at the Galaxy was under way, and no one spared a thought for Christine Walters.

'I've come to London town, my fortune here to seek . . .'

A simply-clad girl in white bought a bunch of violets and placed them with a charming gesture in her bosom, before turning winningly to the 'audience' in order to confide that: 'My fortune is not gold, but the love of a true sweetheart'.

Thirty ladies and gentlemen of the chorus, resting their voices after their lusty opening, 'Piccadilly Parade', melted tactfully into the background, and thankfully away from the direct heat of the gas battens above them, to leave Florence to her discovery of the toyshop.

In the wings Thomas Manley fell in love anew with his wife as she tripped lightly across the stage. Behind the backdrop Herbert dedicated himself once more to her service. In the stalls Robert Archibald nodded approvingly and thanked the gods for the lucky day that had sent him Florence.

Waiting for her cue Edna looked jealously at Florence. She was lucky. She had everything, including Thomas

15

Manley. Not that Edna wanted him. She was far too shrewd to waste time on a married man, and was determined to marry a peer. There was always the Honourable Johnny, of course, if the worst came to the worst, but he was only a younger son so there would be no title for him. Summerfield was a much better prospect. Summerfield – a slight feeling of unease took hold of her. Wasn't there something –? Yes, Christine Walters. Christine and Summerfield. And afterwards Christine had gone away – to Paris, it was rumoured. Strange how unexpectedly she'd gone, after only two performances of *Lady Bertha*. Edna dismissed the thought and concentrated on funny old Herbert's caperings on stage.

'Quickly, young woman, her ladyship's waiting. Get on with you.'

Herbert was in the midst of displaying his comic genius as Mr Hoggis, the toyshop owner for whom Lady Penelope (in disguise, of course) works.

Florence tripped lightly across the stage once more.

Swept away by the tension and excitement of a new Galaxy play, no one was prepared for what they heard next. Not the dainty strains of one of Edward's best tunes but yet another scream and gurgle from Florence's pretty throat as she stared aghast at the thing in her hand. It fell to the floor with a thud. She turned as if in appeal to the darkened auditorium, her hands outstretched, then burst into tears and ran off the stage.

Thomas reached the object first. The doll had its head half twisted off, a scarf viciously twisted round its neck, and for good measure a stage dagger stuck into its bosom in the V left between the two bound, crossed hands.

Chapter Two

For once Auguste was not concentrating solely on the exciting task in hand: preparing a sauce for the chicken *à la belle vue* to be served at the banquet after the first night that evening. He was thinking back to the previous night. Not so much of Maisie – delightful though that had been – but of their conversation after they had returned to his small suite of rooms in lodgings at the end of Wellington Street.

'I don't like it, Auguste,' Maisie had said, sitting on the bed and easing her feet out of their purple satin slippers with a sigh of satisfaction.

Auguste looked at her worried, honest brown eyes and sat down beside her, taking her hand in his own.

'Nor I, *ma mie*. Perhaps it is as Mr Archibald says, a practical joke.'

'That's all smoke, gammon and spinach! We've never had practical jokers before. Why now? Why that? Why Miss Lytton? She hasn't any enemies. Everyone likes her. You should see some of the leading ladies I've worked with. More temperament than a pepper pot. But not Miss Lytton.'

'Jealousy perhaps?'

'Amongst us, you mean?' she asked shrewdly. 'The show girls and chorus girls? No. And even if one of us wanted to upset her, they'd choose something different. There's a ton of tricks you can play, without being gruesome.'

'There are many people in the theatre on a dress rehearsal

17

day: errand boys, telegraph boys, fitters. Any one of them might have –'

'But why?' Maisie asked practically.

'A rejected lover?'

Maisie looked at him indignantly. 'All round my 'at! You know Florence is devoted to Thomas. No one would get close enough to her even to be rejected.'

She stopped suddenly as an unpleasant thought struck her. 'Except – Auguste, you don't think Props might have . . . ?' Her voice trailed off.

Auguste considered. Props, with his well-known fanatical devotion to Florence Lytton. It was obvious he had only taken the job at the Galaxy to be near her, since he had been a furniture maker previously. Yet he never spoke to her, never approached her except to press a posy of violets into her hand. He was accepted as a harmless eccentric.

'He is a little strange, you know. You don't think he could have, well, turned against her?'

'It is possible, yes,' said Auguste. 'He had the best opportunity to do it.' He was beginning to tire of the matter of the dolls. The episodes had left him uneasy, but the day had been long and Maisie was very close. His arm tightened round her. But she had not finished talking, unresponsive for once to the eloquent message of his dark eyes.

'Auguste, what *do* you think happened to Christine Walters? I know everyone thinks she just left for Paris to join the Folies Bergères like she always said, but something worries me . . .'

'What, *chérie*?' asked Auguste patiently, removing his hand from her waist until its reception seemed likely to meet with more appreciation.

'She left her rabbit's foot behind.'

'Her what?'

'Lucky rabbit's foot,' repeated Maisie. 'You wouldn't understand but we all have something. A lucky handkerchief, a lucky scarf. We're a superstitious lot. And

18

Christine had her rabbit's foot. She swore she always had bad luck without it. She'd never have taken another engagement in Paris, leaving that behind. She'd have sent for it if she had really forgotten it.'

'Then what do you think –?'

'I don't know. The Honourable Johnny said the police had come to see him when the Sûreté hadn't been able to find her in Paris. I know he's a joke, but he was quite worried. It was weeks since Christine had given him the "get off me barrer" – it was Summerfield she was seeing, and didn't we know it? She was determined to end up under a coronet. Some hopes, with his mother!'

'His mother?'

'He's a bachelor. Lives with Mama at the ancestral towers in Buckinghamshire. Every so often he sneaks a night away at their town house, and is round here quicker than a duke out of a jerryshop to take one of us to dinner. Doesn't mind who it is, just has to be one of the famous Galaxy Girls.' Her voice was scornful. 'I feel sorry for him, poor old boy.'

'And Christine disappeared while she was the reigning favourite?'

'He told Miss Pearly Queen Purvis that Christine never turned up that evening. He couldn't see her on the first night of *Lady Bertha* because of the party and so arranged to see her the next night. But no Christine. And being a lord and all that, he don't like having a piece of wet cod slapped round his face, so he never bothered to find out why. He likes to be the only cock in the henhouse, does His Lordship?

'And so, my love, do I,' said Auguste, pulling her to him.

'I tell you what, Auguste,' she said after a pause, 'English I might be, but I have to grant you there are still some things Frenchmen do better than Englishmen.'

'The creation of a *timbale*, perhaps?'

'And other things, other things . . .'

Auguste smiled at the memory as he stirred the liaison. Twelve dozen plovers' eggs, three galantines of chicken, lobster salad of course, *poularde à la d'Albutera*, two hot dishes, Soyer's *pièces montées*, the *croquantes*, the *nougats*, the *madeleines*, the *gaufres*, the *bavarois*, the *charlottes*, Maître Escoffier's crawfish *à la provençale*.

Auguste, influenced by his English mother in his upbringing, usually inclined to English receipts, but for a first night celebration he knew the girls would not be impressed by English cooking. They would want the finest French delicacies of which his art was capable, and they would not be disappointed. He would create a centrepiece as magnificent as those of the great Soyer himself, though he would not go so far as had one maître and insist that the ceiling be removed to accommodate it. Instead he had created a sculpted masterpiece in spun meringue and fruit. He thought longingly of the moment when the curtain would be drawn back at the rear of the stage and his creation revealed to the 'Oohs' and 'Aahs' of the company.

First there would be the dinner on stage, then dancing to follow. And so democratic! Stage hands would dance with the Galaxy Girls; he, the cook, might dance with Miss Lytton. He dwelt with some enthusiasm on this idea, but then reflected that Maisie would be watching. Her good nature only went so far. Yet there was something about Miss Lytton's manner that reminded him on occasion of Tatiana. Tatiana, with her black hair and lustrous eyes, was very different, a princess after all, and yet there was something . . . He dragged his mind away from the Paris of his past, and concentrated hard once more on the *farce de foie gras* for the *poularde*.

In the cold light of morning, the high tensions of yesterday seemed far away as he marshalled his small kitchen staff in almost military order for the final preparations. Tonight after the show the theatre restaurant would be left to his assistants while he, Auguste, attended the party for the company. It was hard for them – and a risk for him. A maître should always be present in his restaurant. But perhaps even he might be allowed to see a little of the new musical comedy.

'Didier, I want you.'

With this peremptory summons, Robert Archibald burst through the secret communicating door that he had installed in the wall that had to be built between theatre and restaurant to comply with fire regulations despite his loud protestations. The door, known only to himself and Auguste, since it defied council rulings, was masked by a larder through which he made his entrance. Now he stood menacingly in the kitchen. Auguste bowed to the inevitable. Casting only the merest glance at the ingredients for the *St Honoré crème* as yet unprepared, he followed in Archibald's imperious wake. In the inner sanctum, its owner flung himself into a huge leather armchair.

'You're a balanced sort of fellow. Would you say there's something wrong in this theatre? I'm not an imaginative sort of chap, but it seems to me rather more than first night nerves coupled with a nasty practical joke or two. I've always thought we were such a happy family.' He looked pleadingly to Auguste for reassurance.

Auguste shrugged. 'Even families, monsieur, have their difficulties.'

'But why?' Archibald's tone was outraged. It was clear he was taking it personally.

'I do not know, but have you not observed, monsieur, that one bad egg amongst a gross will render them all useless? Perhaps you too have one bad egg.'

'Eggs.' Archibald's tone implied this matter was rather more important than eggs.

'Very well, monsieur. One dancer out of step.'

'Yesterday it was dolls. Today Florence is huffy, Hargreaves has got a face as long as his own first fiddle, and young Brian is flinging his hair around like a prancing ballet dancer. And it's the first night. My play!' His voice rose in anguish.

'But there has been something wrong, Monsieur Archibald, for some time.' Archibald bristled in denial. 'Miss Walters,' Auguste reminded him.

'Well, what about her?' asked Archibald, bewildered.

'Do you believe she went to Paris?'

Archibald stared at him. 'Didier, you're French. You see these girls as innocent young flowers. So they are, some of 'em. But suppose they meet a bad 'un? What can I do? Only talk about contracts. And much they care for that with a tiara or money dangled in front of them. Christine Walters wasn't one to say no to money. I hope she's now kicking up her legs in the Folies Bergères, but if she's not, there's nothing I can do. Once they leave the Galaxy, that's it. They're not my responsibility. Nothing to do with me. Anyway, what has Miss Walters to do with it?'

'Perhaps nothing. Perhaps much. But it seems nothing here has been quite right since she left. The sauce has been stirred.'

'Nonsense,' said Archibald irritatedly. 'Stuff and nonsense.'

Up in his dressing room Thomas Manley carefully applied his greasepaint and then as carefully took it off again. His dresser watched incuriously. It was a first night ritual. It had happened on the night of his first big success; thus he believed it had brought him good luck, and had done it ever since. Tonight it seemed especially important.

Oblivious to the seething mass of turbulent emotions backstage, the outside world battered the Galaxy with its usual tributes. Bouquets were arriving at such a rate at the stage door that Bates' small office resembled a flower shop. Telegrams were hurtling around the building, clutched in grubby call-boy hands. The box office alone was not busy.

22

The seats for this evening's performance had all been sold many weeks ago. It was not necessary to check the library returns – there were none. Each agency had sold their quota and had been pleading for more.

Would-be suitors were busily thrusting cards in at the stage door, only to be disappointed. None of the young ladies was going out tonight. Tonight was strictly a Galaxy party. There had been no more untoward happenings. The set had been checked and double-checked for practical jokes.

Such was the hectic pace of events that had it not been for a slight hangover of unease from the day before, and a certain alien paleness to Florence's cheeks, Robert Archibald might almost have convinced himself that his fears were unjustified and that the unfortunate events of yesterday had never taken place.

His portly, impressive figure in tailcoat and silk hat was everywhere in the building. He believed in being seen to manage his theatre. He was the host to its many thousands of guests. In the chorus and show girls' dressing rooms, frilled dresses were being carefully lifted over tightly boned bodices, silk drawers pulled over multi-coloured corsets. This latter was Archibald's idea – or rather, his wife's. Let them have silk underwear, she had said percipiently, then they will feel expensive as well as look expensive – you'll see. And he did. Dr Jaeger's best wool might be healthier, but he bowed to his wife, a very sensible woman, and paid for the girls' silk drawers without a murmur. With the gentlemen he compromised on pure silk handkerchiefs and neckties and, once bought with his usual generosity, told them they could keep them afterwards. His generosity to all who shared his family roof was boundless.

'Who do yer reckon did it last night?'

'Must have been someone who don't like Miss L,' commented a newcomer.

Fourteen indignant pairs of eyes looked scathingly in her direction. She flinched.

'There ain't none of us don't like Miss Florence,' explained one, kindlier than the rest.

The newcomer was silenced, but not convinced.

'Ah, Mr Hargreaves.'

Florence was at her most winning. She was by nature charming, but on occasion lent artifice to natural ability. She would be charming but determined, she told herself. Unfortunately womanly charm had little effect on Mr Hargreaves, a fact that she should have realised since she was perhaps the only member of the company who knew about his private life.

'Miss Lytton. All ready?'

It must be quite obvious to him that she was ready, she thought, with an unusual trace of irritation. She would hardly wear a white silk dress with rosebuds down the side and paint on her face for walking along the Strand. But she suppressed a tart rejoinder.

'Quite, thank you.' If only he wasn't so – so – *stolid*, she thought. He made a somewhat unattractive figure with his attempt to add to his face and sideburns the hair he had lost from the top of his head. 'I wanted to ask you again – my song at the end of the second act –' Edward Hargreaves stiffened. 'Do you think just a little slower?' She smiled winningly. 'Such a beautiful tune.' She hummed a few bars. 'I should like the audience to hear, to appreciate the melody. Such a beautiful melody.'

He glared at her. 'It's meant to be fast for its effect, Miss Lytton.' Then he remembered that Florence was the leading lady and added placatingly, 'You sing it charmingly. You always do. Believe me, though, it's not right at that slow tempo. Pa, pa, pa, pa, pa, pom.' He hummed tunelessly. He wished she'd go away. Singers were necessary evils, but he refused to allow them to come between himself and his music.

* * *

'Why did you send flowers to Miss Purvis, Thomas?' asked Florence, already aggrieved after her defeat in the matter of the song. She regarded the bouquet of lilies sent by her husband balefully – it had not escaped her notice that Edna had received late red roses.

'Darling – you wouldn't begrudge a present to her on her first show.'

'Second actually,' said Florence absently, reading the card. Was it her imagination or was the wording a little more offhand than usual? True, he had taken the trouble to ask Obadiah's permission to present the bouquet personally, since it was not usually permitted for a gentleman to visit the ladies' side of the theatre, but he had also taken the opportunity to present Edna's personally.

'Second then,' said Thomas shortly. He had expected more glowing thanks from his Florence. Moreover, he had expected some tribute himself. For the first two years of their marriage each first night had been marked with a small gift from his adoring wife: cufflinks engraved with the name of the play, a silver tie pin, a gold pocket watch.

Florence was studying her face in the mirror.

'As you are obviously not interested in listening to me, I shall return to my own room.'

She smiled to herself. That had put him in his place. But she still felt on edge. Thomas had not been as thoughtful as usual when they returned home last night. She had had to attend to Nanki-poo herself, or the poor little dog would have starved. And then Thomas had been ungentlemanly enough to protest when she felt too tired to let him . . . Really, after a dress rehearsal! Men were quite unreasonable. It was in this frame of mind that she recalled that other unreasonable man and set out to find Percy Brian. If one side would not budge, the other might.

'Mr Brian, about the marionette song –'

'Ah, yes.' He tinkled a few notes on the piano. 'The

25

marionette song.' He smiled at her, and tinkled a few more.

'Please, Mr Brian, not *so* fast.' She tried hard to keep the edge out of her voice.

'But I have to take my tempo from Mr Hargreaves, Miss Lytton.' He continued playing and she was forced to shout at his back.

'Then tell him to slow down. It ruins the whole effect.'

'I can't tell Mr Hargreaves what to do, Miss Lytton.'

Unusually, almost uniquely, Florence lost her temper, tired of facing that elegant, unresponsive back. 'Of course you can. I know you're his molly.'

There was an abrupt silence as his fingers came crashing down in a final chord and he spun round on the stool to stare at her, aghast. Miss Lytton - even to know about such things, much less to say them out loud! For once Percy Brian was shocked. And goodness knew what Edward would say. But he was looking forward to finding out.

Ashen-faced, Edward Hargreaves stared back at him. 'She knows, you think?' His voice shook.

'That's what she said, Edward.'

'But . . . do you think she knows we - live together?'

Percy shrugged. 'Who cares?' He flashed a brilliant smile, a perfect advertisement for Jewsbury & Brown's Oriental Toothpaste.

'Don't be foolish, Percy. We're in danger. Do you want to spend time in prison? To say nothing of our jobs here.'

'No one cares nowadays. Look at Mr Wilde and Lord Alfred. The police aren't interested.

'*I* care,' said Edward Hargreaves vehemently. 'I care, and I shall make sure nothing, *nothing* ruins our lives.'

'You wouldn't leave me?' said Percy in sudden alarm. Boring though old Edward was, he was very fond of him.

Edward looked at him, a peculiar expression on his face. 'No,' he said. 'Oh no, I'll never leave you.'

Herbert Sykes, listening to this absorbing conversation

outside the door, was disturbed as well as riveted. There was a tone in Hargreaves' voice he hadn't heard before, and it boded no good for his Florence, as he always thought of her. But he, Herbert, would protect her.

On the other side of the curtain, anticipation was high. A stream of hansoms was arriving, depositing the theatre-going middle classes, and the pit and gallery queues were in good-humour; at the Catherine Street entrance a warbling baritone, formerly of the Royal Opera House (supposedly), was entertaining them with a song that the august portals of his former home – if it was – would never have recognised. At the Royal Entrance in Exeter Street a discreet carriage, unmarked by a regal crest, deposited a portly but immaculately attired gentleman, with a beautiful lady and an equerry hovering in attendance. The beautiful lady was not the Princess of Wales; the Galaxy had risen to dizzy heights but had not yet received that final seal of royal approval.

It was at the Strand entrance that the excitement reached its peak. The linkman was in his element. A first night was the busiest night of the run; it was not only his job to usher in the scented and opera-hatted and to see that trailing silken trains were not sullied by the dirt of the thoroughfare but also to recognise the faces and, with a muttered aside to a pageboy, inform Mr Archibald that Lord and Lady So and So had arrived, or else pass on a suggestion that Lord X's seats had best be changed forthwith owing to the fact that Lord X's sister-in-law was in the audience and would be somewhat puzzled by Lord X's companion! He would smooth the passage from carriage to door, then hand his charges over to a liveried usher who would ensure that the few steps up to the foyer were negotiated safely before they joined the milling, sparkling, bejewelled throng that was an essential ingredient of a Galaxy first night – or any first night at a London theatre in these carefree days of the nineties. But the Galaxy had one difference: it provided a touch of the daring, but a daring that one could allow one's wife to see – if one so chose.

In the auditorium a thousand pairs of open glasses undulated as aigrette-crowned ladies sought to establish who was present, their ostrich feather fans used more for effect than for air on this chill November evening. A sigh of pleasurable anticipation ran round the audience as Edward Hargreaves took his place on the rostrum.

Hidden from them behind the ornate curtain was the stage manager. He was at the rear of the stage, checking the back set for the umpteenth time to see that all those ruddy dolls were in place. None was missing tonight. Not now that two spares had been hastily acquired from Messrs Hamleys. So nothing could go wrong tonight, could it?

Apparently nothing could. The first night of *Miss Penelope's Proposal* looked set fair to beat even its predecessor. Florence Lytton had never looked more lovely, trilled so sweetly. Perhaps, if one were to be critical, she had been not quite at her best in the song in which she confided her innermost longings to a marionette, but connoisseurs put it down to her not feeling at home with the rather fast tempo.

Watching from the stalls and dress circle respectively, the Honourable Johnny Beauville and Lord Summerfield sat enraptured anew at the sight of all their little darlings.

Lord Summerfield watched the show girls, those stately damsels who adorned the stage with such grace and elegant, tall beauty, not singing, not speaking, simply looking beautiful. His eyes were on Edna Purvis. She had let him kiss her in the carriage on the way back from Romano's last week, and there was a look in her eye that suggested he might go a little further next time, though she had made it clear that she was a lady. Not like Christine Walters! He still smarted from that indignity. Perhaps Mother was right, he should marry the Honourable Jane Biggleswade. But, on the other hand, Miss Purvis was so very pretty . . .

The Honourable Johnny did not confine his admiration to the show girls. He loved all the little darlings – show girls, chorus girls, principals – they were all lovely, and he loved them all. He never noticed if they laughed at him, and would not have cared if he had. He was a humble man with no inflated opinion of his own intellectual powers. But as a connoisseur of female beauty, he rated himself highly.

'There's a little stunner,' he remarked enthusiastically, if unguardedly, to his brother. 'What a big –' Only the stern eye of his boot faced sister-in-law stopped him from further enthusing on the female form. Why did she insist on coming if she disapproved so much? he asked himself. She'd sat poker-faced all through *Lady Bertha*; not a twitch of amusement on her haughty features.

Herbert Sykes as the jealous toyshop owner had never looked more comic as when, in the last act, he faced the handsome Lord Harry, come in search of the lovely-voiced female who, out of his sight, had been operating the marionettes. In fact he played his comic gestures mechanically, and perhaps all the better for his private gloating: he had overheard the quarrel between the real-life Lord Harry and Miss Penelope, and had not missed the coolness between them.

The stage was knee deep in flowers as Florence Lytton smiled over the footlights at her devoted public. The female bosoms in the audience swelled to the fullest extent their whaleboning would permit as Lord Harry kissed his hand towards them. The final curtain had fallen.

Robert Archibald mopped his brow, faint with relief. He could have sworn there was trouble on the way but everything had passed off perfectly, perfectly. It was a marvellous play and he had another success. Musical comedy was established. He had his new formula for the future. And all thanks to darling Florence and dear Thomas. And Mr Hargreaves' music, of course.

Yesterday's traumas were of the past, forgotten in the excitement of wriggling into tight-fronted trained satins and brocades, removing stage paint (reluctantly, for did not the eyes look so much enhanced?), and donning as many jewels as the Galaxy girls could muster. The men had no such exciting transformation to effect. They changed only from stage evening dress to their own: from fashionable white stage waistcoats to their own more modest black ones.

More prosaic work was in progress on stage.

'*Mon Dieu*. Not there, Beatrice!'

Auguste's agonised shout was hardly heard by a staff rushing now not only to accommodate the restaurant but to serve the party dinner. Stage hands, having rushed hither and thither striking the set, were now pressed into service as waiters. Spotless silver and napkins were laid in place by hands grubby with the dust of the wings, but who cared? This was a first night. Auguste cared, but even he was forced to close his eyes from time to time. He need not have worried. The galantines, the cold capon with truffles, the *poularde*, combined with the heady success of the first night, had raised everyone's spirits and the dinner was a success. Now chorus girls fancied themselves leading ladies, for all they might be dancing with the stage hands. For tonight, stage hands were as good as Lord Summerfield. Indeed, in their borrowed finery, they were almost indistinguishable. The Galaxy was one big happy family again.

'Edna, dance with me.'

She glanced at Thomas, tempted. It would be nice to make darling Florence suffer a little. Then common sense reasserted itself. 'No,' she said. 'You know what I said. No more of this.'

'Just a dance. Please.'

She glanced cautiously around. It was true Thomas was a good dancer and, in the absence of stage door johnnies, by far the most interesting man there, even if he did not interest her. But she was anxious not to have Florence's attention drawn to her again. Leading ladies – jealous ones – could make trouble. Luckily Florence, attired in palest blue satin, was busy charming Mrs Archibald, her earlier irritation forgotten. Edna accepted Thomas' invitation. Unfortunately for her, the orchestra chose to strike up with one of Florence's songs from the show in dance tempo, and Florence glanced round for her husband to share this moment of glory with. She was not pleased to see him in Edna's arms. Florence stood still, feeling quite bereft.

How dare he, how dare he dance with someone else? She thought. *My* song, *our* song, on this night of all nights.

'That's a lovely dress, Florence.'

'What?'

'I said,' Herbert cleared his throat awkwardly, 'that's a lovely dress!'

Suddenly she smiled at him. Thomas wasn't going to have it all his own way. She could flirt as well as he could. Better. Even if it was just old Herbert.

'Thank you, Herbert dear. Do you think, I hardly like to ask . . . perhaps there is someone else you'd rather dance with?' She paused diffidently.

Herbert reddened. 'Why, I –' He held out his arms and she slipped into them, gracefully hooking the train of the blue satin dress over her arm, her little evening bag dangling from one wrist. She peered confidingly into his face. He did not know the reason for this sudden warmth from Florence but accepted it unhesitatingly. Where she was concerned, he was blind.

Thomas was not. Normally he would never have been jealous of Herbert. But today was not a normal day. It was a first night, when overstretched nerves, wrought up to

31

extreme pitch, wreaked their revenge. He caught hold of Florence's arm after the dance.

'That's the last time you dance with him. I saw you –'

Florence was pleased. She laughed lightly. 'You're not jealous of a poor old thing like Herbert, are you?'

And Herbert, returning somewhat quicker than expected with the requested glass of champagne, overheard. So that was why Florence had danced with him.

Furious with herself for hurting Herbert, for she did not like to hurt people, Florence took it out on the first person she saw: Percy Brian. She quickly remembered her grievance against him, 'I told you not to play the marionette song so fast. Don't you remember?'

'Did you?' He raised his eyebrows. 'Ah yes, so you did. But Mr Hargreaves thought –'

'I don't care a fig what Mr Hargreaves thought. You are accompanying me, and I'm telling you I want it slower tomorrow.'

'Perhaps.'

Stone-walled and frustrated as rarely before in her life, Florence was close to tears. She said the first thing that came into her head. 'I shall ask Mr Archibald for another accompanist. I don't think he'd like to think of his pianist and conductor living together, do you?'

My happy company, thought Robert Archibald complacently looking round the animated gathering. My family. Yes, the Galaxy was a lucky theatre.

More floral tributes were arriving, dwarfing their callboy carriers, to be greeted by the recipients with coos of delight.

'What *is* that?' whispered Gabrielle, a bright twenty-year-old French showgirl, to Edna. Supported by two stalwart delivery men perspiring more freely than the heat of the stage floods warranted, a huge fruit basket, woven in silver and gold and veiled in delicate pink muslin, was

32

waveringly carried towards them. It was placed with some difficulty – almost dropped – on the table already cleared for the appearance of Auguste's grand centrepiece. A lascivious plaster cupid pointed his arrow towards the writing on the card, which proclaimed "Miss Edna Purvis'. Florence's day was blighted anew. Edna? Why the hell should a mere show girl . . .?

Edna went pink, clapping her hands excitedly. She paused to examine the cupid more closely, hoping to identify the source of this extravaganza. As she bent her stately head forward, the basket suddenly heaved, fruit and chocolate flew in all directions, and a black-suited figure leapt out.

'Good evening, ladies!' he beamed, sweeping off his top hat, to receive his audience's acclaim. The Honourable Johnny Beauville had made good his boast that he would pierce the impregnability of Bates' stage door.

'Dear me,' murmured Mrs Archibald.

'What a dawg!' said Maisie in disgust.

Archibald goggled at the intruder, glanced at his assembled cast and staff, and recollected the occasion. There was only one thing he could do. He advanced with outstretched hand.

'Good of you to drop in, Mr –'

'Beauville's the name.'

The company was happy again. It was *the* moment, Auguste decided, time for his creation. He walked to the rear curtain behind which the *pièce montée* rested, and drew it aside.

Le flanc. The highest expression of a maître's art. There was a concerted gasp – as there should have been. Auguste had never – or seldom – boasted of being a master pâtissier, but on occasion he could excel himself. He had tonight. There in front of them was an exact replica of the Galaxy stage as set for *Miss Penelope*. It was made with the utmost delicacy, the stage hollowed out of meringue and

33

whipped cream. Small grapes and bon-bons represented the dolls, the cast were moulded chocolate characters, the flies sheets of wafer-thin rice paper, scattered with crystallised violets and roses. The top of the masterpiece was still veiled in chiffon, to be ceremonially drawn back by Miss Lytton. The honour belonged only to her, the tribute of one artist to another.

'Mr Didier, it is quite magnificent.' Florence was happy again.

She advanced to the centre of the stage and took hold of the yellow ribbon that would draw the flimsy curtains to one side.

But the shriek that followed was not the usual appreciative acknowledgment of Auguste's genius. Nor were the chorus of cries that followed it.

'Hell and Tommy!' breathed Maisie, as Auguste gazed in disbelieving, stunned horror at the travesty of his art.

In place of the elaborate moulded figures of Florence and Mr Archibald presiding over the Galaxy, someone had removed the female figure and replaced it with the marionette she had sung to on stage. Only now the marionette had its strings drawn tight around its neck, its head twisted round, its eyes gouged out. And the crossed arms were bound tightly to its chest.

Chapter Three

'Why does this have to happen to *me*?'

Correctly interpreting this cry of despair to be rhetorical, Props continued to stare at Robert Archibald blankly. It was all but unknown for him to turn aside from his majestic path to the stage door in order to pay a call on the props room. It was even more unusual to see him accompanied by the chef. But these, Props acknowledged, were not normal times. His beloved Miss Lytton was in distress.

'Weren't my fault, sir,' muttered Props at last, again correctly interpreting the tenor of the remark.

Archibald looked round the vast room stuffed in every cranny with ill assorted dusty objects. What a cavern of memories. Momentarily diverted from his purpose, he spied with pleasure the stuffed unicorns' heads from the last burlesque, set on Mount Olympus, *By Jupiter*. There, too, was the sword from *Mrs Julius Caesar* – ah, what splendid days they were. Daisie Wilton prancing round the stage in her tights . . . He was speedily brought back from his reverie by Auguste.

'These dolls, Monsieur Props. They live in this room when not on the stage?'

'They stay on the set, sir,' Props replied promptly, thankfully. 'I set 'em up for the first full props rehearsal and then they stays there.'

'Don't you check them every day?' asked Archibald severely.

'Well, yes, sir, in a kind of way.' Props fidgeted with

some paper flowers. 'But there was a lot to do before yesterday evening . . .'

'And so anybody could have removed them?' said Auguste. 'And Miss Lytton's marionette –'

Mere mention of *her* marionette was lese-majesty to Props. 'I keep that here, sir. Naturally. It's hers, you see,' he added simply, as if that explained everything. As perhaps it did.

'And last night? The same?'

'I brought it back, sir,' Props replied, looking as if he were about to cry. 'Right after her little song. Or rather, young Edward here did.' He cast a scathing look at his sixteen-year-old assistant, who was busily delving into a large packing case in best ostrich fashion.

'Then how could it remove itself again?' demanded Auguste.

'We went to shift the furniture on the stage, see. For the party. Someone must have come in while we were away and took her –' Props' voice trembled.

Auguste stepped outside. Archibald, who seemed to have handed all initiative to Auguste, followed in his wake.

'Monsieur Bates.'

Obadiah slowly stepped from his cubby hole by the stage door, as though reluctant to leave this position of trust for a single second.

'Monsieur Bates, can you see Props' door from your office?'

'No, sir.'

Archibald sighed. 'So you would not have seen anyone going in?'

Obadiah looked puzzled. 'Only Props, and that young scallywag Edward –'

'And you are sure you never left your office all last evening?'

Obadiah's look changed to one of reproach. 'You know, Mr Archibald, I never leave it, not when the stage door's open.'

'So no one could have come in from outside without your seeing,' said Archibald, hope gone.

'I told Mr Auguste already,' said Obadiah firmly, 'no. And if I can say so, sir, you shouldn't have to ask me that. I've worked 'ere fifteen years, *fifteen* years, and you should know by now, sir, that no one gets past my door. Not the Queen herself, God bless 'er, without she 'as an appointment.'

Seeing he had gone too far, Robert Archibald hastily uttered placatory words and the old man calmed down. Robert Archibald sighed. So it had to be someone from inside the Galaxy. He felt it like a physical blow. What had happened to his happy Galaxy? *Et in Arcadia ego.* A snake in *his* Eden. What had he done to deserve it?

'Yet Monsieur Bates, someone did, did they not? The Honourable Johnny,' Auguste pointed out.

Obadiah cast a hurt look at him, and closed his lips obstinately. They began to tremble slightly. 'I can't go inspecting every cake, every basket of fruit that comes in. It wasn't fair. *Honourable* Johnny – huh.' Obadiah's face registered disgust at this misnomer.

Robert Archibald glanced kindly at the old man. 'You can't be expected to keep up with every trick like that, Obadiah.'

'A cake today, laundry basket tomorrow. Can't do your job fair and square nowadays,' Obadiah grumbled. 'Anyway,' he said more brightly, coming back to the case in point, 'no cakes got left outside Props' room. I'd have noticed if bits of crumbs had been lying around my corridor.'

'No one's blaming you, Obadiah,' said Archibald.

'Only meself, Mr Archibald, sir. Only meself.'

'Think Obadiah's getting too old for the job, Didier?' Archibald remarked some half an hour later, napkin tucked well in round his ample chin, the remains of a pot of tripe and onions (*à la mode de Caen*) in front of him.

Auguste was appalled. This business was indeed making everyone lose their perspective. Obadiah was Archibald's man, interpreting his every wish, closer to him than anyone else, even Auguste himself, in the running of the Galaxy. He had the power to decide on the fate of every caller, not only to visit the cast but to Archibald himself. It was Obadiah who kept creditors away when times were unfortunate; he who summed up the potential of aspiring actors and actresses, who tactfully dismissed the unsuitable, such as the clergyman determined to become Hamlet or the matron of fifty who rather thought she'd like to sing; he who had thwarted the last piece of chicanery tried at the Galaxy by a discharged stagehand, when his sharp eye noted that the caller had turned not towards the wardrobe mistress' domain as befitted the self-termed cobbler's messenger, but towards the dressing rooms.

'You cannot blame Obadiah for last night, monsieur,' said Auguste earnestly. 'The Honourable Johnny is a determined young man.'

'Perhaps you are right. But all the same, it does show that someone could have come in from outside. You can't forget that, Didier. Our joker is not necessarily from the Galaxy itself.'

'But it would have to be someone close to the Galaxy, if not one of us, to know the lay-out of the theatre, our ways –'

'Why?' Archibald burst out. 'Why do all that for the sake of a practical joke? And against Florence of all people. Now why should someone want to upset Florence? It doesn't make sense, Didier.'

He had tried to convince himself it was mere spitefulness on the part of a jealous chorus girl because who else could dislike Florence? No one. He was born and bred to the strange complex world of theatre, where tensions were heightened, emotions intensified, by the claustrophobic world they lived in. As the rehearsals continued, under-

38

currents could build to a crescendo. But this was different. He had always prided himself that the Galaxy was above that sort of thing. Indeed, till now it had been. Perhaps this musical comedy was a mistake. Perhaps he should go back to burlesque.

'Mind you, Didier, I don't think it's anything really. Just a joke.' It was the cry of a drowning man. Archibald regarded Auguste hopefully, seeking the reassurance he could not give.

'*Non*, Monsieur Archibald. I do not think so. You will not easily discover who played this trick with the dolls, I think.'

'I could appeal to their better natures, to come forward for the good of the theatre?' said Archibald hopefully.

Auguste hesitated. 'I think, monsieur, the good of the theatre will not be uppermost in their minds. You must ask yourself first who does not like Miss Florence. For someone does not like her at all.'

'Everybody likes Florence,' said Robert Archibald, shocked.

'Yes,' said Auguste, 'she is like the mackerel.'

'Pardon?'

'The mackerel. As the *bon* Grimod de La Reynière said: "The mackerel has this in common with good women – he is loved by all the world." '

Robert Archibald tried to grapple with the concept of dainty blonde Florence Lytton as a mackerel, and failed.

'Yet, it is not quite true,' Auguste went on. 'Some do not like the mackerel. It is a good fish, yes, but it does not agree with everybody. Perhaps Miss Florence does not agree with some people.'

Archibald sighed. 'I heard about that blasted marionette song. It's a song, just a song.'

'It is an ingredient, my friend.'

'Ingredient of what?'

'Perhaps disaster.'

Archibald blinked. 'Come now, I admit I was rattled by

those blasted dolls – but disaster? Bit strong, isn't it, Didier? Nasty sense of humour someone's got, and it's got to be stopped. But it isn't that important in the long run. Dammit, man, this is the Galaxy!'

'And an hour before the curtain went up last night four of your main people were at each other's throats; Mr Hargreaves would not speak to your leading lady, his pianist was teasing him, your leading man was failing to support his wife who was attacking the pianist. Normally the pianist would hardly be opposing the will of the conductor, Miss Lytton would have been on the best of terms with Mr Brian, and Mr Manley would have been riveted to his wife's side. None of these things happened.'

'Because of a song?' Archibald's voice was disbelieving.

'In the Provençal dialect, Monsieur Archibald, the mackerel is called the *peis d'Avril*. You call that the April fool. It seems that Miss Lytton is your April fool. But you do not know where the joke began – nor, Monsieur Archibald, where it will end.'

Egbert Rose looked round his tiny office in the Factory, as they called the Yard. Books, papers, files cluttered every shelf. He wouldn't have them touched. It was his home. Mrs Rose was a keen housekeeper, perhaps to make up for her culinary shortcomings, and even his den did not remain inviolate. He made up for it here. He liked dust. It made everything feel secure. His. He knew where everything was. He'd had nearly four years now in this new building. It had been an upheaval moving from the Old Scotland Yard, but he was settling down nicely now. The villains could watch out.

He went to the door dividing his office from the lesser fry.

'Constable Edwards, get me the Ripper files.'

Edwards looked up, startled. 'The Ripper files, sir?'

'You heard me.'

'But he's dead, sir.'

Rose regarded him lugubriously. 'You aiming to be a sergeant, laddie?'

'Yessir.'

'Then get me the files, son.'

He returned to his desk, and reread the report on Christine Walters. The corpse had a name now, an identity, and with identification came the prospect of having to break the news to her parents. The girl had lived in lodgings, so it had been two weeks before hesitantly, reluctantly, her parents reported her missing. The theatre had reported her missing after three days, though with no great sense of worry. Nothing more sinister in it than a better job, an ardent beau, or irate parents, they'd implied. These things happened with chorus girls, they disappeared from time to time, but it was not usual at the Galaxy. The theatre inculcated a sense of responsibility in its girls, and therefore the disappearance of Christine Walters on September 27th, flighty though she had been, was a departure from the norm, and thus to be reported to the authorities.

And eight weeks later she turned up, a corpse in the Thames, identifiable only by the dress she wore and the rings on her fingers, details gleaned from her colleagues as a precaution on the Yard's first being notified of her disappearance.

'Here, Inspector.' Edwards staggered in with a mountain of files. 'Had to make Chief Constable's report, sir. They're specials, sir.'

Rose sighed. Of course. McNaughten would want to know about anyone seeing the Ripper files. Half the population of London still lived in dread he would return. They weren't to know, and the Yard couldn't tell them, that the Ripper was dead. Or so they assumed. But they could be wrong, there was the hundredth chance, and he dreaded to think what Her Gracious Majesty Queen Victoria would have to say about *that*. She had made her displeasure at the Yard's handling of the Ripper case very plain – even started to play detective herself. This case had better be solved quickly.

He didn't like those crossed arms. He didn't like them at all. The girl hadn't been touched with a knife, not even interfered with – but there was something about those arms . . . He began to read the Ripper files. Recalling the photographs, the endless reports, the Ripper's eerie letters, it all started to come back. He'd been a sergeant then, not directly involved with the case, but he'd gone along to the room where Mary Kelly had been found – it wasn't a scene he was likely to forget. She had been the last in the series. Series . . . What reason could there have been for those arms to be crossed? Wasn't to keep them out of the way. Done after death, so the report said. All laid out, like a ritual, like a figure on a mediaeval tomb. And that reminded him of something else he couldn't quite bring to mind . . .

Some time later, Rose emerged from the hansom at the imposing Mayfair portals of Summerfield House. He regarded them gloomily and advanced on the entrance. The butler was not impressed, clearly hesitating as to whether to redirect him to another, lowlier entrance. Rose was not impressed by the butler.

He stepped in firmly, ignoring the waves of disapprobation emanating from the doorway.

'Lord Summerfield,' he said firmly.

'He's expecting you?'

'No,' said Rose cheerily. 'Just tell him Scotland Yard, my man.'

From the look on the butler's face, he was clearly now convinced of his error in admitting the inspector through the front entrance. Nevertheless, he vanished speedily through an ornately decorated door.

It was some while before he re-emerged, time in which Rose had ample opportunity to study the Ming vase, the ornate group of Staffordshire figures, and the Cotman watercolour that graced the hallway.

'Lord and Lady Summerfield will see you,' the butler announced in terms of one astounded beyond belief at the honour conferred. Rose handed him his bowler, his cane, his ulster, taking his time, and then maliciously indicated that the butler should take those of Constable Edwards who stuck beside him like a faithful, attentive shadow.

Lord Summerfield rose from his leather armchair in the morning room as they entered. He was a tall, thin man of about forty. It was hard to estimate his age accurately for he had a smooth, impassive face on which emotions played but lightly. Good-looking in a patrician kind of way, Rose decided, if you liked those long-nosed types. He had a pipe in his hand, the barrel of which he stroked constantly with his thumb.

'Good morning, Inspector. You called once before.' The visit had clearly not been a passport to Lord Summerfield's favour.

'Yes, indeed, sir,' said Rose woodenly. 'Same business, I'm afraid.'

'Mother, this is Inspector Rose of Scotland Yard.' He did not bother to introduce Police Constable Edwards. The Countess of Summerfield, holder of that title until such time as her son should marry, a time which would be dictated by her, acknowledged his presence with the merest inclination of her grey, elegantly coiffured head. No Dower House for her, she had determined. She remained seated in her armchair, back erect, eyes piercing, face impassive, hands on the chair arms, waiting. Like a vulture waiting to pounce, thought Rose. Poor devil, no wonder he's nervous. It was the first time he had met Mother. Summerfield had been alone last time, though scarcely less nervous.

'I came to tell you, sir, that Miss Walters has been found. She's dead, sir.'

A flicker passed over Summerfield's face. Then he turned and gazed at his mother.

The stentorian voice spoke. 'As I gather my son

43

explained to you before, Inspector, he is unable to help you. Occasionally, in order not to disappoint friends, he accompanies them to the theatre – the Lyceum. He has no knowledge of the Galaxy or of the persons employed there.'

'And as I explained earlier, ma'am, we have several witnesses who claim that Miss Walters told them she had arranged to dine with Lord Summerfield the evening she disappeared.'

'My son,' said an icy voice, 'does not dine with girls of that class. These *people* are clearly mistaken.'

Rose turned to Lord Summerfield.

His knuckles were clenched white around the pipe stem. 'So you told me before, Lord Summerfield. Is it true?'

'I – well, just that once, perhaps – there were to be several of us, Mother.' He was more scared of revealing the truth to her than to the police, Rose noted dispassionately. 'I hardly knew the girl, however.'

Lady Summerfield said nothing, though her lips grew a little thinner and her stare icier.

Once Rose might have been intimidated. Now he wasn't. 'Nothing wrong with those Galaxy Girls, ma'am,' he said easily. 'Nice lot they are. Why, the Duchess of Stockbery once told me that within ten years' time half the aristocracy –'

It had its effect. Mention of the Duchess mollified Her Ladyship and, though still suspicious, she stayed out of the conversation.

'Now what happened that night, My Lord? Not that fangle dangle you told me before. What really happened?'

Lord Summerfield looked uneasy. 'Nothing, Inspector. Nothing at all. That was it. That was why I felt no need to tell you. She never arrived.'

'What?'

'I had arranged to meet her – with the others, of course,' he added hastily, and manifestly lying. 'My carriage waited outside the Lyceum in Wellington Street at ten o'clock – our usual time,' he said artlessly, 'but she never

44

came. I assumed she had mistaken the day.' And he stared straight at Rose, as though daring him to doubt this.

Oh yes? thought Rose. With a coronet on your head?

The Honourable Johnny Beauville had no mother. At least not one who maintained a presence as did Lady Summerfield. As younger son to the Earl of Ashford, he shared his brother and sister-in-law's, Lord and Lady Charing's, modest Mayfair town house with them while in town.

'The mater thinks it good for me. The folks stay down in the country. They think Jeremy and Gertrude keep an eye on me,' he remarked cheerily. He at least had no idea of keeping Rose at a distance.

'I came to tell you, Mr Beauville –'

'Bevil, not Bowvil,' remarked Johnny casually.

It would take more than that to throw Rose off his stride. 'You knew Christine Walters?'

'The little darling who disappeared?'

'Yes, Mr, er, Bevil. She disappeared after the second night of *Lady Bertha's Betrothal*, and you were heard enquiring after her very persistently at the stage door on the evening before. You were told that the young ladies were at the party and not seeing anyone, so you informed the stage door keeper you'd return the next night. And the next. And the next.'

He looked alarmed. 'Me?' he bleated. Then his face cleared. 'First night of jolly *Lady Bertha*? Oh, yes, I remember that.' He grinned. 'The Dragon was with me. That's me sister-in-law. She and Jeremy came round to the stage door in the carriage, in case I came to harm. They looked after me,' he said wistfully. 'Bates wouldn't let me see her – Christine, that is. So I climbed into the old carriage and they dropped me at my club.'

'And what about the following evening?'

'Oh, the club, too. Overdid the old oysters the night before, so I thought I would give the Galaxy a miss.'

'And then Miss Walters disappeared – only a few days or so, according to my information, after you had asked her to marry you.'

'Really?' Johnny's jovial face suddenly went blank. 'I can't say I remember – but if you say so, it's probably true.'

'You don't remember if you asked the young lady to marry you?'

'No,' said Johnny regretfully. 'Was she the tall ginger-haired one or the small – no, that was –'

'Do you propose to a lot of young ladies?' asked Rose frostily.

'Quite a few,' said Johnny cheerily.

'And do you always say you'll shoot yourself if they won't marry you?'

'Part of the form, you know,' he said apologetically. 'Never mean it.'

'Did you mean it when you said you'd shoot her as an alternative?'

'Eh?' Johnny gaped. 'Seems a bit extreme. Did I really say that? She must be a stunner.'

'Have been, Mr Bevil. She's dead. Murdered.'

'Murdered?' He blinked. 'That's why you're here to see me –' Suddenly, he looked intelligent. 'Oh, I say, you've got it all wrong. I love all the little darlings. I wouldn't touch a hair of their pretty little heads. Oh no, you've got it all wrong.'

Traffic at the stage door was hotting up. The mashers began to arrive, agog to see their idols as they entered the theatre, to make certain of their prey for later that evening; those more dignified approached Obadiah Bates with notes, flowers, chocolates, threats or bribes. The tangible offerings he accepted for their recipients, the latter two he ignored. He gloried in his power. Hadn't Mr Archibald said he couldn't run the theatre without him? Six o'clock and the girls were now arriving: principals, chorus girls, show girls. Funnily enough, the principals would often come in the growlers, the show girls in the hansoms. The men always seemed to arrive later. He always had young Phipps standing by before the show as a kind of stage door linkman in case any of the young ladies needed an escort through the crowd. The scuff, as he inelegantly called it. But it was all under his control.

'Evening, Miss Lepin.'

'Evening, Obadiah.' The girls were on terms of easy familiarity with him for he was their confidant. He knew their escorts, every stage and nuance of their romances, he fostered where he approved, otherwise discouraged. He would rid them of unwanted admirers, encourage the others.

'Evening, Miss Maisie.'

'Let Mr Beauville through tonight, Obadiah, will you?' She sensed his disapproval. 'Now then, Obadiah,' she said robustly, 'Auguste isn't going to mind. Nobody in their right senses could be jealous of Johnny.'

'Very well, Miss Maisie. If you say so. But I don't hold with his goings on.'

'Evening, Obadiah.'

'Evening, Miss Edna. Who is it tonight then?'

'Lord Summerfield.' She was scarcely able to contain her pride.

'Oh ho, looking up, are we? Evening, Miss Julia.'

'Good evening, Obadiah. If that Captain Hoskins calls here, I am not available. Not tonight, not at all. Is that clear?'

'Perfectly clear, miss. He won't get past me.'

Business was back to normal, the matter of Trojan cakes and such dishonourable behaviour swept under the carpet.

Edna came into the show girls' dressing room glowing with triumph. The other girls were duly impressed.

'Aren't you worried though? Christine Walters disappeared when she was going out with him.' Gabrielle pointed out.

'He's a *lord*,' said Edna definitively. 'He wouldn't do anything. I mean, he's *English*. Not like that Italian count who went off with Angela. Or that Frenchie. Never trust a Frenchie.'

Maisie, who had rushed in to borrow some hair-tongs, thought of Auguste and kept her own counsel. She tried to keep apart from the others. They were a good bunch, but she had been brought up in the hard school of Bethnal Green where it was everyone for himself. If you wanted to keep what you had, you kept quiet about it. And she wanted Auguste at the moment. Not that she'd marry him. There was time enough for marriage. Meanwhile, she might as well enjoy life to the full. Johnny Beauville would suit her down to the ground. The other girls might laugh but she never saw anyone turn down a date with him. Except Christine. And Edna, of course. He had plenty of money. Knew how to treat a girl like a lady. He knew all the right places to take you to. Oh yes, Johnny was all right.

Florence entered, glancing round her dressing room nervously, half expecting to see it full of mangled dolls. But it presented its usual flower-filled aspect, and the neat orderliness imposed by her dresser. She relaxed. Perhaps it had all been some horrible first night prank. She slipped off her heavy dark day dress, and into the satin robe held ready by her dresser. She sat before her mirror and examined her paint carefully. No, she was getting ridiculous. As though anyone would tamper with that. She shivered at the thought of anything ruining her looks, and had to calm herself with a great effort before, with a trembling hand, she began to apply the greasepaint.

There was a tap on the door which made her jump. Her dresser opened it. Edward Hargreaves and Percy Brian

She stared in amazement, for it was all but unheard of for men to call at the dressing rooms on the ladies' side. Even Thomas. They must have sought special permission. It boded no good.

'Miss Lytton,' said Edward firmly, 'it's about that song.'

Florence stiffened.

'Percy and I just don't think we can throw that song away by slowing it down like you want. We slowed it a little last night but we won't any more. We've got our integrity to think of.'

Florence went white. How could they, just before a performance? She summoned up all her courage. 'I've got to sing it,' she said firmly. 'And you hardly slowed it at all last night. You can't do it faster still. Not after' – there was a catch in her voice – 'not after all I've been through.'

'Just a little,' said Percy Brian persuasively.

'No,' said Florence obdurately. 'I'll do it like last night, if I have to, but not like you want it. It's too fast. I'll lose the feeling. "If you could but hear",' she trilled, ' "what I sing to you . . ." It should be slow, slow, *slow* –' To her horror, she found herself stamping her foot.

'We'll tell Mr Archibald how we feel. Both of us.'

'Tell him,' said Florence recklessly. 'See what he says when his leading lady resigns as a result. Because someone is carrying out a vendetta against me. First this song, now the dolls. I wouldn't be surprised if they were connected, would you?' she said with a viciousness that appalled her.

'Do you mean –?' Hargreaves gaped. Bloody woman! Women were trouble, he knew that, not like men. They couldn't be relied on. 'As if Percy and I –'

'Not me, my dear, not me.' Percy was strangely quiet.

'What?'

'Well, you never asked me. I think dear Florence is perhaps right, wanting it slower.' His bright eyes were innocent, his face angelic, but he carefully avoided looking at Edward.

Hargreaves stared at him.

'But, Percy – you –'

Florence smiled. Percy was on her side. Quite rightly. He would defend her against that horrid Hargreaves. Graceful, restored, reassured, Miss Penelope swept out, billowing wafts of perfume, closely followed by the dresser, still vainly attempting to adjust the folds of the dress gathered over Florence's retreating victorious backside.

The two men faced each other.

'You've betrayed me, Percy,' said Edward Hargreaves hoarsely.

'Just because we live together, Edward,' said Percy softly, 'it doesn't mean you're right all the time. I've got my integrity as a pianist to think of.'

He was like a stranger to Hargreaves, this boy he'd lived with, loved, for three years.

'Percy, take care,' Hargreaves said suddenly. 'Don't let this go on. You persuaded me to come up here. Now you're stirring things up. Take care. If this gets to Archibald, if he finds out about us –'

'Phooey,' said Percy, tossing back his hair petulantly. 'He'd never take any action. It's all the rage in London now. The police don't care. You're just a fuddy duddy.' And he walked off.

'But what about those dolls?' Hargreaves called after him.

Florence tripped happily down to the stage. Percy had been an unexpected ally. Now everything was all right. The last little thing had been attended to.

'We've won, Herbert,' she said gaily, seeing him in the wings.

'Won, Florence?' he replied, his expression unreadable under his clownish make-up.

'The song, silly. We're going back to the original tempo. Slow, all the time. Percy supports me, so now it's three of us against Mr Hargreaves.'

'No,' said Herbert, matter-of-factly, his expression strangely remote. 'Two.'

'Two,' said Florence, puzzled.

'Yes,' he said, not looking at her. 'I told Mr Hargreaves I liked it faster. Like this: "Pom, pom, pom, what I'd sing to you. How I'd sing to you, my dear".'

She stared at him, speechless.

'You never asked me, you see. I do have to sing a verse too.'

'But I thought –' She stopped. How could she say she took his devotion, his acquiescence in what pleased her, for granted? So in the normal way she could. But not tonight. Herbert, in his own way, intended to pay Florence back.

The performance flagged. Perhaps this was inevitable after the triumph of last night. It was not noticeable to any but the cast; to the audience it would seem another triumph, perhaps a little pale by the side of *Lady Bertha*. But to the cast, and more particularly to Robert Archibald, it flagged: it was lifeless, it was uncoordinated; a chorus girl was out of step here, a beat missed there, the orchestra's playing a trifle ragged, a wrong note on the piano, a top note insufficiently held, a humdrumness about the comedy. But not noticeable to the audience. Not, that is, until Florence's solo at the end of Act 2, in which she was joined by Herbert for the last verse.

Miss Penelope clutched her marionette to her, and gazed fondly into its wooden face. She was riding on a pinnacle of exultation; she was adored by the gods, by the stalls, by the pit. She had forgotten she was apparently not so adored on her side of the Galaxy footlights.

'If you could only hear what I'm saying to you,' she whispered to the puppet's calico-clad body. 'If only *he* could hear –' throwing a wistful glance towards Lord Harry, at present lingering in the wings beside Edna Purvis. 'If only, if only . . .' A tinkling note sounded on the piano. A chord from the orchestra.

> 'If you could only hear,
> What I sing to you –'

Alas, no one *could* hear. Least of all the audience. For Florence, having reverted trustingly to the slow tempo set by Percy at the piano, was completely drowned and overtaken by the orchestra reverting to the fast tempo of Edward's choice, a tempo in which Herbert joined with gusto, advancing two verses early from behind his toyshop counter.

It was disaster. Florence, overwhelmed, stood openmouthed, still automatically singing on. The orchestra leader, belatedly remembering his duty to his audience, increased the volume to drown the piano, then since Florence's mouth was no longer moving, softened it for Herbert to finish the song in triumphant solo while Florence stood like a dumb thing.

Watching from the stalls, Robert Archibald permitted himself to relieve his feelings with one single oath culled from his Hoxton childhood.

With masterly presence of mind, Lord Harry swept on one scene early, took his wife by the hand and gazed fondly into her eyes. Then he bravely began to no accompaniment whatsoever his final love song, to a Miss Penelope about to reveal to the audience, for the sake of their delicate susceptibilities, that she was after all no shopgirl, but the daughter of a viscount.

The episode had lasted perhaps two minutes, but it was a lifetime for the Galaxy. Twenty years of patient tradition-building might never have been.

Not for nothing was Robert Archibald a theatre manager. With great self-control he merely sent round a note by the call-boy, requesting the presence of certain principals and musical staff in his office the following morning.

'Let them stew in their juice, eh, Didier?' he said thickly, mournfully mulling over his problems in the kitchen of the restaurant.

'That is generally a good thing, monsieur,' said Auguste. 'But there is one problem – the meat is tough if allowed to stew without great care. You must be careful, *hein*?'

Robert Archibald regarded him balefully. 'Might have known you'd drag the kitchen into this.'

'*La cuisine* is the epicentre of the world, monsieur. As Brillat-Savarin so rightly says: "The destiny of great nations is directed by what they eat".'

But Archibald was in no mood for Brillat-Savarin. He could not bear even to walk through his beloved theatre that night so, locking the communicating door, he donned his bowler hat and ulster, and walked out into the gaslit night.

'I saw you,' shouted Florence. 'I saw you laughing with her – with that show girl in the wings. Laughing at me, your own wife.'

'Dearest, I wasn't laughing,' said Thomas patiently. Indeed he wasn't; he was horrified. His muttered aside to Edna (who had indeed been laughing) was for her to mind his gloves while he rushed on to save Florence from ignominy. He gazed, helpless and aghast, at his wife's pretty face now distorted with an anger he had never seen on it before. Was this the quiet girl he had married, whom everybody loved? He tried to reason with her.

'Everyone's against me. Mr Archibald, Mr Hargreaves, Percy – because he only wanted to get back at Mr Hargreaves – even Herbert, and now you. It's too much. Making eyes at a show girl while I'm in trouble.'

'I wasn't –'

'Yes you were. You can't wait to get near her. Touching her, cuddling her.'

It was so unfair. 'I wasn't –'

'You were. You know you were. Just like you were with

Christine Walters. If you prefer them to me, just tell me. Just tell me.'

'I don't.'

'I daresay she's waiting for you now. Waiting for you to take her out to dinner. Then you'll see her home. And then you'll – you'll screw her.'

Appalled, Thomas gaped at his wife as if seeing her for the first time. That she even *knew* these words. His gentle Florence. He was shaken and hurt by the injustice of it all. After all, he hadn't yet taken Edna to bed. She'd refused him – so far.

'Very well,' he managed to say coolly, 'if that's what you think of me, I *will* take her out to dinner. Edna thinks more of me than you seem to . . .'

Alone, Florence burst into tears. She wept for a long time. How could they? Nobody loved her. They played horrible jokes on her. Now they'd gone and left her alone. All was quiet in the corridor. Deathly quiet. She must be the last one left. She called out to the girls but there was no reply. She looked at her little French clock. Even Obadiah would have left now. The night watch should be here, but suppose he wasn't? She might be alone in the building.

She was suddenly scared. Usually Thomas was with her. He came to the theatre with her; he went home with her. They had dinner when they got home. Now she'd have to summon a hansom and go home alone. Could she do it? She'd never summoned one before in her cosseted life. She supposed she could. It was just a matter of pulling herself together, of getting out of this horrible empty place. Just a matter of walking down that corridor, down the stairs, and finding her way out.

She began to wipe the paint from her face, then to bathe her eyes, to remove the tearstains so that she could leave. She realised she was still in her costume. Rapidly, illogically nervous, each sound she made seeming magnified in the empty room, she stripped off her costume. Fool to tell her resser to go home, because she couldn't bear to face her ⋯ fter the disaster! She slipped the mauve woollen day dress ⋯ ver her head and began to fasten the many buttons, fingers ⋯ ervously fumbling. She pulled on her boots, picked up the ⋯ ong button hook, her stays digging in viciously, and began ⋯ he tedious task.

She stopped and straightened up. Quite clearly through ⋯ he door, which was ajar, she heard the sound of footsteps ⋯ oming up the stairs. Heavy footsteps. Her heart in her ⋯ nouth, she tried to subdue her rising panic.

'Watch?' she cried out interrogatively. It must be the ⋯ reman who kept guard during the night once Obadiah had ⋯ one home. 'Watch?'

But there was no reply.

The footsteps advanced along the corridor. A male ⋯ nadow fell across the doorway. Petrified, Florence sat ⋯ nere, steel button hook in hand, and watched the door ⋯ owly open . . .

⋯ n early morning butcher's boy whistled cheerfully ⋯ nrough his short cut from Newcastle Street to Wych Street ⋯ the back of the Olympic Palace Theatre, a favourite ⋯ oute since he often found old programmes amongst the ⋯ ash thrown out by the theatre. There was an extra large ⋯ le this morning. Kicking it in the way of all errand boys, ⋯ e felt something hard and, curious since the litter was ⋯ enerally paper, bent down to find the reason for this ⋯ ardness.

It was only relatively hard. It was a woman's body.

He gurgled, then gagged. At his feet, eyes bulging in a ⋯ urple face, was the body of a woman. Her hands, neatly ⋯ olded across her chest, were tied into place with thick rope.

Chapter Four

Robert Archibald had risen on this Thursday morning with a new determination. A night's sleep and the calm ministrations of Mrs Archibald had restored to him his sense of proportion. One mistake in a performance did not mean the end of the Galaxy. Something was undoubtedly wrong in the state of Denmark, but it should not be beyond his powers to discover what and put it right. There was a bad 'un somewhere, but close questioning of those involved should reveal who it was. You could always trace these ripples back to their source. With these cheering thoughts, he entered the Galaxy with more or less his usual sprightly step.

'Morning, Mr Archibald.'

'Good morning, Bates.'

'Gentleman waiting to see you.'

'What?' Irritation replaced geniality. 'Good God, Bates, you know my rule. Not before eleven, and particularly not today.'

'Police, sir,' replied Bates with some relish.

It says much for the state of Mr Archibald's preoccupation with the problem of Miss Penelope's marionette song that it was a little while before his brain could diagnose any possible reason why the Law should wish to see him. Then, as he strode along the corridor to the office, he recalled the disappearance of Christine Walters and the subsequent routine call by the police.

His worst fears were realised as he entered his office to find Egbert Rose studying the photographs of Daisie

Wilton (in her tights) adorning the walls, his bowler laid carelessly on the desk on top of the box office returns for the first night. Two things came to Archibald's mind: this was clearly not a police constable, and it was clearly going to be a bad day

Just how bad neither he nor Egbert Rose could possibly imagine, but Rose's present mission was quite enough for the moment.

'Murdered?' Robert Archibald was aghast. 'Poor girl, poor girl,' he said, shaking his head sadly. He felt it as a personal loss. The girls were his concern, his family. After they left the Galaxy he might lose all interest in them, but while working under its portals everything about them – their health, their happiness, their private lives – were all part of the Galaxy so far as he was concerned. And if she had died while in Galaxy employ, then Christine Walters was most definitely his concern.

'When?' he asked abruptly. He thought of the dreadful probability that the girl must have gone straight from the Galaxy to her death.

'Can't say, sir. Been in the water, you see. About the time you reported her missing, though. That was' – Rose glanced at his notebook – '30th September, and you said you last saw her on the 27th.'

The 27th, the day after the opening of *Lady Bertha's Betrothal*. Such had been the excitement, the ferment at the Galaxy at the unexpected popularity of this new piece, of the possibilities for an entirely new kind of entertainment, that so far Archibald had scarcely spared a thought for the missing girl. To him she was an empty place in the show girl line. Even though he reported it as a matter of form, since she had sent no explanation of her disappearance, he had assumed that she had gone off with a man. She was a flighty little filly. Lived in lodgings on her own. He always discouraged that among his girls. But all that time she had been dead. Strangled. There was a pause while Archibald's mind conjured up unpleasant pictures.

'I'll have to talk to your staff, the cast,' said Rose, watching conflicting emotions run over the manager's face. His hand was absent-mindedly stroking the large drooping moustache, the pride of his life after the Galaxy and Mrs Archibald, carefully preserved with Oldridge's Balm.

'It's changed,' said Archibald. 'We've a new show now. But you talked to them at the time.'

'Not me,' said Rose. 'Different department. Missing girl, thousands go missing every year. They don't all end up murdered in the Thames though,' he said matter-of-factly. 'And since bodies tend to go into the Thames at night, and it's a noticeable fact that the old river runs mighty close to this theatre, we'll have to do a bit of investigation. Talk to the men in particular. And I'd like a list of any of the gentlemen who were here then, who aren't here now. Any you remember as being special friends of hers, if you get my meaning.' He stood up and clapped his bowler on his head. 'One more thing, Mr Archibald. Do you keep rope around this theatre?'

Archibald blinked. 'Rope?'

Rose produced a short length of rope from his pocket. 'She was tied up, you see. Hands bound across her chest.' He glanced up to see Archibald's face slowly turning paler. 'Ah, I see that means something to you, sir.'

Half-an-hour later found Rose walking gloomily along the Strand. It was a mild day and the pavements were crowded with workers and shoppers. Ah, he could remember the days when the Strand really was something, a majestic sight with the old Temple Bar dominating it. He was just a young police constable then, all eyes, long gangly limbs, and far from the heftiest lad in the force. But Williamson had spotted him. 'An eye for the villains, you've got, lad,' he'd said when Rose proudly brought in that bit faker.

Now Temple Bar was long since gone, and the Strand was losing its dignity to progress – traffic, traffic and more traffic. Mind you, St Mary's in the early morning was still worth a dawn rising to enjoy its quiet before the rush of London's workers poured out from Charing Cross. What was it Dr Johnson had said? "The full tide of existence is at Charing Cross." His eyes would have popped out of his head if he could have seen Charing Cross Railway Station today. But the Old Thames never changed . . . Rose brought his mind back to the unpleasant case ahead of him – the girl, poor lass, and now these dolls.

They might just be dolls, but it was too close to what had happened to Christine Walters for his liking. Archibald seemed to think them just a joke directed against Miss Lytton. His superiors might scoff, but all the same it didn't look like a joke to Rose. In a sense it made his job easier, though, for it looked like someone inside the theatre. A nasty business. Menacing. Something not quite sane about it. He greeted a crossing sweeper with surprising cheerfulness considering the nature of his thoughts and made his way to the Yard.

Reports had been piling up on his desk, but he did not get past the first one. Young girl, body found in Maypole Alley. He sighed. Another courting couple, passions flaring, too much force . . . He read on. He'd been wrong. The description of the clothing did not sound like a market girl. Nor the fur. By the time he got to the end of the report, his worst fears were confirmed. Her arms had been bound across her chest. So as news of the first murder had not been released, it was odds on it was the same villain. He hardly bothered to read the rest of the report for he knew what would be in it. The contents of her handbag revealed her to be a member of the Galaxy.

Edna Purvis would never fulfil her ambition to become the wife of a lord.

Auguste Didier had been right in his analysis of the stew. The meat had grown tough. Overnight the principal actors had become entrenched in their positions. They were not speaking to each other. Percy was now convinced of his rightness in supporting Florence. Edward Hargreaves was implacable about defending his integrity as composer and conductor. Thomas Manley found it impossible even to face his beloved Florence. Florence felt persecuted by the whole world, while Herbert Sykes now had no option but to commit himself wholeheartedly to the support of Edward Hargreaves.

Their first sight of Robert Archibald was not reassuring. The interview was clearly going to be tough. Each mentally wriggled more firmly into position. Lesser deities in the presence of Jupiter, they waited for Archibald to speak.

'Our Miss Walters, it appears, did not disappear.' He smiled deprecatingly as though reluctant to give such bad news. 'She was, I regret to say, murdered.'

Herbert replied first. '*Murdered*, Mr Archibald?'

'Drowned, strangled. And in circumstances which – ah – look as if the matter might have something to do with this theatre.' He forbore to say exactly what circumstances. There was little point in alarming Florence unnecessarily.

'The theatre!'

Edward and Florence spoke with one voice, the marionette song, if not forgotten, laid aside.

'But surely –' Florence paused delicately, 'Miss Walters was well known to – ah – have a wide variety of gentlemen friends.' She did not look at Thomas. 'Why is the Galaxy involved?'

Robert Archibald shifted uncomfortably.

Herbert could hardly remember Christine Walters. Tall, he remembered, classical features until one looked more closely and saw the mean jaw, the insufficient space between the eyes – the coarse mouth that had spoken slightingly of Miss Lytton. Florence. He closed his eyes briefly. The horror of last night still filled his every thought. He would never forget. How cruel women were.

Edward Hargreaves was too preoccupied with his present

falling out with Percy to cast his mind back to Christine Walters. He took little notice of the show and chorus girls, except when they got in his way. They were a series of numbers, in his mind, to be arranged, rearranged, reprimanded, moved about to complement the perfection of his music. Music was the only reality, the only integrity. You could trust nothing else. No one else. He stole a glance at Percy, whom he had thought he knew through and through. But Percy had not come home last night. The fear went through his mind that he might have gone back to his old life, picked up someone . . .

'The police will be calling. Coming to talk to you all – just about Miss Walters, movements again and so forth,' Archibald added hastily. 'And in the case of the gentlemen' – he looked uncomfortable – 'about their own movements. Just routine.' He stared at his staff unhappily, little knowing what effect his words had on his audience.

Florence was looking at Thomas and wondering; Herbert blenched at the thought of having to think about Christine Walters, particularly after last night; Percy studiously avoided Edward's eye, and Thomas looked straight ahead.

It was left to Edward, as Archibald seemed inclined to dismiss them, to raise that other important matter: 'Ah, Mr Archibald, the song. Um – tonight –'

'The song. Ah, yes.' The carefully rehearsed sentences and subtle approaches he had planned on the way to the theatre seemed to have deserted him. But inspiration took over.

'I've decided,' he said (two seconds before if truth be told), 'I think it would be effective if verse one were slow, as Miss Lytton desires. Then we speed up a little, and for the last verse, as Mr Sykes joins in, we are at Mr Hargreaves's tempo.' There was a note of finality in his voice as he beamed at them. There was nothing like compromise. And after all, the Galaxy had always been a unified happy theatre. The unpalatable thought that this might well be a thing of the past briefly crossed his mind – and was firmly dismissed.

'Ah, Monsieur Sykes, *bonjour*.'

Herbert watched Auguste in the midst of puréeing peaches for a *vol au vent au pêche*. Herbert liked his food.

Auguste had always had a soft spot for the comedian who made no close friends, though the girls treated him like a cross between an elderly uncle and a eunuch in a harem, with his inoffensive soft ways. But even Auguste did not quite understand what went on behind those mild eyes. He had the impression sometimes that Herbert was using his wit as a defence against something quite different. 'You look like a souffle that has failed to rise, *mon brave*. What has happened?'

'Murder has happened, Mr Didier, murder.'

'Murder.' Auguste blinked. '*Ma foi*. Over a song?'

Herbert giggled. 'No, Mr Didier. But that poor chorus girl, the one that disappeared, seems she disappeared right into the Thames. Strangled,' he said, almost with relish, picking up the strainer and neglected masher from where Auguste in his horror had let them fall. 'Here, let me do some. I've always enjoyed a bit of kitchen work.' After a moment, 'Strangled,' he repeated, his large, strong hands grinding down the fruit. 'Not pretty, but quick. Like your mixing machine, eh? And there's something funny about it, too. Mr Archibald says it's to do with the theatre, but wouldn't explain why. Myself, I think it has something to do with those dolls. That was nasty, don't you think? Poor Miss Lytton,' he added rather belatedly.

Auguste looked at him sharply. Something strange there. Herbert's head was cocked to one side, a gleam in his eye – an expression, Auguste suddenly recollected, he put on on stage when he had, as he put it, done something 'a little naughty'.

So Maisie was right, and murder had entered the life of

Auguste Didier again. One should not be surprised in this large city, especially so close to the old rookeries of Clare Market whose reputation lingered long after the market proper had disappeared, and but a short distance from the East End where men and women vanished every day and few noted their absence. But this affair would be different because it was a girl from the Galaxy, and the Galaxy affected everyone's lives. From the aristocracy to the middle classes and to the services, the Galaxy was known everywhere. Auguste sighed. This place of entertainment, magic and beauty, was a strange setting for murder. Yet was it any more strange than Stockbery Towers, the ducal residence where he had been instrumental in solving two murders?

The hearts that beat under ermine, whether real or stage, had the same passions, if not the same daily preoccupations, as those that dwelt under rags and tatters or the stockbroker's top hat.

Rose entered the restaurant somewhat unwillingly. He wasn't one for fancy restaurants as a rule, but he couldn't deny a spot of lunch was welcome. The morning had been gruelling, to say the least. Over to the Galaxy to break the news of Christine Walters' death, back to Scotland Yard to find the report of the Maypole Alley murder, conferences with the Superintendent, then the Chief himself, despatching constables to Miss Purvis' lodgings and to the lady's parents in Shoreditch, then back to the Galaxy to face Archibald with the shock of the second death. His second interview with Archibald had been even worse than the first. Rose had been to the Galaxy burlesques a few times himself, and had even taken Mrs Rose for a rare night out, to see *Lady Bertha's Betrothal*. She'd enjoyed it very much. 'Not so, well, rude, Egbert, as some of them others I've heard about.' He'd even spotted a rare tear in his good lady's eye.

Now he had to break the news to Archibald not only that

it seemed very likely that the murderer was connected with the theatre, but that the possibility existed that he might kill again. The nightmare dreaded by public and Yard alike: another Ripper. True, this one hadn't yet ripped – but there was that element of 'nastiness', as Rose termed it, that could turn in any direction. He could see the newspapers now: the *Pall Mall Gazette* screaming: 'What are our police doing?' The *Thunderer* thundering on: 'Police admit possibility of Ripper's return.'

Archibald took the news surprisingly calmly, as one whom nothing could further surprise or horrify. Almost as if he'd been expecting it. Indeed he had been, for once concentrated on the possibility of disaster for the Galaxy, his intelligence was remarkable. He'd even courteously suggested Rose might care to partake of lunch in their restaurant before tackling his official duties. The restaurant, as it was a matinée day, was open, and if he took an early luncheon he could have time to see at least the stage staff before the performance.

Rose sat at a table next to the window overlooking Wellington Street. It was a pleasant restaurant, lighter than some. He liked a nice comfortable heavy red decor himself, with good solid chairs. This was more ornate than his taste allowed. All the same, it was very pleasant. He ran his eye down the menu. It would make a change from the offerings of Mrs Rose at any rate.

His eye fell on something familiar. He studied the menu more closely. Then he glanced once again at the decor. An evil look came over his face and there was an anticipatory gleam in his eye as he gave the order. '*Sole au chablis*,' he said firmly, pronouncing the final 's' with relish. 'And a nice cup of tea,' he added wickedly.

When the dish was presented to him ten minutes later, he inspected it carefully. Then he sent for the waiter. 'Take it back,' he said peremptorily.

'Sir?' The waiter was disbelieving.

'Take it back. Tell the cook that's not chablis in that sauce.'

A look of stark horror crossed the waiter's face. It was probably the first time anyone had questioned the authenticity of one of Auguste's dishes, certainly anyone who ordered a nice cup of tea to accompany it. How to face the maître was clearly the waiter's dilemma.

'Take it back. Give the cook my message. Head cook, mind.'

Retribution was swift. Auguste erupted from the kitchen door within twenty seconds, red-faced and quivering with hurt indignation, bearing the scorned *sole au chablis* in his own hands, clearly with the intention of forcing it down the unfortunate customer's throat.

Egbert Rose looked at him with a bland smile of satisfaction.

'Morning, Mr Didier.'

'Ah.' Auguste Didier's face changed instantly from a mask of rage to one of great pleasure, ruffled feathers subsiding as quickly as they had arisen. 'Inspector Rose. It is the joke then. And the cup of tea also?' he asked anxiously.

'Now that I wouldn't say no to – afterwards, of course,' Rose added hastily. 'Wouldn't ruin your dish by mixing the two. You taught me enough at Stockbery Towers not to do that, Mr Didier. I didn't expect to find you here.'

'Ah, Inspector, the Towers. It is delightful, your English countryside, but a maître must broaden his horizons and bestow his gifts widely. I came here two years ago – I left the Towers a year after we met.'

'Never the same afterwards, that it?'

'Ah, no, it was exactly the same. That is the trouble with your big houses.'

Rose laughed. 'And now you're running the Galaxy restaurant. Rather a comedown, isn't it?' he said without meaning to cause offence.

'Ah no, Inspector. I make this run-down restaurant into one of the best in London, then *the* best, and when it is the best, I will go elsewhere. Perhaps have my own restaurant. Perhaps not. It's too much of a tie. There are other things in life to be experienced before a maître can run a restaurant that is worthy of him.'

'Like a spot of detection, eh?'

'Perhaps, Inspector. We agreed once that our crafts are very similar, the cook – the maître, that is – and the detective. The assembling of ingredients, the marinating, the selecting of the main flavours, the mixing, et *voilà le dénouement*. But I am right, Inspector, that your visit here is not because of my art but because of yours, is that not so?'

'Yes, Mr Didier, that's quite right.' Rose cast a longing glance at his *sole au chablis*. Appalled, Auguste stepped aside. He had broken his own rule, never to allow an interruption when *le plat* has been served.

When Rose had finished, he sat back and wiped his lips, then summoned an anxiously hovering Auguste. 'Lost none of your touch, Didier,' he said kindly.

'It is the dolls then,' murmured Auguste. 'And poor Miss Walters.'

'And another,' said Rose sombrely. 'Edna Purvis, her name was. Found early this morning in Maypole Alley.'

Auguste's thought flew instantly to that girl who only yesterday had been boasting . . . 'A late night reveller from the Olympic?' asked Auguste slowly. 'It has not a high quality clientele, that place. If she took a short cut home –'

'With her hands bound across her chest?'

'Ah.' Auguste sighed. 'So the poor Galaxy . . .'

'Funny, that's what everyone says,' commented Rose. 'Not poor girl, but poor Galaxy.'

'It is how we feel about this place,' said Auguste simply. 'While we are in it, we think of it first. Outside, we have our lives, our loves, our thoughts, but here – it is *the* theatre, the Galaxy. And now we have lost one – two – of its members. Not good. There is something wrong in the theatre, Inspector. You must find what, and quickly, or more girls may follow Edna.' His thoughts were with Maisie.

'There already, are you?' grunted Rose. He took a sip of tea. 'Good,' he said. 'Not so good as that *verveine* stuff you call tea, though. I remember that.'

'It is not the restful *verveine* you will need, Inspector, but borage "I, borage, bring courage". That is the saying. I think we will all need courage in the Galaxy. And we must all unite against this murderer?' There was a note of query in his voice, which Rose picked up.

He thought for a moment, then nodded. 'I reckon so, Mr Didier. I could do with your help. Behind the scenes, information, that sort of thing. The ingredients, you'd term it. Within the same limits, of course.'

'*Entendu*,' said Auguste. 'Now there is one thing, Inspector, from what you have told me that I do not like. Christine Walters disappeared. *Bien*, someone does not like Christine Walters. Now, two months later, we have three nasty jokes played against Miss Lytton. *Bien* again, someone does not like Miss Lytton. It is difficult to understand but perhaps there are reasons. But today you tell me Edna Purvis is murdered. Not Miss Lytton, but Edna Purvis. And that tells me something quite different.'

'Yes, indeed, Mr Didier.'

'It tells me that it is possible this murderer did not kill Miss Purvis because he did not like her, but because perhaps, just perhaps, he does not like women.'

'Not necessarily, Mr Didier. I see your point, but it could be the same person trying his luck with one after another.'

'It comes to the same thing, Inspector, in the end,' said Auguste slowly. 'When there is a next – if there is a next – if you do not catch him – it could be any of the ladies here. It could be my friend Miss Maisie.'

'Ah.' The inspector fastened on this. 'You didn't marry Miss Ethel then?'

'Miss Ethel is married long since to the good Constable Perkins,' said Auguste with dignity. 'My heart is – ' he paused.

'Bespoke. To that Miss Tatiana,' said Rose, remembering the gossip.

'Princess,' said Auguste shortly. Tatiana was not a subject he wished to dwell on unless it were expedient.

'If it wasn't for the dolls, of course,' said Rose, reverting to the matter in hand after a swift glance at Auguste's face, 'it could be one of these stage door johnnies wanting to take the girl out, pressing his attentions, girl won't give, and there you are. But those dolls suggest it is someone inside the Galaxy. And someone with a grudge against Miss Lytton. We'll have to keep an eye on her.'

'You have met Mr Bates?'

'Bates?'

'Mr Obadiah Bates, the doorkeeper. The most important person in the Galaxy after Mr Archibald, and some would say without that qualification. He will know who goes in, who goes out. It is his proud boast that no one gets past his front door. And yet, Inspector, two nights ago one did.'

'The murder was last night.'

Auguste impatiently brushed this aside. 'I tell you this, Inspector, so you may see that the Galaxy is not impregnable. Two nights ago the Honourable Johnny Beauville was smuggled in inside a cake.'

'Oho, was he indeed?' murmured Rose. 'A cake, eh? Not one of yours I hope, Didier?'

'This will put the cock in the hen house all right,' said Maisie, summoned in the interval to the small office assigned to Rose, and surprised to find Auguste also present.

'Your language is colourful, *ma petite*, but correct as

69

always. For that reason I suggested to the good inspector here that you would be the person to tell first. You can tell the other ladies and gentlemen without spreading undue alarm.'

'It seems to me, Auguste, that undue alarm is just what we should be spreading,' replied Maisie vigorously. 'Two of us? They're all going to say, "Who's going to be next?" And so do I! And what about them dolls? Creepy. If I were Miss Lytton, I'd be out of 'ere faster than a costermonger on Lady Day. What if Edna were killed in mistake for her?'

Rose glanced at Auguste. 'It's possible, miss. But I want to know now everything you can tell me about Edna Purvis and Christine Walters. I'll be seeing everyone individually of course, but Mr Didier here seems to think I should begin with you.'

Maisie was in the exotic stage costume of a society lady at the home of Lord Harry. Under the paint standing out starkly on her face, she was very pale. The unreal world of the stage had been brought face to face with the grim realities of murder.

'I didn't know either of 'em really. They were show girls, you see. I'm chorus.'

'What's the difference?'

'We chorus girls have to look all right too, but our acting and singing are more important. The show girls don't have to sing, dance, act, nothing. They just come on, stand around, and look beautiful.' She sounded scornful. 'It's a new idea – Mr Archibald thought it up for Lady Bertha. So they were all new in September. At least, Edna was. But Christine was a failed chorus girl and, as she was very handsome and had a nice figure, Mr Archibald took pity on her and made her a show girl. They're chosen for their looks, not for our voices.'

Looking at Maisie's generously proportioned bosom, lovely face and flaming red hair, Rose thought the show girls must indeed be wonderful creatures to outshine her.

'The show girls tend to keep to themselves, so I don't know them too well. Both Christine and Edna had the reputation of hawking their mutton around, though.'

Auguste blinked. Rose, whose beat had been the Radcliffe Highway, understood her perfectly. 'Do you know who in particular they hawked it to, miss?'

'Edna, yes. She wanted everyone to know. She was that sort. But Christine kept herself to herself. But Edna . . . news travels fast within these walls. She was escorted when she first arrived by Johnny Beauville, the Honourable Johnny Beauville that is,' Maisie said, smiling faintly. Then she laughed. 'Being new, you see, she didn't know. She thought it was a catch, him being a Hon. Then she found out he was a joke around the dressing rooms – that he'd had a go at all of us and didn't care which one he took out, and she said goodbye quicker than a bishop in a brothel.'

Auguste winced. Rose laughed. 'And who came next, miss? And last night in particular.'

Maisie said slowly, 'She was shouting last night – wanted us all to know – that she was seeing Lord Summerfield. But that may just have been talk. He –'

'Was she indeed, miss?'

Maisie stared at Rose. 'You're thinking that Christine Walters was going to see him too. But it don't mean a thing,' she said robustly. 'What time was she –?'

Rose finished the question. 'Killed, miss? Between ten-thirty and eleven, we think. Before midnight anyway.'

Maisie was quiet, then asked awkwardly, 'Was she all right?' She could not bring herself to put it more directly. Rose understood what she meant.

'Yes, miss, not interfered with in any way. Strangled.'

Maisie let out her breath. 'Funny thing, that awful do yesterday at the performance over the song. It seemed like the greatest disaster in the world. And now –' Her voice trembled.

Auguste put his arm round her comfortingly. There were

matters other than the purely culinary in which he could be useful.

Florence's nerves were taut. The news of Edna's murder, broken to them all by Archibald after the performance with a plea for unity and every co-operation with our gallant police force, had served as an all too unpleasant reminder of her fright the evening before. Not that she could ever forget it. Herbert, of all people! She shivered. Clutching her, kissing her, then when she pushed him away, on his knees declaring his devotion, tears pouring down his face. Such passion, such emotion. Florence preferred her devotion kept at a distance. She recalled her panic at the realisation that she was alone in the theatre with him; the watchman must have been out of earshot or not there, or he would have answered her earlier cry. She had been alone with someone she hardly recognised as the usually quiet, gentle Herbert. He was a complete stranger, and it was all Thomas' fault . . .

And then there was the wretched song! They'd called it a compromise, but she knew Edward had won. No one loved her any more. She'd probably be the next one to be murdered. Perhaps they had intended to murder her all the time, not Edna. This frightening thought took hold of her. After all, they would assume the woman with Thomas to be *her*. And Thomas had been with Edna Purvis. Thomas . . . Suppose . . . her panic grew. Then there were those dolls. A joke, everyone had said comfortingly. They weren't saying that now though, they were murmuring in corners and discussing who could have got at those dolls, and why? They were even saying Props did it himself. As though he would! He was devoted to her. She knew that. Everyone knew that. But then she had thought Herbert devoted – till yesterday.

The door opened after a tentative tap and Thomas came in.

'You know you're not supposed to be here,' she said

stiffly, turning away. 'Mr Archibald asked you not to keep coming. It sets a bad example.'

'I think today's special, don't you?' he said firmly. 'Anyway, I asked Obadiah and he said it was all right. Look, Florence, about last night.'

She shrank from his touch, and her fears came flooding back. 'Where were you last night?' she whispered. 'Where were you? You didn't come home till one o'clock. You said you were going out with her.'

'What?' His mouth fell open. She couldn't be thinking that *he* had anything to do with it. 'Florence – I was just walking, just walking – I wanted to forget our quarrel, dearest. We'd had words and I couldn't bear it. So I went for a walk to get rid of my silly old bad mood. Your old moo-moo lost his temper. And you must have been mistaken, dearest. I was back *much* earlier than that.' He smiled at her pleasantly.

'You said you were going out to dinner with Edna Purvis,' she said obstinately. 'Didn't you?' Her voice began to rise in hysteria. 'And Christine, you liked her too, didn't you?' She began to sob, while he stared at her, his face curiously blank.

'Where were you last night, Percy?' Edward Hargreaves stared at his lover, white-faced.

Percy was shaken but did not intend to show it. Not after Edward had won over the music. They said it was a compromise but Edward had won really. Percy took that as a direct insult. Archibald meant to show him up in front of everyone. It was unfair.

So he said nothing. Just smiled. Let Edward wonder if he'd been escorting show girls again . . . He had to have *some* fun. And he couldn't go out with Edward.

'You didn't have anything to do with her, did you, Percy?' asked Edward in a low voice. 'You wouldn't. Not now, surely?'

'Do you see me as a strangler, Edward?' said Percy contemplatively, stroking one arm of his velvet smoking jacket lovingly. 'My dear, I am flattered. But think what it might do to my hands.'

'You've got the strength,' said Edward, looking at his pianist's broad hand, with the long, sensuous fingers.

Percy's eyes widened. Dear Edward *was* serious. He actually meant it. It was time he teased him a little more.

'They're pretty little things. Besides, a little variety in one's life –' he paused, 'if you see what I mean, is a good thing. Anyway I'm only thinking of your reputation. We mustn't let rumours start that we're –' he paused again, delicately, 'pansies.'

Edward Hargreaves winced. How could he? It made their love sound like one of those awful rendezvous places you heard about. Their love was above that. It was pure, as pure as his music.

'But when you take them out, what do you –' he swallowed, 'do you –?'

Percy raised his eyebrows. 'What a question, Edward. Surely you know that Mr Archibald's girls are ladies. You don't think I would dare tamper with their virtue.'

Edward relaxed.

'Unless invited,' Percy added, admiring his beautifully manicured hands.

Herbert sat brooding in his dressing room, alone save for his dresser scurrying to and fro preparing costume and adornments for the evening performance. But he did not interfere with Herbert's thoughts, which were not on the performance at all. Nor even on murder. He felt bruised, hurt, wounded as never before. Something like this always seemed to happen when he told a woman how he felt. Something seemed to go snap in his head and there he'd be, pouring out his devotion to a pair of unresponsive feet.

He'd never forget the sight of Florence, her lovely face

74

distorted into ugliness, that ridiculous button hook in her hand, threatening to strike him with it. Was he so unappealing to women? He looked in the mirror. He wasn't that unattractive, surely? Late thirties, slightly balding, but everyone told him he had a kind face, so he must have. So why wasn't he attractive to women? He'd heard of men who were attractive to other men. He couldn't understand that either. He wasn't attracted to them anyway. He liked women. He liked their softness, their prettiness, their daintiness, their shape, everything about them, the things they talked about. Yet somehow he couldn't get near them. Florence would never speak to him again, at least not alone, and after last night he wasn't sure he cared. Women weren't such angels beneath their smiling paint. Not such angels, after all.

Property man William Ferndale's devotion to Florence, however, remained unchanged. He was a simple man. He had come to work at the Galaxy because Florence Lytton adorned its stage. It did not matter to him that she was married, since he entertained no thoughts that she might ever notice him, let alone bestow feminine favours on him. It was enough for him that he was able to see her every day, was allowed with the tacit connivance of Mr Bates to deliver his posy of flowers, with no message, no label, before every performance. Sometimes, with great daring, he would place it in her hand himself as she entered the stage door. Sometimes she smiled at him. That was enough. Or it had been till the other day, when she had been in such distress at discovering the doll on the stage, and he had been able to bring her a glass of water. He still had the glass her lips had touched, and longed for such an emergency to occur again.

'You'll be Mr Ferndale,' said the gentleman.

Props looked up. He rarely heard his name in the theatre. It was usually just Props.

'Yes,' he said simply.

'Inspector Rose. Scotland Yard. A few questions if you don't mind.'

Mr Archibald had told him this inspector man would be coming round asking questions. Silently he led the way into his sanctum. Amazed, Rose walked through the Aladdin's cave. He recognised the throne that had held King Zeus in *By Jupiter* and was surprised to find it simply plaster and wood, a crude image, yet to the audience it had seemed a thing of magic when it descended from the clouds. Illusion, that's what it was. Like Mr Maskeleyne and Cooke's House of Magic at the Egyptian Hall. Murder was like magic. You couldn't see at first how it was done. But, at the end, there was usually a reason and a pattern behind it. And if you knew the tricks like he did, knew what to see and what not to see, there was always a solution.

'Do you see much of who's coming and going in the stage door?'

Props shook his head. 'Oh no,' he said. 'My door's facing wrong way, you see. That's Mr Bates' job.'

'How old are you, Mr Ferndale?'

Props looked as if even this question was too personal. 'About twenty-eight, me mum said. P'raps twenty-nine. Don't remember.'

'Like working here, do you?'

Props nodded cautiously.

'What time do you leave at night? Last night, for instance.'

'Lock up time.'

'When's that?'

'Depends. When Mr Bates knows the cast is out of the theatre, or nearly all. He decides when he locks the door and hands over to the night watch.'

'And when was that last night?'

'Mr Bates will tell you that,' said Props matter-of-factly, and turned away to complete what appeared to be the stocktaking of gentlemen's canes.

But Rose was not ready to go. 'Ever seen this before?' He produced from his bag a coil of rope. Props turned back reluctantly and took it without comment.

'Yes,' he then said carefully, and handed it back.

'Where, lad?' Rose said impatiently, cursing all literal-minded dolts.

'Over there.' Props nodded towards a corner. 'It's a bit off one of them special coils for the battens the gasman leaves here.' For the first time he displayed some animation. 'What is it?' he asked.

'Rope found tied round Miss Purvis, lad,' said Rose. 'Looks bad for you. Dolls, rope – all out of your room.'

He got an unexpected reaction.

'Dolls?' said Props slowly. 'Them dolls? Bound with my rope?'

Chapter Five

Auguste sighed in exasperation as the leason of eggs curdled for the second time. Some days even the simplest thing could go wrong, even in the hands of a maître chef. It was symptomatic of the theatre itself. Currents of unease ran through the corridors of the Galaxy – in and out of the dressing rooms, the green room, the carpenter's shop, the painting room – like sand in an egg timer. A heightened awareness of something not quite right.

The leason failed. He frowned. Two Galaxy Girls dead and Miss Lytton threatened, perhaps the next to fall victim to the strangler. A policeman could not guard her all the time. Against the sudden attack by a stranger, yes, but what of those nearest to her, her friends, her fellow actors – her husband?

He thought of Rose's parting words: 'I think we have to look for our joker inside the Galaxy. That rope came from Props' room – he don't deny that, Mr Didier. And those dolls, not much doubt they must be linked. But how – well, I reckon that's your job to find out. You know these people, Mr Didier.' Yes, he knew them. Or thought he did. Until yesterday he had thought them all straightforward, simple people, a mistake Rose never made. Today, he was not so sure.

'No one gets past my door,' said Obadiah firmly. That appeared to be the end of the matter as his eyes flickered from one to the other of them uncertainly. Yet it was a statement made more by rote than from total conviction. His wrinkled face peered at them, incongruously framed by two enormous baskets of fruits built into pyramids with flowers.

Egbert Rose grunted, eyeing the old man for a moment to get his measure. 'You think our villain's one of the Galaxy then,' he said finally. 'No doubt about it if you're right. There's the rope the poor lasses were bound with. Came from here.'

Torn between his own pride and his loyalty to the Galaxy, Obadiah was constrained to say reluctantly: 'I don't say it couldn't ever happen, mind, that someone sneaks past.'

'But a risk, eh?' supplied Rose for him jovially, now that he had won his point. 'But no one could blame you, Mr Bates, not with the watchful eye I've heard you keep. Heavy responsibility, isn't it? All these lovely ladies about.'

'Look after them like they was me own daughter, sir, God rest her soul,' replied Obadiah gravely.

'We must make sure there are no more murders, Obadiah. For the Galaxy's sake, as well as the girls',' said Auguste, noticing the look of anguish on Obadiah's face. He was taking it hard, as a personal failure. Cerberus had been circumvented.

'It's got to stop, Mr Didier. Oh, yes.'

'So no one gets past your door, Mr Bates.' Rose kept a grave face. 'Except for the Galaxy ladies and gentlemen. That it?'

'And the regulars, of course,' said Obadiah.

'Regulars?' enquired Rose resignedly.

'Oh yes, sir.' Obadiah was eager to please. 'There's Charles Baker Morning Coats. Then Archie Spenser – that's the sandwich boy – brings in the sandwiches for the young ladies and gentlemen. Mr Archibald, he always tries to get them to eat a proper meal, but they won't, not even when he paid for them to have cheap lunches at Romano's – before you came that was, Mr Didier,' he added hastily, seeing the thundercloud pass over Auguste's face. 'He's that generous, Mr Archibald' – his eyes moistened – 'that generous.'

'And Madame Swaebe's Dressmakers,' he continued. 'Miss Fortescue, hats and millinery. And, of course, Willie Clarkson the wigmaker. And there's the delivery men. Wood, paints, properties, that sort of thing.'

'In fact, half of London,' said Rose sourly.

'Oh no, sir, they wouldn't get past me. Except that Mr Beauville,' Obadiah added disgustedly. 'Came in here in a cake, he did.'

'When these – er – regulars have passed your door, with your say so of course, Mr Bates, do you see where they go?'

Obadiah's face brightened. He was on firmer ground here. 'I see what you're getting at, sir. There was that case of the young lad pretended he was from Blurtons Gents Shoes, but he weren't no bootboy – turned towards the dressing rooms he did. It was that Johnnie Perkins the Guv'nor sacked for making improper advances towards one of the young ladies. Very strict, Mr Archibald is.'

'So you would recognise most of the regulars.'

'Not the delivery men of course,' said Obadiah doubtfully. 'I wouldn't recognise them.'

'And could they go straight into the property room?'

'He runs a tight ship, does Props. No one crosses his threshold without his say so. You'll have to see him about that. Bright lad. Got the makings.'

'Anyone else cross your threshold, Mr Bates?'

'Mr Archibald's callers, sir. I looks after them. He gets a powerful lot. He looks to me to turn them away. "Bates", he says, "I can just make the two o'clock at Epsom" – fond of racing is the Guv'nor. No callers, mind. Soft heart, the Guv'nor. Knows it too. So he looks to me to sort out the deserving from the undeserving. We understand each other all right.'

'Any such callers on Monday, the day those dolls were attacked?'

Obadiah considered. 'There was that vicar thought he'd like to go on the stage. Guv'nor saw him. There was Miss Fawcett, poor lass, down on her luck. Used to be in the chorus but thought she could do better. Went off with this so-called lord. Didn't marry her, of course. Came to ask for her job back. Not two pennies to rub together. She learned the error of her ways. Pearls and coronets ain't everything.'

'Now about the ladies' gentlemen friends. Do they wait inside or outside the stage door? Those they're expecting.'

'I let them stand in the hallway if it's raining, sir. If I know them, that is.'

'Including, I assume, the Honourable Mr Beauville and Lord Summerfield?' Rose shot at him.

'Lord Summerfield? He waits in his carriage round by the Lyceum in Wellington Street. Thinks no one'll see him there. Just one of his little ways.'

'And Mr Beauville?'

'He comes in often, sir. Very chatty gentleman. When he's not in a cake, that is.'

'And what about Monday, the day of the dress rehearsal? Or Wednesday when Miss Purvis disappeared?'

'I don't recall, sir,' said Obadiah, with a note of finality in his voice. 'But he wouldn't have got out of this hallway. I'd have been after him.'

'You're a friend to these young ladies, Mr Bates. In their confidence, that sort of thing. Do they tell you who their escorts are?'

'I keeps my eye on 'em, sir,' said Obadiah. 'Part of my job. I warn 'em against the bad 'uns. The Galaxy looks after its young ladies.'

'Not well enough,' said Auguste unthinkingly until he saw Obadiah's reproachful eye on him and added hastily: 'It's not your fault, Obadiah. You are only responsible for the stage door, not what happens to the girls after that.'

'That's right, sir. I have to go home, sir.'

'When do you leave? When everyone has gone?'

'Not always, sir. Watch sometimes sees the last one or two out. Door's locked, of course, when I go.'

'Did you see Miss Purvis leave on Wednesday evening, the night she died?'

'Yes, sir. I delivered His Lordship's bouquet earlier, and Miss Purvis was that pleased about meeting him, but as I said, sir, His Lordship waits in Wellington Street. I understand he has a mother and likes to keep his life to himself, so I don't know whether Miss Purvis met him or not.'

Egbert Rose sighed. 'And how about Miss Walters? I understand His Lordship had arranged to see her too.'

'Very probably, sir. Some of the young ladies like titles very much.' He shook his head in disapproval. 'Keep to their own class, they should. Nothing but bad will come of it. That's what I say.'

'And you're sure Lord Summerfield did not come in to the theatre on either occasion?'

'Quite sure, sir, unless he was disguised as a chrysanthemum!' Obadiah laughed at his little joke.

'Would he or Mr Beauville know where Props' room is?'

'Most likely, sir. Always a lot of comings and goings to Props' room. You can't see the actual door from here, of course, it's round the corner, but there's no mistaking what it is.' He hesitated. 'Beg pardon, sir, but this rope – no doubt it came from Props' room? Not from the wings or flies?'

'No doubt at all,' said Rose. 'Why?'

'No reason, sir. No reason.' Obadiah was paying great attention to the bouquets and telegrams in front of him.

'Obadiah, if there is anything, *anything* that seems strange to you, – just a little fact, perhaps, that seems unimportant – you must tell us. After all, the whole future of the Galaxy is at stake perhaps,' Auguste added as the surest way to impress Obadiah.

83

Obadiah raised his head and looked Auguste straight in the eye guilelessly. 'There's nothing, sir, nothing. I've told you everything.'

'Interesting,' said Rose.

'Ah, yes,' said Auguste putting the finishing touches to a Mephistophelean sauce. 'You understand, the final addition of the bay leaf –'

'Lord Summerfield and those two girls,' said Rose firmly.

'You are right, Inspector. I remember Maître Escoffier saying, "Seek the obvious solution, the simplest course". And the simplest course is Milord Summerfield.'

'But the dolls, Mr Didier, don't forget the dolls. He'd have to be popping in and out all day. Unless they are just a nasty coincidence, which don't seem at all likely to me.'

'Unless –' Auguste broke off and stared thoughtfully at the plate of raw liver in front of him.

'That's a nice looking colour,' said Rose, momentarily diverted.

'*Mais oui*, not many people like the sight of raw meat but to a chef it is poetry. What ballads can be composed from it. What songs –'

'Not that. The bottle. I like a nice drop of rosé.'

Auguste stared at him, then with a smile said: 'Then you'll take a glass, Inspector.' He whipped down a glass from the shelf and filled it. 'Côtes de Provence, Inspector. From my home village.'

'And very nice too. I just like a sip –'

A sip was all he took. He coughed and spluttered as the harsh liquid found its way down his throat.

'What in the name of thunder is that?' he said reproachfully. 'None of your deadliest poisons known to man, I hope?'

'Forgive me, Inspector. No, it is simply raspberry vinegar for the marinade *pour la foie de veau*. My own recipe. It will do no harm. Indeed, much good if you have a cough.'

'I haven't, or rather I didn't,' Rose grunted, still spluttering. 'French concoctions!'

'No, Inspector, an old English remedy. Your own Mrs Beeton recommends it. A lady of whom I greatly disapprove in most matters – but with this I concur. But enough of cooking – you see how this helps our case? You believed it was Côtes de Provence because you saw what looked like a rosé wine and because I told you it was Côtes de Provence. Now Obadiah believes these delivery men are delivery men because he is told so, and because they look like delivery men. They have the uniform. But suppose it is not a delivery man. Suppose it is Lord Summerfield.'

Rose was unforgiving. 'Here we go again, Mr Didier. You and your complicated ideas. Just you look at the commonsense side of it. It ain't just a matter of stealing into the theatre past Obadiah. Our villain's got to find his way into Props' room when it's unoccupied, creep around the theatre behind the scenes, wander all over the stage.'

'Once past Cerberus at the stage door,' said Auguste, 'it is not difficult. This theatre is an ant heap teeming with people. One ant is much like another. They are all so busy keeping their own place in the line they will never check anyone else, provided he seems to know where he is and what he is doing. Come, I will show you.'

He led the way to his own special larder where none but he was allowed and which was therefore concealed from the gaze of the curious. Once inside he swung open a false set of shelves to reveal the secret door.

'I show you this, Inspector Rose,' he said grandly, 'because I know you will not take advantage of it. It is possible but unlikely that someone other than myself and Mr Archibald knows of the existence of this door and could perhaps have used it. But I, I am a greater Cerberus than Obadiah. No one comes through my kitchen without my knowing it.'

'Contravening the Licensing Act, 1872. Have to remember that, Mr Didier,' said Rose, coughing slightly. 'Raspberry vinegar.'

Auguste cast him a suddenly nervous glance and decided to proceed down the steps and along the corridor running under the foyer to the other side of the theatre. It brought them past Props' room and the corridor to the stage door, and through a door into the wings. 'Now, Inspector, I will show you how easy it is to be one of these ants. Take off your hat, and your overcoat, and roll up your sleeves. *Voilà*! You are a workman with business to do in this building.'

It took a moment to accustom themselves to the dimly lit wing space, and in that time Rose managed to trip twice over the paraphernalia of theatre; the prosaic facts behind the magic. Auguste took his arm and led the way on to the Galaxy stage lit by a solitary gas tee light. Rose stood as one bemused, gazing over the darkened footlights into the cavernous auditorium.

'Fancy,' he said at last in an awed voice. 'You're standing where that enormous cloud came down in *By Jupiter* and roughly where Bluebeard's Castle stood. Yet it's quite small when you look round. Where does all that scenery go?'

Auguste pointed up, way up, to the roof fifty feet above them. 'Up Inspector, or down to the cellars.'

'How do they get it down?'

'I will show you, Inspector.' Down on the mezzanine floor a dozen or more cellarmen were moving around, busily oiling machinery, greasing traps, hoisting ropes. It was a vast underground factory of industry. No one took any notice of them.

'This is the star trap,' whispered Auguste, pointing to a star shape in the floor above their heads, and the machinery underneath it. 'For the demon king – or the villain. We don't use it now. But in the burlesques it was invaluable. The down traps also. And others.'

'Could someone hide down here, and get up on stage when all was quiet?'

'It is possible, yes,' said Auguste, considering. 'But you would have to know a lot about the cellar and how to remove the rebates to clamber on to the stage. And then you could not shut it behind you. In theory it is possible. The stage is one mass of moving parts. Most of these boards remove to make sloats for raising scenery. And down traps. We even have a grave trap. Our villain could shoot up like the demon king through the star trap, or he could go up to the flies, strap himself to a travelling iron and fly down.'

Rose regarded Auguste severely. 'You're being fanciful, Mr Didier. At my expense. I'll have you know we regard contravening the Licensing Act most severely at the Yard.'

'Ah, but I do not entirely jest,' said Auguste, laughing. 'You will see. You have a head for heights?'

Up at the first level of flies, Rose stepped gingerly between ropes, windlasses for the curtains, borders and gas pipes, trying not to look below him. He was none too easy about heights if truth be told.

'You see, Inspector, travelling irons.' Auguste waved his arm towards the narrow bridge linking the flies of both sides of the stage. 'Now, how easy to hide up here and float down like a god. The Nemesis of the Yard – the *deus ex machina*.'

Rose grunted. He could not see Summerfield up here. But Auguste was inexorable. The flies were nothing to the gridiron floor which formed a roof to the stage. Up, up and still up until they were nearly fifty feet above the stage. Up here another small army of ants beavered away.

'Lie down on the floor, Inspector. Look through the cracks.' He could see the small twinkling glitter of the tee lights, far far below, and between them a chandelier ready to be dropped for the scene in Lord Harry's home. It was hot here already. What must it be like with all the gas lights lit for the performance? Rose's respect for the performers' cool poise grew.

Off the far side of the grid a ladder led down to another room, this one full of bespattered men, furiously painting a huge canvas in a frame.

'Reminds me of that scene in Mr Carroll's book,' grunted Rose. He was a zealous father where reading was concerned. 'Painting the roses before the Queen found out.' Indeed, such was their concentration the painters might well have had their heads at stake.

'This is small beer, Inspector, compared with the world of the pantomime. I had a *petite amie* in the chorus at Drury Lane. Ah, the effects there! It is magic, fairyland. But how many men slave to get that effect? The transformation scene is unforgettable there, yet many girls have burnt to death in the process. It is like our case here, Inspector Rose. The glitter of the Strand, the romance of the Galaxy. But behind the Strand lie the old rookeries, and after the curtain has fallen at the Galaxy two girls are strangled.'

'But all the same,' said Rose. 'I don't see Milord Summerfield gallivanting around up here just to strangle a few dolls. It would have to be a man of the theatre. Used to it,' he said, wiping the sweat off his face with the white handkerchief impeccably ironed by Mrs Rose. 'Yes, a man of the theatre.'

Lord Summerfield clearly did not enjoy his obvious role of suspect-in-chief in a murder case. Lady Summerfield relished it even less. She regarded the purlieus of Scotland Yard as she did her own outhouses – as evils necessary for the continuance of society. As she was conducted with her son into the higgledy-piggledy clutter of Rose's office, she looked around as if she had stepped for one misguided moment beyond her own green baize door and found herself in an alien and unwelcome world.

'Good morning, Inspector,' murmured Lord Summerfield in a desperate attempt at patrician graciousness, which failed dismally.

'Sit down, My Lord.'

He blinked at the somewhat peremptory tone. Rose was carefully prepared for his lordship this time. Lady Summerfield had already seated herself in the chair of honour, if the shabby leather chair which faced Rose's desk could lay claim to such a name.

'Got bad news for you, sir. Miss Purvis was found dead yesterday. Circumstances were very like Miss Walters'.'

Lord Summerfield's face blanched to the colour of his own embossed writing paper.

His mother spoke for him. 'Why should this concern us, Inspector?'

'Not you, ma'am. Lord Summerfield. Anything you'd like to tell us, sir?'

Lord Summerfield glanced at his mother. 'No,' he ventured.

'Try again, sir. We understand you'd arranged to meet the young lady the night she died.'

'No.' A definite squawk this time.

'Now that you have your answer, Inspector, we shall depart,' Her Ladyship stated, rising to her feet, eight yards of purple alpaca falling submissively into place behind her.

'Not yet, ma'am. You can leave if you wish, but not Lord Summerfield. Someone I want him to meet.' He rang a bell on his desk.

Maisie Wilson was a bright light in that small office, bringing with her a sense of exuberant life as she swept in on a waft of Floris perfume and rose soap. A bright green dress battled with flaming red hair to bring a rare exoticism to the Factory. Auguste, in her wake, was almost overlooked.

'Lady Summerfield, I'd like you to meet Miss Wilson.'

Her Ladyship stared through her lorgnette, making no attempt to return Maisie's bow.

'Who,' she demanded indignantly of the world at large, 'is this young person?'

Auguste was about to intervene when Maisie saved him the trouble.

'This young person,' she said cordially, 'is Miss Maisie Wilson, in the chorus at the Galaxy. What are you playing? The Empire?'

Auguste snorted and hastily turned it into a cough. Lord Summerfield looked frightened. Lady Summerfield regarded Maisie once more through her lorgnette and when this failed to achieve the desired result, compressed her lips and regarded Inspector Rose sternly.

'And this, Lady Summerfield,' that gentleman said, 'is Maître Didier.'

'Ah, a lawyer,' said Lady Summerfield, gratified that the proceedings were at least graced by one acceptable human being.

'No, a cook,' said Rose, enjoying himself immensely.

Lady Summerfield paled, then rallied. 'Somewhat unorthodox, Inspector. We do not meet cooks.'

'So's murder unorthodox, milady,' murmured Auguste.

What dull lives these English lived – how much in life they were missing, ignoring the riches that the gastronomic art could bestow. For as they treated the practitioner, so they regarded his product. Now in France . . .

'Tell Lord Summerfield what you told me yesterday, miss. He don't seem to remember,' said Rose, surveying his little group with glee. That's right. Make them uneasy and they'll come clean. Just like that bit-faker down the Nichol. That heaving cesspit of crime in the East End had once been Rose's territory, after which few places held terrors for him.

'About Edna and him, you mean?'

Lord Summerfield went white.

'It's true, isn't it?' she appealed. 'Why, she was shouting all over the place that night about meeting you. But you've got nothing to worry about. Unless you killed her,' she added encouragingly.

Lady Summerfield slowly turned her head towards her son, but for once his mother was not his main concern. It was the inspector he must convince.

'She didn't come,' Summerfield said desperately. 'She didn't come. You must believe me.'

'Must I? So now you've remembered, you tell me what happened.'

'I took the carriage to Wellington Street, as I always did,' he said miserably, ignoring the swelling of Her Ladyship's bosom. 'But she didn't come.'

'Didn't you go round to the stage door to find out if she'd left?'

'No, I thought she must have left with someone else. They sometimes do, you know,' he added disarmingly.

'Anyone see you in Wellington Street?'

'Not that I am aware of. I –'

'Why do you bother to do it?' asked Maisie indignantly. 'Why not come to the stage door like everyone else? Not ashamed of being seen with us, are you?'

'My son clearly realised what was due to his position as head of the house of Summerfield,' said a glacial voice.

'Like the Galaxy ladies, do you, sir?' said Rose, ignoring this offering.

'I – er – have the greatest respect for them, Inspector,' said Summerfield, mustering what dignity he could.

'I'm sure, sir. See all the Galaxy shows, sir? Just to show respect?'

'Every one.'

'Like Miss Lytton, do you?' Rose shot out.

Summerfield flushed red, clearly annoyed. 'Ah, I have the greatest respect for –'

'Ever taken her out – just to show respect, of course.'

Lord Summerfield muttered, 'She is a married lady, Inspector.'

'But you'd like to get friendly with her?'

'Miss Lytton – Miss Lytton is' – he had some difficulty

in framing his words – 'an angel, Inspector, an angel,' he said fervently, his tongue suddenly unexpectedly loosened. 'A light in this dull world. She is far, far above me – I am unworthy – I would not presume - I have the utmost reverence for – She is all that is most lovely in woman, a pearl among swine.'

He stopped, now conscious that his audience was looking at him in amazement.

'You like Miss Lytton then,' said Rose stolidly.

Poor old sod, thought Maisie to herself. Fancy thinking women are like that!

Lord Charing and his wife flanked the Honourable Johnny Beauville like Nelson's guardian lions. Not that they regarded Johnny as a saviour of the nation's honour. They were clearly there to ensure that the family honour was not impugned.

Johnny did not look grateful for this attention. Lord Charing, a serious-minded gentleman as befitted the bearer of the family title, was in his mid-thirties, a more sober version of the Honourable Johnny himself, with rounded face, sideburns, and a carefully nurtured moustache. His wife, of similar age, was a handsome statuesque woman. Her blond hair was swept up Grecian-style and her brown walking dress was severe – as was her expression.

Reminds me of someone. Ruby James at the Albion? thought Rose. But Lady Charing did not behave like Ruby James.

'We,' Lady Charing said severely, 'do not approve.' It was not clear whether she was using the royal we or whether she spoke for all Beauvilles, past and present.

'Of what, ma'am?' enquired Rose blandly.

'Sin.'

There Rose was essentially in agreement with her, but the relevance of the statement at this moment was not clear to him.

'The occupation of the devil, theatre,' she graciously explained.

'Yet I understand you were with Mr Beauville here at the first night of *Lady Bertha's Betrothal*, and again at *Miss Penelope's Proposal*. Keeping an eye on the devil, eh?'

She frowned.

Her husband intervened hastily. 'My wife feels that my brother should not attend these places alone, you understand.'

'And you stayed with him, I understand, until he appeared somewhat unexpectedly in a cake backstage. You weren't with him then, ma'am?'

'I seldom appear in cakes, Inspector,' replied her ladyship frostily.

Johnny shuffled uneasily.

'And did you see your brother-in-law on Wednesday evening, too?'

'My brother-in-law was at his club that evening. May I ask why this sudden interest in his movements?'

Johnny seemed about to say something, but was quelled by one look from his sister-in-law.

'Miss Edna Purvis has been found dead,' said Rose.

Johnny looked blank. 'Dead? That long girl? Thin? Handsome filly. Talked like a –'

'It's come to my attention you were acquainted with the young lady.'

'Perhaps,' said Johnny cautiously.

'You don't know?'

'Can't remember 'em all,' he said apologetically.

'And you were a friend of Miss Walters too.'

'Yes, but I say – you know –' Dimly it dawned on the Honourable Johnny that this was more than a friendly chat. 'I hadn't seen the little stunner for a week or more. She – Edna, that is – gave me the old boot. Had her eye on better things. They all do,' he added sadly.

'So you admit you were friends with them both?'

'Love all the little darlings,' he squeaked. 'Miss Lepin – little French stunner; Daisy Applechurch; then there's Ethel Love, and Gladys Milling – that's the one that kicks her legs up.' He laughed nervously till he saw his sister-in-law's eye on him.

'And what about Miss Lytton?'

'Florrie?' Johnny beamed. 'Lovely little girl. Pity she's married. Mind you, I wouldn't do them any harm. Safe as houses. But she wouldn't look at me. You'd think she'd like a change after acting with that dull old stick all the evening. She likes all the fuss, but she doesn't like it when a chap tries to get close.' His face clouded, and he seemed to have forgotten his audience as he whispered, 'No, she don't like it at all.'

Chapter Six

'Didier, where are you, dammit?'

Archibald's roar could be heard even from Auguste's kitchen. He interpreted the roar correctly as being one of the ilk that brooked no denial. Delaying merely to add the shredded truffles to the Francatelli's most interesting *salade à la Rachel* he hurried once more to Archibald's office – there was no doubt as to the direction of the shout, nor of the offender. Florence Lytton was once more having hysterics.

'Ah, Didier, Miss Lytton – under the weather – get one of your drinks – stop her –' The big man looked helplessly and beseechingly at Auguste.

'Oui, monsieur. But – might I suggest – her husband?'

It was the wrong suggestion; it merely brought forth a new wave of hysterics.

Auguste vanished, wondering where he could suddenly produce an infusion of valerian – it was not a product in which the market at Covent Garden specialised. He produced the next best thing.

Florence sipped gratefully at the soothing concoction Auguste held to her lips. The tears began to flow less rapidly, the red to subside from her cheeks, the hiccups to grow less raucous.

'Ah, that's better, my dear, isn't it?' said Archibald, rubbing his hands together heartily and a trifle briskly. 'Nothing to beat Didier's special brews, eh?'

Nothing indeed, thought Auguste, laughing to himself.

Nothing to beat Brillat-Savarin's simple panacea of sugar and water for such emergencies.

'Thank you, Mr Didier.' Florence smiled gratefully at Didier, her poise restored, and her image of lovable leading lady redonned. 'It's just so - well - *horrid* knowing that someone is trying to kill you.'

'Kill you, madame?' said Auguste slowly. 'You think that?'

'Well, of course,' said Florence indignantly, determined to maintain her centre stage position. 'Those horrid dolls - it's obvious. For some reason,' she said hesitantly, 'Edna Purvis was killed in mistake for me.'

'But Florence, my dear, who would want to kill you?' asked Robert Archibald, bewildered. 'Now the girls have admirers, we all know that, but here you are, happily married -'

Auguste Didier noticed the tightening of Florence's fingers, and wondered.

'There are others,' said Florence mysteriously, dabbing at the corner of her eye with an exquisite Brussels lace handkerchief.

'Who are these others?' asked Auguste urgently. 'You must tell us, and then make it known that you have told us. And then - pouf! There is no reason to kill you because everybody will know.'

'Mr Hargreaves doesn't like me,' Florence blurted out with no hesitation at all.

'Because of a song? Oh, come, my dear, you took it too seriously.'

'No, not because of that,' said Florence slowly. Her big moment had come. She had always wanted to play in tragedy. 'It's because -' she drew a deep breath, '*I know.*'

'Know what?' said Archibald, lost.

'About him and Percy.'

'Him and Percy?'

'They *live* together.' She waited for her effect.

'Do they?' said Archibald without much interest. 'Very good of Hargreaves to give a home to the lad. Look after him.'

'No.' Florence grew pink, while Auguste watched with more interest than shock. 'They – they *live* together – as if they – well – as if they were married.'

Archibald slowly registered the fact that Edward Hargreaves and Percy Brian were homosexual lovers. In ordinary times he might have exploded into wrath. But these were not ordinary times. It seemed a small issue besides murder. Anything that did not immediately threaten the Galaxy paled into insignificance so Florence was deprived of her effect. Robert Archibald, sensing her annoyance but not understanding its reason, declared placatingly that he would 'have a word with them'.

Auguste returned to the restaurant, a puzzled man. It was clear to him, and he therefore assumed it must be clear to all those who worked within its portals, that someone closely connected with the Galaxy was a double murderer, and perhaps the worst kind of multiple murderer – one who kills to a pattern. Those arms were crossed for a reason. Were both Christine Walters and Edna Purvis killed because they were mistaken for Florence, or because they were substitutes for her – much as in the days of ritual killing of kings, they retained the right to nominate a substitute? An interesting idea that. He thought about it as he raised the crust of a game pie.

And yet to everyone else it was almost as though murder were not the central issue at the Galaxy. It was like a nightmare where instead of seeing the danger in front of them, they were preoccupied with other matters – the song, the discovery of Edward and Percy's secret, the dolls, and Herbert. He too was noticeably preoccupied, and so was Thomas. Why? Auguste frowned. Discipline must take over. He was a maître chef. He needed order, reason.

What does a chef do? He looks at the receipt, assembles

the ingredients, prepares his *batterie de cuisine*. This was the important part. The technique was the preparation, his art the essential that came later. Who was it who said that genius is an infinite capacity for taking pains? As the good Mrs Acton had said: 'Only the genius cook could afford to ignore the precise instructions of a recipe'.

Auguste gathered together the snipe, the onions, the parsley, the nutmeg (as he grated he noted that unauthorised use had been made of this precious spice), salt, white pepper, the lemon, the sherry and the broth, and bread. One *entrée* was ready for the evening. Were the dolls the *entrée,* the murders the *plat*, the crossed hands the *flancs*? He reproached himself for thinking so frivolously then decided it was not frivolous. It was a method of discipline. He concentrated again on the receipt. The good Alexis Soyer – Auguste did not always approve of his methods. In this, for example, he preferred a little less sherry, a little more lemon. Once his hands were moving, his brain too began to react. It was necessary for him to take control. Too much had been happening all round him at the Galaxy without his directing events. A maître should control. These murders had to be solved – not only for the victims' sake but for the survival of the Galaxy. The crowds were flooding in now because of the notoriety, but any more incidents and they might quickly turn. He had seen it happen before. Inspector Rose was good, very good, but he, Auguste, was in a position to discover things that Rose could not.

'A leg of mutton,' he said triumphantly.

'Who are you calling a leg of mutton?' Maisie bounced indignantly into the kitchen, furs surrounding her laughing face.

'Not you, *ma mie*. I was just thinking to myself that these murders are like a leg of mutton *à la provençale*, garnished with mushrooms *au gratin*, stuffed with a complicated forcemeat, yet when you take away these accoutrements, *voilà*, a leg of mutton. What we must seek, *ma pigeonne*, is the leg of mutton in this case! And I, maître detective *extraordinaire*, will discover it!' In his enthusiasm, forgetting the salamander in his hand, he seized her in his arms and waltzed her round the kitchen.

'Tell you what, Auguste,' she said when they stopped, breathless, 'if you don't stop being so modest we'll all forget you're a master chef.'

'No,' he said simply, twinkling at her, 'that will not happen. I will not forget.'

'Anyway, what I've decided we need is not a master chef, but a maîtresse. I was watching old Egbert' – Auguste laughed to himself – 'he's good but he hasn't got the right touch with the mashers of this world. Now I got the measure of the Beauvilles of this world long ago. And I've always fancied myself as Lady Molly of Scotland Yard. I'm going on the hunt.'

'No,' said Auguste in alarm. 'No. This murderer has a penchant for Galaxy girls, even if only as a substitute for Miss Lytton. No, you must not do it.'

'I'm not daft,' she said lightly. 'Anyway, you can't stop me. If I want to accept a dinner engagement, I'll make sure it's Romano's or somewhere else public. You don't catch me walking through an old rookery.'

'But it might not be Summerfield or Beauville. It could be Hargreaves or Percy or any of the other male principals or chorus. Or stage-hands. Props even.'

'Or maybe Obadiah?'

'He'd never leave his door long enough, not even for murder.'

'Now didn't you tell me, Auguste, that a good cook never overlooks anything?'

'You are so right, *ma mie*. We must look for the leg of mutton underneath the garnish.'

'Now is Miss Lytton the leg of mutton? The dolls were intended for her, no doubt of that.'

'So do you think she was the intended victim for the murder. Someone clearly hates her.'

'Very careless of the murderer to kill two other women in mistake for Florence,' commented Maisie scathingly.

Auguste cast her a look. Delightful though Maisie was she did not understand the power of pure logic. He was not sure he approved of the New Woman, he decided, then dismissed this unworthy thought.

'Yes, indeed. But the dolls,' he said hastily, seeing a way round this problem. 'The person who arranged those wished to upset her, to play a trick on her. And then' – Auguste's detective instincts were fully warmed up now – 'the murderer follows his example, and binds the arms of his victims across the chest to make it look like part of the same thing.'

'Bravo, *mon maître*,' said Maisie, clapping her hands. 'Only Christine was killed two months ago.'

'True, *ma mie*,' said Auguste, crestfallen. 'But,' brightening, 'suppose the leg of mutton is the *girls*. The murderer wishes to kill Miss Walters and Miss Purvis, and uses the dolls as a red herring.'

'Why?' said Maisie practically.

'To make it look more complicated than it is,' said Auguste. 'Some cooks thrive on this. There is Francatelli, who in his recipe for *boudin à la reine* –'

'Auguste,' said Maisie, dangerously quiet.

'As I said, like the art of theatre, it is all appearance.'

'It doesn't seem rational to me. Perhaps you're right and Miss Lytton *is* at the heart of the mystery.'

'And where the hen pheasant is we must look for the cock, *hein*? Monsieur Manley who is so in love with his wife. Yet perhaps he is not quite so in love?'

'That's what they're beginning to say,' said Maisie slowly, 'in the dressing room. A bunch of red roses arrived for Miss Purvis on the first night. The handwriting looked familiar, and the way she was looking at Florence! Like a

Band of Hoper with a new convert. *And* he would have more opportunity to put the dolls in Florence's dressing room than anyone else.'

'What about Herbert?'

'I've never seen him there. Florence wouldn't like that. Besides, he is hardly likely to want to upset Florence. He wouldn't have a motive, would he? You know how devoted he is to her.'

'*Ma fleur*, I always hear how devoted people are to Miss Lytton – her husband, Obadiah, Mr Archibald, Props, Herbert – and yet someone dislikes her. Dislikes her very much indeed. Besides, look what happened to the song. Herbert showed no sign of devotion to Florence then. He's a strange man.'

'And this is a strange crime,' said Maisie thoughtfully. 'All this crossed arms business. It means something, I'm sure.'

'What?'

'A sort of farewell, perhaps?' suggested Maisie. 'I mean, crossed arms. Like those brasses in churches.'

'And paintings of angels, too.'

'Yet if he thought they were angels, why murder them?' asked Maisie practically.

'I don't know, my love, I don't know.'

The performance was somewhat muted that evening; the show girls conscious of the one that wasn't there, the artistic groupings that had to be carefully redone to make up for the absentee until a replacement could be found. But expectation on the other side of the footlights was all the keener. The Galaxy, its girls, and murder too! Perhaps by one of the people on the stage. It was a heady mixture. Pure escape.

The murder seemed real enough, however, to Inspector Rose, poring over files of interviews, reading and re-reading the Ripper files in case something should give a clue, an idea as to procedure, the mistakes to avoid. One mistake had already been avoided. No mention had been made in the newspapers of the ritualistic nature of the crossed hands. The strangling was bad enough, giving rise to fears of another wave of garrotters. Yet Edna Purvis had not been robbed. Her silver purse had been found by her side. Would the murderer stop at crossed hands? Or, if unstopped, would he progress further, like the Ripper? Would Florence Lytton be another Mary Kelly? Not if Rose could help it. Ignoring Twitch's clear signs that enough was enough for the day, he began to read the files again.

Enviously, Gabrielle watched Maisie drop the heavy yellow silk dress over her head.

'It must be someone special, yes? Not Auguste?' Had she been less ambitious, Gabrielle would have been a keen rival for Auguste's favours. Being French herself, she saw herself as the natural choice of any Frenchman.

Maisie smoothed the folds, pulling the fullness to the back over the heavy petticoat, arranging the lace sleeves beneath which her rounded arms emerged, enticing and lovely, and above which her shoulders were a match for any of the show girls; she was well aware that this dress complemented her auburn hair to perfection.

She took a deep breath. 'Summerfield,' she said carelessly.

There was a sharp intake of breath round the room. What on Wednesday would have made her the envy of the room was now clearly seen as madness, to all perhaps save Gabrielle.

'What if he does to you what he did to Christine and Edna?' breathed one. 'They both went to dine with him. Bluebeard! I wonder the police ain't arrested him already. Aren't you scared, Maisie?'

'No,' she lied, for there was no doubt she was not quite so brave about it as she had pretended to Auguste, who had in any case forbidden her to go, happily confident that as her lover his words would be obeyed.

'We're going to a restaurant, not for a long walk.'

'It's that meek and mild type you have to watch,' declared a worldly wise eighteen-year-old as Maisie donned her wrap, picked up her dorothy bag, crammed her hat a little harder than she meant to on top of her piled up hair with the French hat pin Auguste had given her, and sallied forth. Quite what she hoped to find out she had not yet asked herself, but had she analysed it she would have said that these crimes had to be stopped at once and one way was to eliminate the possibilities. The Galaxy was important to her, and Robert Archibald even more so. He had discovered her in the Britannia at Hoxton, brought her back to the Galaxy and transformed her life. There was no way she was going to let him suffer.

' 'Night, Obadiah!'

She had insisted that Summerfield meet her not round the corner but in the entrance hall. No skulking round the back for her. He seemed nervous. Very nervous. It was the first time his preference for Galaxy girls had been laid open to public inspection. Yet with the obstinacy bred into him by centuries of aristocratic assumption of superiority, it did not even occur to him to change his habits for the sake of Scotland Yard. Though Mama might be a different matter . . .

The Strand was twinkling with lights, London was waking up ready for the evening now that the theatres had emptied. The bourgeoisie was surging to Charing Cross to catch homeward trains, but London's beau monde was just starting its evening. Across the road Romano's was brightly lit, the cupids over its canopy looking knowingly down as carriages drew up, one after another. The Galaxy restaurant was under the eye of an Auguste blissfully oblivious to the whereabouts of his beloved. Across the road at the Savoy, another Auguste, Escoffier, slaved in similar fashion in happy partnership with César Ritz. But the Savoy was not to be Maisie's destination.

Kettners, with its discreet private rooms yet utter respectability, was his lordship's choice.

She had a momentary qualm as Summerfield escorted her up the staircase into one of the many private rooms. It was all very well the Prince of Wales entertaining Lillie Langtry here, she thought to herself, but despite the rumours about his son having been the Ripper no one could accuse the future king of England of being a possible strangler. She gulped, and tried to look a great deal more confident than she felt.

The table was set for two, and she had few illusions that after the coffee had been served, and doubtless a large liqueur, the service would be as noticeable by its absence as by its assiduousness during the meal. She patted her hair and was reassured to find the hatpin safely in position. With a weapon within reach, she felt more secure, and turned a beaming smile on her escort.

'Have you noticed,' she said, 'all the best cooks are called Auguste? Auguste Escoffier, Auguste Kettner – and Auguste Didier.'

Summerfield blinked. He had not given the matter much thought. He had been thinking, in fact, how soon he could decrease the distance between himself and this desirable creature.

'Who's Auguste Didier?'

'The cook you met at Scotland Yard.'

'I don't see why they need a cook at Scotland Yard,' said Summerfield, with some disdain.

'He's a detective as well as a cook,' said Maisie. 'And he's at the Galaxy – he keeps an eye on things there for Inspector Rose. I think,' she said tremulously, lying with practised ease, 'he suspects *me*.'

'Of being a strangler? My dear young lady, you exaggerate, surely.'

'Of that trick with the dolls – and perhaps of luring the girls into the murderer's trap. Oh, Lord Summerfield, you *know* what it's like to be suspected, don't you?'

'Yes,' said His Lordship bitterly.

'And it would be such a *help* to me to talk about it with you. To have a *gentleman's* advice.'

Lord Summerfield's ego burst forth from the shelf where it had lain neglected for so long, and leapt to meet this unaccustomed challenge with as much eagerness as Auguste would greet a long-buried truffle of Perigord.

As the plovers' eggs were arriving in the private room at Kettners, Auguste was in the midst of serving evening dinner at the restaurant, an experience that never failed to challenge, exalt, uplift him. Whether for solidarity or out of sheer bravado, an unusual number of the cast had chosen to eat in, thus filling the restaurant. This was fortunate, for while murder had brought a larger audience even than usual to the Galaxy theatre that Friday evening it had deprived the restaurant of anything like its normal clientèle.

'Perhaps they think, Mr Didier, that a murderer that strangles can also poison,' remarked Herbert. He was dining on his own, having feigned not to see when Thomas had held out a beckoning finger for Herbert to join him and Florence. Anything to avoid a tête-à-tête with Florence, Thomas had been thinking, yet short of sitting at another table there was little he could do but endure his bravely smiling wife.

Herbert's grin at Auguste's pained reaction lit up his face. 'Not that you would be serving poison, Mr Didier, but some folks have odd ideas.'

'Miss Lytton does not seem to regard me as a poisoner. She looks happier, *la petite*.' And so she should, he thought to himself. That is my best soufflé of orange-flower.

Herbert continued to savour the raspberry charlotte on

his plate as though it were the most important thing in the world. This to Auguste seemed perfectly natural, but he acknowledged it was not natural for Herbert to ignore a reference to Florence. 'But then,' he continued exploratorially, 'she has little reason to fear. She has no enemies. Everybody loves –'

Herbert put down the spoon and looked squarely at Auguste. 'There isn't anybody doesn't have enemies, Mr Didier. Even Miss Lytton. There's several of the girls don't care for her, if you can get them to confess it. They tell me sometimes. Jealousy, of course. Very nasty about her they can be. Spiteful, women,' he remarked bitterly to the raspberry charlotte.

'Ah, there I agree with you,' said Auguste quietly, quickly changing direction, sensing something of interest was coming. 'Women can be fickle, false-hearted creatures, not like we men. Why, my own Tatiana did not hesitate to play the coquette with other men, conscious that I as a mere cook could not object. She did not mean to be cruel, but liked to use her power. She will be true to me forever, my Tatiana, but –'

'That's as may be, Mr Didier. Your Tatiana might not have meant to be cruel,' Herbert burst out, 'but others do. They make use of people. She likes people to be devoted. Oh yes, she likes that. But doesn't like it when you try to tell her how much you – I didn't want anything, Mr Didier, not really. I wouldn't hurt her, she couldn't have thought that. So she had no cause to do it. No cause at all.' He gazed now at the raspberry charlotte as if it were responsible for all his woe, then with an effort picked up the spoon and began to eat as if nothing had happened. Auguste knew that the charlotte was wasted on him. It could have been Mr Soyer's Maids of Honour for all Herbert would have cared (a receipt that, in Auguste's opinion, might as well have vanished along with the ladies at Queen Elizabeth's court who inspired it.)

Herbert pretended to take no notice when Florence rose, making her intentions plain. She departed alone, donning her wrap and summoning a hansom from the linkman without one word of farewell to Thomas Manley.

He was left staring into a large glass of Napoleon brandy. 'Women,' he remarked moodily to the passing Auguste, with a disillusionment that did little credit to the leading man of the Galaxy whose face adorned so many postcards, whom gods and stalls swooned over, who wore his evening tailcoat to perfection, who kissed a hand with more sensuousness than a Keats' ode. 'I tell you, Didier, I don't understand her. Sweetest little thing, dearest little woman' – it was possible that he was a little drunk – 'turns into a vixen, all because I –'

'Because you –?'

'No harm in telling another woman she's pretty, is there?' said Manley belligerently.

'Indeed not, monsieur, indeed not. But perhaps the trick is not to let the dearest little woman find out, eh?'

Manley glared at Auguste, then became mournful. 'There wasn't any harm in it, I tell you. She didn't come. It wasn't Edna Purvis I escorted on Wednesday evening. She didn't arrive. She had her eye on that lord. She told me she'd come, then she must have changed her mind when Summerfield offered to escort her. She didn't even bother to tell me. So I hung around for a while, went over to Romano's and met Gabrielle. I couldn't leave her sitting alone, could I?'

'Indeed not, monsieur,' said Auguste, fascinated, wondering whether Egbert Rose was aware that one so close to Florence Lytton was not impervious to the charms of the other Galaxy Girls.

Egbert Rose was not dining on plovers' eggs or *foie gras*. He had dined some hour or two ago on Mrs Rose's boiled tripe and was now feeling the after effects. Mrs Rose was not a good cook, and thus the one maid-of-all-work was a worse one. Whether Mrs Rose's was the hand that rocked the cradle of the stove or merely its superintendent, she apparently passed on her lack of prowess by osmosis to their succession of maids over the years. Nevertheless Rose had made a valiant effort.

'That was a splendid supper, my dear.'

'Thank you, Egbert,' said Mrs Rose, gratified.

'*A la mode de Caen*, was it?'

'Pardon, Egbert?'

The dinner in Kettners had reached its finale. As usual Maisie had to waive the *crème georgette* in favour of the consommé and bypass the *turbot à la crème et au gratin*. Ample her proportions might be, but there was a limit . The Galaxy kept a stern eye on such matters.

'Miss Wilson.' She saw with sinking heart the gesture that dismissed the lingering waiter for the last time. 'I want to ask you something very difficult, very personal.'

Maisie kept the hatpin firmly in mind.

'Do you think that policeman really suspects me?'

She relaxed. 'Sure to, I'd say,' she answered cheerfully.

'But I'm a peer of the realm,' said Summerfield, outraged.

'Same size neck as the rest of us.'

He gave her a shattered look. 'But neither of them came,' he bleated in anguish.

'What did you do then?'

'When?'

'After they didn't come, what did you do? Eat your way through this mountain of food alone?'

'I walked around.'

'Go on. A swell toff like you. Walk around?'

'I went home.'

'Then the servants will testify.'

He went red. 'Not right away. That is – I went home, but not immediately.'

'Look, my old cocksparrow, what *did* you do?'

'I – I walked around.'

She shut her eyes. 'Gawlimey, give me patience. No wonder they think you're guilty. I never seen anyone look so guilty in my life. If you mean you took a stroll up the Haymarket for a spot of the local produce, why not say so?'

Lord Summerfield went red, then white, upbringing warring with relief.

'And,' said Maisie, warming to her subject, 'if I were you, I'd keep to the Haymarket for a while, and forget the attractions of us Galaxy Girls.'

But, despite her warning words, she noticed with alarm that his eyes were fixed on her with a dog-like devotion, and that he seemed to be getting closer.

'Mr Didier,' Percy flashed his charming smile, 'perhaps a little more goose liver – since it's in season. From the Dordogne, I trust?'

Edward frowned. Trust Percy to cement their re-established rapport by ordering the most expensive thing on the menu.

'Just that and a little Château Margaux to wash it down. A little *dégustation* before we go to bed.' He flashed a smile at Edward.

Auguste had never seen a middle-aged man blush like a maid before, and watched in amusement.

'Percy,' Edward rapped.

'Sorry, little *pichets* of Château Margaux have big ears,' Percy giggled.

'Monsieur,' said Auguste, anxious to safeguard Florence, 'you would perhaps wish to know that' – he prayed to St Christopher for safety on this perilous journey – 'that Mr Archibald is aware – um – of your generosity in providing a home for Mr Brian.'

Edward Hargreaves turned the colour of Auguste's sweetmeat of currant jelly.

Even Percy looked alarmed.

'The bitch!' he hissed. 'He'll sack us.'

'I think not,' said Auguste soberly. '*Le bon* Monsieur Archibald has other things on his mind. He is concerned with keeping the Galaxy together, not tearing it apart.'

'I'll resign,' said Edward resolutely. 'I will not have everyone knowing.'

'Ashamed of me, darling Edward?' asked Percy sweetly.

'Of course not, Percy,' said Edward, abjectly.

'I beg that you will not,' said Auguste, serving the *noix de veau demi-grasse à la purée de concombre*. The cucumber was a masterstroke by Soyer, one small part of his mind was thinking. He could not always admire Soyer's work and disagreed with his flippant approach, but in this he was irreproachable. 'The Galaxy needs you.'

Edward set his lips mulishly. 'I cannot work with Miss Lytton after this.'

'I beg you to reflect, *mon ami*, that she will be feeling much the same thing. Remember, she is in fear of her life, that one.'

'But those dolls were a joke!'

'Perhaps the other girls were killed as a preparation for her, much as it has been claimed the Ripper's victims were all a preparation for Mary Kelly. It has even been thought that you yourself, monsieur, had a motive for harming Miss Lytton. Now that is disposed of. You and Mr Brian have now no reason to wish her dead.'

Edward said nothing, and Percy inspected the *noix de veau* with great interest.

'But, *chérie*, what next, what next?' asked Auguste, hopping with impatience as he ripped off his clothes to don his night chemise.

Maisie removed her silk drawers and struggled ineffectually with the top hooks of the red corset. 'Ouf,' she said as the first one gave way. The black lacing parted to reveal another two inches of Maisie's white skin. 'Then he said he just walked around, but –'

'No, *chérie*, the *minute* – the menu – what came next?'

'Oh, Auguste, really! I told you, there was this *filet piqué japonaise* – of quail it was – and salad.'

'Salad?' said Auguste, pausing in the act of jumping into bed. 'Salad,' he repeated suspiciously. 'Describe this salad to me, *chérie*. This Sangiorgi – pouf, he lives on Kettner's reputation. And Kettner was not a maître cook – he was a great restaurateur, he wrote cookery books, but it is my belief he is not the genuine cook at heart. He was taught, not born a cook. The great showman, that one.'

'Do you or do you not want to know what Summerfield said?'

'In a moment, *chérie*. The *salade* – describe the dressing.'

'How can I describe a dressing? I'm supposed to be *un*dressing,' she said impatiently, tugging at the centre hooks. 'It's no use, you'll have to help.'

Auguste, his mind inconsiderately elsewhere, tugged at the recalcitrant corset then stopped. 'Only if you describe this dressing.'

She sighed, defeated. 'It was good, I'll say that for it. Had a bit of onion –'

She felt Auguste's fingers stiffen behind her.

'And anchovy – there was anchovy in the dressing?' he asked, almost viciously.

'Now you mention it there was a slight touch – oh, Auguste, what *are* you doing?'

He had sprung away, yelping as if in pain. 'Not the Sydney Smith dressing again! This Kettner was so proud of it but it is Miss Acton who should have the credit for bringing it to public attention. "Fate cannot harm me, I have dined today," they say the epicure remarked after eating it. But it is overdone. It is interesting, yes, but a meal in itself, no no no! The Chevalier d'Albignac who, you may

111

recall, travelled the length and breadth of England to demonstrate his salad dressings –'

'Auguste,' said Maisie, offhandedly, 'then he put his hand on my thigh –'

'He was the maître of salad dressings and he would not include so harsh a taste as anchovy. The tarragon, chervil, but not –'

'And moved it till it was stroking both thighs and his other hand on my bosom, the left one, that is –'

'Even that of the Maître Ude was too subtle for his master, your Duke of Wellington –'

'And slid it between my –'

'Who sacked – *what* did you say?' Maisie had Auguste's full attention. He was purple with indignation and not from the ingredients of Sydney Smith's sauce. 'He did *what*?'

'No, he didn't. I just wanted to see whether you were listening to me.'

'But you wore your yellow dress,' said Auguste suspiciously. 'And you know it is my favourite.'

'And I shall wear the second favourite tomorrow when I go to Romano's with Johnny Beauville,' said Maisie serenely, extricating herself at long last from the corset, removing her chemise and clambering into bed where she settled herself on the pillows. 'Now come on, my old Sherlock Holmes, you can talk to me of clues and motives and all sorts of things.'

'I have no wish to talk of clues and motives,' said Auguste with dignity, settling in beside her. 'It is not *comme il faut* in the circumstances.'

'What circumstances are those?' enquired Maisie interestedly.

'These circumstances,' said Auguste, turning to take her into his arms.

'And another thing,' he added, some considerable time later, 'I wish to inform you, *chérie*, that you are not in the least like Dr Watson.'

112

Chapter Seven

At first, Sergeant Wilcox was disinclined to let Auguste in. He was disbelieving of Auguste's claim that the inspector would wish to see him. Inspector Rose was well known for his dislike of casual callers. Moreover, this one was clearly foreign, and it was them foreigners that tried to blow up Scotland Yard. Or was that Fenians? Much the same thing anyway. Only the name Galaxy produced a positive response, and a constable was despatched to escort the Froggie to the hallowed sanctum.

'Come to confess, most like,' the sergeant consoled himself.

Auguste found Egbert Rose, hands clasped behind his back, standing at the dormer window of the cubby hole of his office high up in Scotland Yard, staring out over the River Thames.

'Ah, Didier.' An informal greeting that impressed the accompanying constable, who threw Auguste a look of respect before scuttling off to spread the report below that Rose the Nose was going all Frenchified.

'Look at that river,' he went on, 'just been thinking to myself there's a tidy lot of villains depend on that river. What it could tell us! Always fancied being with the river police. That river hides more crime than the Nichol. Look at that down there: pleasure boats, cruising along as happy as mudlarks, not knowing what's underneath them. Found out anything, have you?' he continued without pausing for breath.

'Some things, Inspector, but I have had many thoughts also. I think the Galaxy is like a splendid dish of toad in the hole.'

'I thought it would be, somehow,' said Rose gloomily. 'You see everything in terms of food, Mr Didier, that's your trouble. I don't doubt you see me in terms of food.'

Repressing the temptation to compare Egbert Rose to a Herodotus pudding, Auguste continued: 'It presents to the world an harmonious whole, pleasing and simple.' He paused for effect, while Rose listened indulgently. 'Inside, however, what a mass of complications! This toad in the hole prepared from so many ingredients, not always harmonious – where else could salt beef stand side by side with guinea-fowl? – and yet within this toad, they rejoice together.'

'And now you're going to tell me someone has tipped the balance of ingredients and, pouf, the recipe is ruined.'

'Indeed, Inspector, it is a fact that Monsieur Hargreaves is at odds with Percy Brian; Herbert no longer follows Florence as a King Charles spaniel, and that the Manleys do not get on as once they would. And it is not the mere fact of murder which makes everyone uneasy. It is true that Edward Hargreaves, Percy Brian, Herbert Sykes and Thomas Manley all had some reason to wish Florence Lytton harm.'

'But not those two chorus girls surely?'

'But,' said Auguste, 'I was discussing a leg of mutton with Miss Wilson –'

'I've heard you Frenchies have a way with women,' murmured Rose.

Auguste tried to quell him with a look and, having failed, continued hastily, 'And we believe Miss Lytton is *not* the intended victim. We believe he is a maniac, or someone who hates all women, or –' he paused, 'someone who hates the Galaxy.'

'Then we don't have to restrict the field to those who had

a grudge against Florence Lytton,' observed Rose somewhat drily. He had covered all this ground in his own mind some time earlier. 'If you ask me, Mr Didier, we're making this all too complicated. My thinking's along these lines: we've got Summerfield and Beauville, both acquainted with the young ladies, Mr Sykes who seems to have been a great favourite with all the girls, Mr Manley whose eye roves further than it should, and even more obviously, there's Props and Bates. Who better placed to know all the girls' comings and goings than those two?'

'Bates?' said Auguste. 'As well suspect Mr Archibald himself. He adores those girls.'

Rose shrugged. 'Just pointing out the possibilities, Mr Didier. Nice and handy for him. He can look up when he likes, for instance.'

'You are right, of course,' said Auguste. 'But if it were Obadiah then he would have to be a madman. And why, when he has worked at the Galaxy so long, does he suddenly take it into his head to start murdering girls? In fifteen years there would have been a sign of unnatural interest in them, and I have never heard one word against him from the girls. Even a madman needs a motive. And poor Props – what reason?'

'Props is interesting,' said Rose. 'A sort of fanaticism there already, wouldn't you say, Mr Didier? Didn't you tell me he works there just to be near Miss Lytton? Never speaks to her. Just gives her flowers every day.'

'Yes,' said Auguste unwillingly. 'He is gentle. He finds it difficult to speak to Miss Lytton, let alone touch her.'

'All the more likely that, if he were sick in his mind and thought himself spurned, he might turn the other way. Take it out on innocent chorus girls first, then summon up the courage to attack Miss Lytton.'

The two men looked at each other. 'It is possible, yes,' said Auguste. 'They are good ingredients, Inspector. But will they make a good *plat*?'

115

Gabrielle Lapin (or Lepin as she preferred to be known, in case her escorts were acquainted with the French language) entered the underground train in thoughtful mood. She was also thinking of food, of the dinner she would have on Tuesday evening with Lord Summerfield. She wondered whether she were taking a risk. After all, the other two girls had disappeared. But she, Gabrielle, knew how to look after herself, and the chance of ensnaring Lord Summerfield could not be missed. If she had refused, then he would not have asked her again. They were proud, these *aristos*. She drew her coat around her. It was an expensive one, for Archibald expected his girls to be well dressed and paid them extra to do so. He also expected them to travel by hansom cab. But a rumour had run round the dressing room last evening that the murderer was a hansom cab driver whose post was on the Strand.

Gabrielle was not an over-imaginative girl. She was pert-faced with an elfin charm that would not last past her thirtieth birthday, and she was clever enough to be aware of it. The puckish smile and kittenish appeal would settle all too quickly into ageing lines and vixenish frowns. She had only three years left to fulfil her ambition – and that of her parents – of making a suitable marriage. Archibald was generous to his girls, but even he had to face the fact that age overtook them, and gradually their faces, their figures and their dancing abilities fell below Galaxy standards. The call to his office would come. The increase in salary to show how valued they were – and then, a week or two later, an embarrassed chat with the stage manager. *Fini*.

Gabrielle glanced at the kid boots peeping out from under her blue merino wool skirt and thought of the price she had paid for them at Messrs J Sparkes Hall & Son of Regent Street, Bootmakers to Her Majesty. It was unthinkable that she should not be so shod for the rest of her life.

Yes, she was glad she had accepted Lord Summerfield's offer of dinner.

By Tuesday evening, the theatre seemed to have settled down to a permanent state of edginess. There was little general conversation. Ignorant of their starring roles in Inspector Rose's surmises, Obadiah was busy with callers and messages in his cubby hole, Props was organising his team in the props room. Obadiah Bates was also sorting out the tributes for the Galaxy Girls. Not many tonight – the mashers scared off by the publicity. It was all bad for the Galaxy and that worried Obadiah. Worried him very much. Mr Didier had said he should tell the Inspector everything he knew, that any little detail might be important. That the future of the Galaxy might be at stake. For the umpteenth time he wondered what he should do.

The Green Room of the Galaxy was an oasis, a limbo between the outside world and the world of illusion. After the performance it became a place of relaxation where friends might gather to greet the cast, to bathe them in sweet adulation; here they were gods to receive their worshippers, only gradually metamorphosising once more into human beings – albeit larger than life human beings. Here they were cosseted, enshrined in their own immortality by the playbills, photographs, oil paintings and sketches adorning the walls.

Like all oases, it offered also more material comforts. Robert Archibald provided in the Green Room not only health-restoring refreshments after the performance, but pre-performance sandwiches, tea and coffee, with one of Auguste's minions to serve them. Archibald was a keen observer of human nature, and percipient of its frailties. Far too easy for his ladies and gentlemen of the chorus, even for the principals, to wait until dinner for nourishment and not bother to eat before the performance. So here it was

117

for any that were too poor, too miserly or too lazy to partake of supper before they came. For all it had been meant as a democratic institution where Galaxy unity might flourish, and chorus eat with principals, it was noticeable that Florence Lytton and the other principals rarely indulged in Auguste's best chicken pâté sandwiches.

Tuesday, however, was Herbert Sykes's housekeeper's afternoon off, and the sustaining qualities of the stale angel cake she had left for Herbert's tea were not great. Thus he was alone in the Green Room – like all free offerings it was not patronised as it should have been – and was interrupted in the midst of a Roquefort sandwich, addressing a vicious and unrepeatable remark to the portrait of Florence Lytton painted by a latter-day Pre-Raphaelite who had seen her through rose-coloured spectacles as 'Golden Innocence'.

'Why, Herbert! What a thing to say! *Quelle bêtise*!' There was a giggle behind him. They always called him Herbert, he thought, even as he spun round in alarm. They had no respect for him, these girls. They just treated him like an old slipper.

'It was the sandwich I was talking about,' he muttered. Luckily Auguste was not in earshot.

Gabrielle Lepin had come to partake of some food before the performance in order that her stomach might not rumble unbecomingly whilst in the confines of Lord Summerfield's carriage. She could also thus pretend that she had a bird-like appetite. First appearances were important.

'Ah, has the nasty Miss Lytton been unkind to poor little Monsieur Herbert?' she twitted unwisely. His changed attitude had not gone unnoticed in the dressing room.

'No,' he said sharply. Then he looked at the little kid boots peeping out under her skirt. And thought about Gabrielle Lepin, not Florence Lytton.

'But she's not a patch on you, my dear,' he said gallantly, though insincerely. 'How about supper? Rule's, perhaps?'

'Ah, not tonight. I have an engagement. But perhaps one

118

day, I will. You are so funny, Monsieur Herbert.' Quite why she should imagine this would endear her to Herbert was not clear. It did not. His face darkened, but he said nothing. She watched the shadows creeping over it and said uneasily, 'I was only joking about Miss Lytton. I expect she's ever so nice when you know her and ever so fond of you.' Herbert was, after all, a principal.

He seemed not to hear her. Then his face grew red, and he burst out angrily, 'Funny! You think I'm *funny*!' Then he spun round and looked at 'Golden Innocence' again. 'You think I'm funny too, don't you?' he said viciously, 'Oh yes, funny old Herbert. Second best. You're not worth it, none of you. Cock-chafers. Harlots. *Florence*!'

Unfortunately the lady's husband was standing in the doorway. Florence had elected to travel separately. Futhermore there had been no supper for him at home. Florence had been served tea in her boudoir. It had been locked to him. Unwisely he took exception to his wife being thus referred to, however much he might privately agree with the bitterness with which the insults were hurled. But ladies were always ladies in public.

'Florence is my *wife*, Mr Sykes,' he said with dignity, one hand on the door handle, playing as he had in so many provincial melodramas the injured husband.

Cornered, Herbert went white, then lashed out: 'And I'm sure you're to be pitied.'

Manley's eyes bulged. His repertoire did not allow for this retort. 'Pitied!' he exploded. 'Are you mad, Mr Sykes?'

Herbert was not, so he claimed. 'She's a bitch. She leads people on. Look how she led that Lord Summerfield on, even Johnny Beauville. Didn't you know? I did. Led me on too. Promised me everything, everything. Cock-tease –'

Gabrielle listened fascinated. They seemed to have overlooked her presence and she was not going to remind them. This was better than the day at the Folies when Gaby had attacked Jane with a knife.

'You're no gentleman,' Manley replied weakly, taken aback by this new Herbert.

He laughed.

This was what Manley needed. 'You can laugh,' he said, firing up. 'You'd laugh on the other side of your fat face if you knew what she said about you. "Poor old Herbert," she'd say, "poor old roly-poly. Clown on stage and clown off. And he really believes I'm fond of him." When you try and sing that song –'

At that unfortunate moment Edward Hargreaves, determined not to surrender and cook Percy's tea, arrived to take his own repast. The word 'song' and he was off. Moreover, his new ally seemed under attack.

'Charming though Miss Lytton is,' Hargreaves hissed through clenched teeth, 'she is hardly a musician. Look at that song, for instance. Now you, Mr Sykes, have a true sense of the poetry of music, but Miss Lytton is merely a *performer*!' He uttered the word with disgust.

Thomas Manley, perceiving himself in the minority, lost his self-control. 'My wife,' he shouted, 'is the leading lady. Adored by the gods. *The* star in the firmament of the Galaxy. The dearest little woman –' He almost choked.

Gabrielle leapt in, mindful that he was the leading man at the Galaxy. She fluttered her eye lashes. Herbert remembered that gesture. She had done it to him once in happier days. To dear old Uncle Herbert.

'I think you're so right, Mr Manley. Dear Miss Lytton. It did ought to be *un peu*' – being deliciously French – 'slower. Her charm deserves it.'

'You see,' said Manley triumphantly. 'Now we shall finish the row about that stupid song once and for all. After the show, we shall remain behind and we shall play it at the piano and *all* decide the best tempo. And after that, I could perhaps offer you supper perhaps, Miss Lepin? My wife retires early.'

'Not tonight,' said Gabrielle with pride. 'I'm dining with

Lord Summerfield tonight.' Suddenly she had all three men's full attention.

'Do you think, um, that's wise, Miss Lepin?' said Hargreaves diffidently. 'Don't you think you are being rather foolish, all for the sake of trying to get a coronet on your head?'

Gabrielle glared. 'No,' she said shortly. 'But do give my love to Percy,' she added spitefully. 'Tell him how much I enjoyed the other night.'

'Percy?' bleated Edward 'Percy? You've been out with Percy?'

'Why not?' she asked innocently.

'You're lying – he wouldn't. He wouldn't.'

'Steady, Hargreaves,' said Thomas well-meaningly. 'The lad's only young. He has to have some fun. He often goes out with the young ladies. Keeps them up very late, but then he's a bachelor! Lucky dog, eh?' He winked, and then stared, aghast, as Edward burst into tears.

Standing on the threshold, an observer of this revealing scene, was Obadiah Bates, come to deliver a message. What was the Galaxy coming to? Now he was even more worried. The future of the Galaxy might be at stake, Monsieur Auguste had said. He should tell him anything that might help the Galaxy. Where did his duty lie?

Now the principals were grimly concentrating on their pre-performance routines, and even the chatter in the chorus dressing rooms was muted.

Florence, tired of being marooned on an island of persecution, managed to direct a weak smile at Thomas as she passed him in the corridor. After all, he couldn't really want to murder her, could he?

Herbert stumped morosely around his room, wondering how he was going to summon up courage to make a fool of himself before Florence on stage without thinking of the real life scene the other night, and wondering how he could ever have felt such slavish devotion to her. His eyes were open now, he told himself.

Props, however, remained faithful where Florence was concerned. This evening, indeed, marked a new departure for him. The posy of violets had been clutched a little more tightly than usual, and instead of being thrust into her hand by a rapidly retreating Props, they remained in his possession as he barred Florence's path through the wings.

'Sorry about those dolls, miss,' he said to an alarmed and nervous Florence as he pushed the violets towards her, still avoiding her eyes. It was the longest speech he had ever made to her.

'Dolls?' Florence cried. 'You mean – you – it was *you*?' Her voice rose alarmingly.

Props gaped at her. 'Me? What, miss?'

But he spoke to thin air. Florence had fled, screaming. Props tried to think what it was he had said to upset her so much.

Her precipitate passage ended on the floor, together with a glass, a bottle of whisky, and the remains of a gratin of lobster. She had run full tilt into Auguste on his way back from Archibald's office with his supper tray.

Auguste supported her as best he could, while she sobbed at him: 'It was Props, Props all the time!'

'Now calm yourself, madame, what was Props?'

'Props is the murderer?' The door to Archibald's office had flown open, and Authority stood on the threshold – albeit a panic-stricken Authority with only ten minutes before the curtain went up, and a leading lady apparently once more in hysterics.

A glance was exchanged between Auguste and Archibald, and Florence was lifted bodily off her feet and transported once more to the leather-covered chair in Archibald's office.

'Now, dear, what's all this about Props being a murderer?'

'He,' she gulped, '*told me*!'

Auguste soothingly and somewhat absentmindedly stroked her back. These were no ordinary times. 'He said he murdered those two girls, madame?'

'No, but he said he was responsible for those horrible – things – those dolls –' She gulped again, her beautiful face distorted with tears.

'If that's so, I'll – I'll have a word with him. Now don't you worry. You run off and have a nice –' Archibald paused, his tongue was running away with him, performance.' He glanced covertly at the Albert watch on his desk before him. Curtain up in nine minutes.

'Very well,' she hiccuped. 'But I want him out of this theatre, Mr Archibald, *tonight*.'

Robert Archibald duly loomed awkwardly and unhappily at the door of Props' room.

Props looked round, startled, wondering what possible calamity had brought the great man himself hither, the mountain to Mahomet.

'Props,' said Archibald kindly, 'is there anything you want to tell me?'

It appeared from Props' gaping expression that there was nothing to communicate.

'It wasn't a very nice thing to do, was it?' said Archibald helplessly. 'What made you do it, my dear fellow?'

Props looked wildly at him. 'It wasn't my fault,' he ventured.

'I daresay, daresay, but all the same it won't do. You admit you did it?'

Props looked ready to admit anything if only this unwelcome glare of limelight would go away. 'Them dolls,' he muttered.

'Then you'll have to go, Props – just for a short time. Edward here can carry on. Just stay away a week and we'll see what we can do.'

Props said nothing, just twisted a piece of paint-smeared rag in his hands, his face growing pinker and pinker. At last he managed to say something: 'Leave, Gov'nor? Because of them dolls?'

As had been noted before, Props was a simple man.

This was what happened when he left his post, Obadiah brooded. He was going to have to do something with the future of the Galaxy at stake. You had to stand firm, like before the Pathans at the Khyber Pass. But Tommy had shown them all right. Tommy never left his post and nor would he now. Fred – pah! These youngsters had no idea of what was involved in controlling a stage-door. Especially the Galaxy's. That brought his worries flooding back. Yes, he'd better have a quiet word in someone's ear before the curtain went up. Then tonight he'd think things over.

It was amazing that, despite her tribulations, Florence Lytton could present such a smiling untroubled face to the world across the footlights. Miss Penelope tripped across the stage as if she had no thought on her mind other than her next Worth gown.

In the wings Thomas Manley studied this stranger, his wife. Would he ever feel the same way about her? She used to be his little Florence, who needed protection. She needed protection like a tiger cub! His masculine pride was bruised, but he was undaunted. Florence, he guessed, would never tell the police about Edna Purvis and his own interest in her because it would make her look foolish. He had several ideas for ways of getting his own back on her, he thought, and ran on to the stage hallooing to the reverberate gods 'Women are the devil,' in the baritone that sent delicious shivers up the spine of half of London's population. 'But the devil may care, for I've not a care, tra la la . . .'

Florence clasped the marionette to the bosom that eschewed the same attentions from her husband. 'Oh, for a love,' she trilled, 'a love to cherish. Ah, if you could but hear, what I say to you . . .'

Were her ears deceiving her? Surely that orchestra had speeded up again? It was a vendetta. She caught Herbert's eye where he stood skulking behind the desk. It seemed to her he was smirking.

Another performance over, and all things considered it hadn't been bad. Robert Archibald breathed a sigh of relief. One day at a time. This one was over and all was well.

But he was wrong. The day was not yet over so far as the fortunes of the Galaxy were concerned. Obadiah Bates locked the door behind him, leaving Watch in charge. Another day over. Obadiah walked along Wellington Street, noting with disapproval the Summerfield carriage waiting outside the Lyceum, and turned towards the maze of streets behind Covent Garden where he lived. The night was foggy again, and he never liked fog. It got in his throat and aggravated it where the spear had got him out in India. At least it had been warm out there. A man could be himself there; a good life, the soldier's. Valuable. Of course, he was doing an invaluable job now, guarding these girls. But two he had slipped up on. He had to be vigilant, very vigilant.

He was not quite vigilant enough. The sound of his footsteps echoed on the flagstones. The noise of the market was deadened by the fog. Once he thought he heard footsteps. He paused. There was nothing. Fog was queer, it distorted things, yet he had this feeling there was someone following him. An old soldier always knew. Nearly home now. He quickened his step as he turned the last corner, shrouded by the fog, only pierced by the occasional gaslight. As he fumbled with the lock on the door, he had a fleeting impression of an outstretched arm and a heavy black shape descending out of the choking mist. He slumped to the ground. The Pathans got me after all, was his last conscious thought.

'The Inspector won't want to be bothered with that, lad.'

'But, Sergeant Twitch – er – Stitch –'

'I said hoppit, Edwards, hoppit.'

Edwards hopped.

It was thus another hour before Rose, who had spent three days interviewing the Galaxy company and sifting the results, learned that its stage door keeper had been attacked on the Tuesday evening. Egbert Rose prided himself on his mildness, but on occasions his roar could be heard from the Thames.

'It was a dipper,' said Stitch indignantly. 'His money was gone. You mustn't see coincidences in everything,' he added kindly.

It was the wrong thing to say to Rose. 'Laddie,' he said insultingly, 'when I say I want to know everything to do with the Galaxy, I mean everything. And that means straightaway.'

'He don't know nothing about who hit him,' said Stitch defiantly to Rose's retreating back.

At the Galaxy he found Robert Archibald wearing the expression of a much tried man. The deputy stage door-keeper, whose services had never been so required before, had first let in a major's wife from Cheshire who thought she'd like to be an actress. What the major thought was not mentioned. Second, a young lady from a ladies' seminary who *insisted* on being one.

'You've heard the news, Rose, then. God knows why. He's not a show girl.'

'No, sir, but perhaps he knew a bit too much for his own good. I'd like a word with Props, he being the nearest at hand like.'

'Props has left us,' said Archibald unhappily.

'Then I'll trouble you for his address. He might well have seen something of what happened last night.'

'I believe I did also,' said Auguste, coming in, having

seen Rose arrive. 'I chanced to look out of the restaurant window and saw Obadiah go past – he always goes the long way round the Strand in front and then down Wellington Street, in the hope he might bump into Henry Irving en route. Even if he's not billed to appear, he still does it. Poor Obadiah.'

'Henry Irving?'

'It is Obadiah's one sadness that the Galaxy does not put on what he calls "real plays", like Mr Irving, and *King Lear* – not his greatest part, in my view. Nevertheless it made a deep impression on Obadiah. Since the never to be forgotten day he saw Irving perform, he always walks down Wellington Street in the hope that the great man might venture forth at the same time.'

'I wonder he don't go there as stage door keeper,' remarked Rose.

'There is such a thing as loyalty, Inspector,' said Archibald stiffly. 'He believes he has a mission to look after the Galaxy. He's taking these murders very personally. I wonder if he wasn't doing some investigating on his own, and his attempted murder is the result.'

'Was it meant to kill, Inspector?' asked Auguste.

'It certainly wasn't a friendly tap, Mr Didier. Fortunately your Mr Bates has a strong head, a strong bowler and a strong constitution. Bit of an amateur, our head knocker. A professional dipper wouldn't have attacked – and if he did, he'd have made a better job of it.'

'There is something else I must tell you,' said Auguste slowly. 'It means nothing, I'm sure. After all, we all have to go home, but I did think I saw someone I recognised walking after Obadiah.'

'And who might that be?'

'Herbert Sykes,' said Auguste reluctantly.

'I can't say, Inspector.' Herbert was clearly unhappy. 'No, I can't say I saw poor Mr Bates in front of me. I was going home,' he said obstinately, blinking through short-sighted eyes at Rose. 'No Romano's for me, you see.'

'Your home's in Bayswater, sir.'

'I walk part of the way, Inspector,' said Herbert obstinately. 'No law against that, is there? Look in at the market. Go to my club on the way. If I was going to hit Bates over the head, I wouldn't walk up Wellington Street for everyone to see, would I?' His eyes were cold as he glanced at Auguste. 'Now would I?' he repeated, pulling a face and cocking his head on one side.

Auguste saw the smile involuntarily cross Rose's face. He had seen that effect before too. He had seen Herbert play clown in the Harlequinade more than once. It was the grin he gave after stealing the sausages. He had never seen him do it offstage.

Florence Lytton stepped confidently from her front entrance towards her carriage. Her coachman opened the door, and she clambered in. There was someone in there already. Before her screams had died the intruder had gone and a posy of violets resided in her hand.

Obadiah lived on the top floor of an old house in Floral Street. The stairs were cold and unwelcoming, and it was with surprise that Auguste and Maisie saw the inside of his lodgings after they were admitted by the woman downstairs who 'did for him', as she put it.

They were not expensively furnished, but warm and comfortable, a cocoon against the world. Above the small fireplace was a mantel crowded with photographs; an aspidistra stood before the window together with a table with more knick-knacks and photographs, including one of a severe-looking woman in crinoline and bonnet with a boy and a girl at her side, the latter a female edition of her father in embryo, the former roly-poly in sailor suit. Also displayed there were the older generations of Bates, in daguerrotype, their clothes suggesting a more opulent style of living than that enjoyed by their descendant.

'How are you, Obadiah?' said Maisie, removing her muff and coat and going to sit by the old man, who was lying on a chaise longue, a large bandage round his head.

'As well as can be expected, Miss Maisie,' he said. 'It's the Galaxy I'm worried about. I've been thinking it over. What are they to do without me?' His face crinkled up as if with physical pain.

'Don't worry about that, Obadiah,' said Auguste. 'They've got young Fred –'

It was a red rag to a bull. 'He don't know how to run a stage door,' Obadiah shouted. 'I'd best be getting back.' He swung his legs to the ground and had to be forcibly restrained by Auguste.

'You must remain here. You don't want him to have another go at you, do you?'

The old man glared at him obstinately. 'You Frenchies don't understand the English. I'm an old soldier, I am. I've got to get back.'

'Perhaps and perhaps not. But the inspector wants you to take no risks,' said Auguste.

'I'm going back,' muttered Obadiah, struggling to his feet. 'The Galaxy's all upset. Ladies and gentlemen quarrelling, shouting at each other – it ain't right. It's got to stop. And I'm going to stop it.'

'But, Obadiah, suppose your attacker tries again. Do you have no idea who it was?'

Obadiah shook his head. 'Like a thunderbolt it was, Mr Didier. Made me think, I can tell you. But I'm going back all the same. Tomorrow.'

'But –'

'And that's all I'm going to say. None of this, "It may be him, it may be her." We've got the Galaxy to think of. I'll speak in my own good time.'

It was not the first occasion that Auguste had been forced

to grit his teeth when faced with the obstinacy of Obadiah Bates. Even the Afghans had proved no match for him!

The awning above Romano's had never looked so welcoming. Maisie stared at it from the Galaxy restaurant window. 'You will not go, *ma mie*.' Auguste had said firmly.

'I will,' she replied robustly. 'You detect your way, I'll detect mine.'

'Do you not trust your Auguste to solve these crimes? Did I not solve the affair of the Duke of Stockbery? Do you think you are Mrs Paschal? Are you going to write more *Revelations of a Lady Detective*?' he demanded.

'I don't see the Honourable Johnny inviting *you* out to dinner,' said Maisie matter-of-factly. 'There are some things that need a woman to carry them out successfully. And don't wait up for me. I'm going back to my lodgings this evening.' And with this parting shot, she had sallied forth to meet her masher.

The Honourable Johnny had not booked a private room, the Honourable Johnny liked to be seen with his escorts. He was amazed that Maisie should condescend to come out with him again; he'd rather got it into his head that he was persona non grata with the Galaxy Girls. As though the pretty little dears were in any danger from him! He wouldn't touch a hair of their heads.

Luigi, the maître d'hotel, advanced towards them, smiling. The Honourable Johnny was a regular – and generous – customer. He was shown to his usual table.

'Now, what are you going to eat, Miss Wilson?' Johnny said, gulping slightly. Maisie's blue dress, although not so devastating as the yellow one, was nevertheless considerably lower in the décolletage. She glanced at the menu. Her corsets could not stand too great an onslaught.

'What do you tell your brother and sister about these evenings out of yours?' she enquired inquisitively.

Johnny's face paled a little. 'Go to my club,' he said cheerfully. 'Good fellows they are there. They'll say anything. Tip them decently, you know.'

Maisie studied Romano's menu intently. Had the Honourable Johnny not been at his club the night of Edna Purvis' murder? *And* on the night Christine Walters had failed to keep her rendezvous with Lord Summerfield? Suddenly the *cailles farcies* looked much less inviting.

Chapter Eight

'This is the yeast that rises too much. No, no, *non!*'

'Why, Auguste, I've never seen you in a temper before,' marvelled Maisie, helping herself to a large portion of kedgeree and two of Auguste's brioche rolls. Her waist-line's demands were apparently only mandatory after ten o'clock. Auguste had almost refused to serve her, but he was a maître chef and it was a crime against his honour for anyone to profess hunger and go unfed.

'I am not in a temper,' shouted Auguste, eyes flashing dangerously, his hair unruly after an agitated hand had been thrust through it, a misdemeanour for which he had so often to reprove *la petite* Gladys. 'I am merely astounded that you wish to go out with murderers.'

Maisie paused in mid-mouthful to cast a look at him.

'People who may be murderers when I, your – your – *alors*, I say no, it shall not be.'

'Your what?' asked Maisie interestedly, applying black pepper to the kedgeree.

'What are you doing?' he cried out in horror once more. 'You think I do not know how to season food? Is that it? You doubt my judgement? *Ma foi*, you betray me. First with gentlemen, then with pepper.'

'Now, now,' she said appeasingly. 'You know I have no palate.'

'That is true,' he said, partly mollified, 'but to do so in front of me, your –'

'Your what?' she enquired again.

'Your beloved, Your *bien aimé*,' he said, glaring at her.

She laughed. 'That doesn't mean you can order me about, as though I were Gladys. I never promised to obey you when you carried me over the threshold of your bed.'

'I regard my duties to you as those of a husband,' said Auguste firmly.

'Do you indeed?' murmured Maisie. 'Then why aren't you?'

With straight face she watched Auguste turn as pink as his own shell-fish dressing. Then his French ancestry reasserted its dominance over his English blood. He waved his hands in Gallic expressiveness. '*Ma mie*, would that – but I explained about my Tatiana – that I could not marry any but her, impossible though that is –'

'That's all right, Auguste,' said Maisie. 'So I'll continue to see such gentlemen as I wish.' She stirred her cocoa vigorously and gave him a charming smile.

'*Non*,' Auguste gulped, torn in a decision even greater than whether to serve carp *à la poulette* or in a *matelote*. 'If you wish it, *ma mie*, I will marry you.' It was out. The decision was made. Tatiana was far away. That betrayal he put firmly aside for the moment. He would square his conscience later. At the moment all he could think of was Maisie, sitting there so serenely, high-necked yellow and white lace blouse tucked into a wide belt beneath that entrancing . . . He gulped.

'I'll think it over,' said Maisie composedly.

'Think it over!' he exploded. 'But I have asked you to *marry* me.'

'Very wise of you, Miss Maisie,' said an approving voice from the doorway. 'Takes a lot of thought, wondering whether to marry a Frenchie.'

'Inspector,' said Auguste, turning in fury, 'this is a private moment.'

'You come in, Inspector,' said Maisie. 'Don't take any notice of Auguste. He's upset. It's the shock of having

134

signed his life away. Have a brioche. The quince marmalade is good.'

'It may be usual for you, Maisie,' said Auguste bitterly, 'to receive proposals of marriage, but by me, these matters are taken more seriously.'

'I can testify to that,' said Rose cheerily. 'Remember Miss Ethel, Mr Didier?' Auguste gave him an outraged look and was strangely silent.

'How did you find Mr Bates? He wasn't too good when I looked in,' said Rose, eyeing the coffee pot hopefully. Mrs Rose preferred her cup of tea.

'Obadiah insists on coming to work. He is so convinced no one can man the stage door but him,' said Maisie.

'I'll have to give him a guard,' said Rose. 'Our friend isn't going to leave it at that. He'll try again – and quickly. Ain't he any idea of who hit him? Or why? He wouldn't say anything to me.'

'We asked him to think, think, think of everything that happened that day,' said Auguste. 'It must be something that neither we nor he see the relevance of.'

'Unless he's keeping something back,' said Rose. 'He reminds me of someone I've met.' He paused. 'Perhaps it's Fingers Field. He kept something back when he split on the Radcliffe gang – and landed up another case for the Thames Police Mortuary as a result. You're quite sure he cannot remember more about our young lord's or Honourable's movements?'

'No, but I can tell you more,' said Maisie, not looking at Auguste. A carefully edited account of her last two evenings was passed on to an interested Rose.

'His club'll back him up in anything, eh?' commented Rose. 'Very handy that. Very.'

Gabrielle Lepin woke up on Thursday morning in her highly respectable Bayswater lodgings and stretched her arms with feline contentment. Indeed, she looked very like

135

the cat that licked the cream. And this evening she would again! She did not breakfast on kedgeree; being French she was breakfasting on stale muffins, spread with jam, provided grudgingly by her landlady. It was the last time she'd have a foreigner in the house. She hadn't realised that Gabrielle was a foreigner till too late. She didn't look no different. And some nights she didn't come home at all! That suited her landlady. She saved on the breakfasts.

Gabrielle was happy despite the stale muffins. She had dined with a lord and, despite all the dire warnings given her, she was still alive. She had been nervous when Summerfield took her to that private room in the Hotel Cecil, and had firmly refused the offer of a walk by the river – and yet here she was, alive! How she had boasted at the theatre yesterday. How silly they had looked now that their warnings had come to nothing. And how jealous they would be when she told them that he was taking her out this evening also, to dine and dance. She could have done without the dancing after the show, but she'd got his measure. He wanted to hold her close – that was all right by her. *Anything*, in fact, was all right with her. But he was not going to know that. She had determined not to give in to him till stage five of the game; then, when she allowed him to seduce him, as a man of honour he would have to marry her. Would the coronet have pearls or diamonds? she pondered.

In a somewhat grander home in Curzon Street, Florence Lytton and Thomas Manley were sharing a somewhat grander breakfast of breadcrumbed kidneys on toast. They were eating in silence. The façade of friendliness mandatory at the theatre took all their energies.

'Florence, listen to me.' Thomas laid down *The Times* which he had been only pretending to read.

Florence continued buttering her bread.

'You must believe me,' said Thomas vehemently, 'I did

136

not, *not*, see Edna Purvis that evening, whatever I may have said to you. And, yes, I did take Christine Walters to dinner, but not that evening, and I am *not* a murderer.'

Florence's beautiful face was unresponsive.

'And another thing,' he shouted, 'I'm tired of sleeping in my dressing room. I'm moving back tonight. And if you don't like it, *you* can sleep in the dressing room.'

That got a reaction. Her face registered fear.

Gratified by this sign of animation, he went on: 'And I shall take whom I please to dinner, since you no longer appear to desire my company at your table or in your bed. In fact –' he paused, thought wildly, then remembered that delightful bosom he had so often admired, 'I have arranged to take Miss Wilson to dine this evening. 'I don't know what time I'll be back. Or *if* I'll be back.'

Herbert Sykes was breakfasting off broiled black pudding and hot chocolate. His housekeeper, as he made no demands or complaints, served him what she liked. Auguste would have been horrified had he observed this assault on the stomach and would have urged a glass of white wine as the only thing that could possibly render black pudding acceptable to the stomach at such an early hour. But Herbert came from the North and had brought his taste-buds with him. When you have started life at the Newcastle Empire, and travelled England and much of Scotland with touring companies, you developed an iron stomach. His present affluence had not changed his habits.

He was wondering how he could summon the courage to go to the theatre to face the horror once more, present a cheery face on stage, make people laugh. He was tortured by nightmares that one day he would find himself before an audience who wouldn't laugh. A sea of faces would stare at him, completely blank, while he fooled around, jokes falling on deaf ears, the clowning more and more desperate as the silence grew heavier. He would make a fool of himself just as he had the other night before Florence. He scraped some butter viciously on to the cold toast. To walk into the Galaxy now was to walk into an atmosphere of hostility and distrust. Once it had been a cosy home, a cocoon of warmth. Now everything was at odds, and Florence was part of it. He'd thought she was different. Not like the chorus girls and show girls who would do anything for a good time – some of them – even with him, Herbert. Well, the ones who were getting worried about their future anyway. He could tell. He had no respect for them. None at all. But he'd thought Florence an angel, unsullied by the commonplace. Until a few nights ago. She deserved everything he'd said about her when Thomas Manley upset him so much.

Edward and Percy were speaking to each other only stiltedly. In Percy's case this was because his thoughts were elsewhere. In Edward's the reason was more complex. He had for a day or two now been unable to rid himself of the dark fear that Percy might leave him. It was a fear he was unwilling to put into words, lest it bring about the very thing he dreaded. He was indispensable to Percy, he knew it. But did Percy? He must please him. Pamper him. He had fried some nice little sole this morning and served them with thick cream on top, but Percy had hardly touched them.

'It's those women, isn't it?' Edward said at last, pouring the coffee which had been peacefully infusing for five minutes.

Percy looked up quickly and smiled. It was not a nice smile. 'What women, Edward?'

'They get in the way,' said Edward bitterly. 'They're always after you, aren't they? I've noticed them,' he said, warming to his theme, as now he had Percy's full attention. 'Those chorus girls are always after you, and you do nothing to discourage them. I sometimes think you like it.'

'Jealous still, Edward? One has to be seen around for the look of the thing, don't you agree?'

'Why?' said Edward. 'Aren't you happy here? You've got the Steinway I bought you. Why do you need to go out?'

'I'm younger than you are,' answered Percy, smiling charmingly. 'I have my way to make in the world.'

'I'm your world,' said Edward fiercely. 'You said you didn't need anyone but me – ever.'

'Did I?' said Percy, carelessly. 'How very romantic of me.' He pushed the spurned sole to one side.

A dull ache in his head, Obadiah Bates rose from his bed and dressed, slowly and painfully. Those doctors weren't going to keep him away from the Galaxy. It was his home. No upstart from the stage staff was going to take his place.

He'd lain there all the morning, worrying and worrying about what would happen if he weren't there, and finally, after lunching off the thin gruel that Mrs Higgins deemed fit food for invalids, he decided to do something about it.

It was raining outside, a biting cold rain that chilled him to the bone as he cut through Burleigh Street. It was not the quickest way to the stage door but possibly Mr Irving might be arriving at his special entrance to the Lyceum, for a rehearsal perhaps. *King Arthur* was to be his next production. That sounded good. The sight of his hero would cheer him on, strengthen the resolve which was diminishing somewhat on this cheerless last day of November.

Obadiah was to be disappointed. Mr Irving was not to be seen. The Strand was a dull, muddy, uninspiring sight. Late luncheoners were leaving Romano's, well-cosseted guests climbing into hansoms outside the Savoy Hotel. But such opulence was no part of the world of Obadiah Bates. Nor would he wish it to be. Stick to your own class, was his maxim. And stick he did. On the occasion Mr Archibald had taken him to the Hotel Cecil to celebrate his fifteen years at the Galaxy, he had been stiff and monosyllabic. The experience had been an ordeal for both and was not repeated.

Auguste, who had noticed him passing the restaurant windows, huddled into an ancient Inverness cape, frowned.

'You do not look well enough, Obadiah,' he said later, when he found the old man restored to his rightful position at the stage door, sitting down on the familiar chair. Bates' face brightened.

'Couldn't stay away, Mr Didier,' he said. 'Couldn't let Mr Archibald down now, could I? Who's to look after those girls if I'm not here? Something horrible might happen to 'em.'

Auguste forbore to point out that even Obadiah Bates had been powerless to prevent a great deal of harm coming to two of them.

Props shifted miserably from one foot to another. He was sheltering ineffectively in a doorway near the stage door. To his right the pit queue, even wetter than he was, was being entertained by a double shuffler, accompanied by an execrable hurdy-gurdy. Even their zest seemed dampened by the weather. He had waited here for an hour already, in case she should arrive early at the theatre. Newsboys with placards reading 'Latest on Murder at the Galaxy' were doing a roaring trade. He stiffened, the queue forgotten. The Manley carriage had arrived outside the stage door. The ripples intensified as the queue, reluctant to cede their places, executed a 180° turn. Props remained hidden.

Thomas Manley was first to step out, stern-faced despite the chorus of 'Ooohs', and then came Florence wrapped in white furs, a high crowned toque perched over her golden hair, smiling and graceful. This, after all, was part of the performance.

A figure darted forward, eel-like in its litheness, long slim fingers urgently seeking to push the violets into her hand.

Florence looked up and screamed.

Manley turned, cursed, and rushed his wife into the theatre.

The queue was left staring at Props, as though the murderer stood before them. Bewildered, then frightened, he hurried away into the rain. If only he could explain to her, that it was all for her! But she seemed so frightened of him. He could not understand why. He must make her understand. He would try again after the performance.

Miss Penelope's Proposal sparkled that night, as if to compensate for the dreariness outside. Imperceptibly the spirits of the cast rose. Perhaps these murders were nothing to do with the Galaxy after all, the dolls a regrettable coincidence. Robert Archibald saw the improvement as a culmination of his optimism that the spirit of unity would prevail. He could almost persuade himself that the Galaxy had been unaffected by the tragedies. Yet there was a certain curious expectancy on behalf of both audience and cast that the performance somehow failed to satisfy. It was as though the Galaxy held its breath.

Props was now unhappy as well as wet. He had not been able to explain to Florence. His nerve failed him at the last moment, and he remained in the doorway watching as she left in her carriage – alone – and was whisked out of sight. It was over. She would never smile at him again. The reason for his living had gone. His grief and distress at his own inadequacy grew. It was not that anyone had ever said he was a failure, but no one had ever told him otherwise, even Archibald.

He clenched his fists in fury. He would get his own back. He would not be spurned.

Gabrielle Lepin excitedly dressed for her evening out, to a chorus of disapproving murmurs. A message had arrived while she had been waiting in the wings that His Lordship would be meeting her not outside the Lyceum but the Royal Strand Theatre. She drew on her best silk stockings with the

141

black clocks, determined that despite the flounces of her petticoat Lord Summerfield should have every opportunity to admire them. She thought up one or two remarks which might advance her cause, and decided that her accent might be permitted to become a *leetle* more pronounced. She gave Maisie a triumphant look. She knew all about the trip to Kettners. Clearly Maisie had now been spurned.

Maisie, surprised by an invitation from Thomas Manley and telling herself how convenient it was, and that Auguste could not possibly object, had also dressed with care. Her preparations included her usual hatpin, and a spare one somewhat uncomfortably lodged in her garter. She hobbled painfully to the stage door where Obadiah was glaring at the companion foisted on him by Inspector Rose.

'I've got my reputation to think of,' he expostulated. 'You wait outside. I'm an old soldier. Don't need no police to look after me . . .'

'Inspector Rose's orders,' said Police Constable Edwards. Sacrosanct, as far as he was concerned. 'Someone's tried to kill you once. Got to get you out of the way before he can start ripping – er – killing again,' he said untactfully.

Obadiah thought about this. 'Ripping?' he said.

'That's what Rose the Nose thinks,' said Edwards, his tongue running away with him. 'He'll turn to ripping. That's what he's leading up to,' he added with relish. '

'Not me.'

'No, not you, Mr Bates. But he's trying to kill you. You know something – or he thinks you do. That's why I gotta protect you. I'll be waiting outside, if you're locking up now,' and Police Constable Edwards went out.

'Waste of time,' grunted Bates, producing his keys.

Sykes popped his head into his office. 'Have you seen Miss Lepin, Obadiah?'

'Not yet, Mr Sykes. Not down yet. Any message? I'll write it on the board.'

'No, I'll come back in a few moments.'

142

Herbert Sykes went out into Catherine Street, his feelings of unease growing. Then he rejected them. After all, she had *promised* to come out with him.

'I ain't having no policeman walking along beside me,' said Obadiah obstinately. 'You can walk behind if you like, or in front, but not with me. And take that helmet off. I ain't going to be made a laughing stock.'

Faced with the centuries-old intractability of the Londoner when he has had enough, Police Constable Edwards gave in.

Intent on getting the journey over with, Obadiah walked quickly for a man of sixty-odd. By the time they reached Bow Street Edwards was having a hard job keeping up, following the sound of Obadiah's footsteps in the misty dark ahead, lit only by the occasional gas light, the muted sounds of the market in the distance.

As he turned the corner into Floral Street, all was silent. 'Mr Bates!' he shouted, his voice echoing in the fog. Before Obadiah could answer, Edwards was aware of footsteps behind him, then a hand round his neck, tightly, pulling him backwards, choking, strangling. Then all was silent, save the sound of his helmet hitting the cobbles as it left his hand. A short pause and the footsteps continued relentlessly in the direction of Obadiah Bates. This time they were almost running.

Maisie sat impatiently in the lobby of the Hotel Cecil. Comfortable though it was, she was getting very irritated at waiting for Mr Thomas Manley. He was over half an hour late, and had it not been that she was very hungry she would have departed. Auguste never kept her waiting. She could not imagine why Thomas Manley should want to murder several girls, but it was undoubted fact that those dolls had been directed at Florence, and Thomas was not on good terms with his darling wife. In any case, she reminded herself with a shiver, they were dealing with a maniac, and one of the symptoms of a maniac was that he had none to the outside eye. Assuring herself that she was not about to dine with Jack the Ripper, she decided to wait just five minutes longer.

Gabrielle was scornful of anybody who was scared of their mother, for such was the rumour about Lord Summerfield. But for a coronet she would overlook even that. She supposed she'd have to walk. It was not far to the side entrance of the Royal Strand Theatre, but humiliating to be walking without an escort in the Strand, and her dress of pale blue would be filthy even though the rain had stopped. She was considering this prospect outside the theatre, when a familiar voice accosted her. She explained her dilemma and was much relieved at the offer of an escort.

It was a fine morning. Mr Postlethwaite-Higgins, a middle-aged lawyer of impeccable background, on his way to his Temple chambers in Hare Court as had been his wont for the past twenty-five years, stopped, as was also his wont, to look at the old Roman Spring Bath for the purpose of admiring the Roman brickwork. In more clement weather he sometimes took a bath, since the water coming from the miraculous well of St Clement was said to have chalybeate properties. He was a gentleman of healthy leanings. In view of the time of year he took a cup of the waters instead. He did this because his father had done so before him, and superstitiously he felt that if he were to follow his father's ritual then he might also acquire his father's gift for the successful defending of villains.

This morning, however, was a milestone for Mr Postlethwaite-Higgins. He was about to earn himself immortality in the annals of Scotland Yard. He wandered into the second brick vaulted room, to view the disused Roman bath. It was thirteen feet long, six feet broad and four foot six inches deep. The corpse of Gabrielle Lepin took up very little of the available space. The sangfroid for which Mr Postlethwaite-Higgins was famous at the bar deserted him as he rushed screaming into the street, to the amazement of one milk roundsman, one ten-year-old crossing sweeper, and an early rising organ-grinder.

'Mr Didier!'

Auguste turned round, surprised in the midst of making a salmon pie. 'Inspector Rose, you are early.'

'I want you to come with me.'

Seeing Rose's expression, Auguste was suddenly grave.

'Not a word to anyone,' the Inspector said warningly. 'Don't want to start the rumpus before we have to.'

Auguste cast only the briefest glance around him to see that preparations for luncheon were proceeding reasonably smoothly and did not even pause to check the Erasmus soup.

'Come on, Didier,' said Rose impatiently.

'It is another one, then? Not Obadiah again?'

'No, Obadiah's all right. No thanks to himself. It's poor PC Edwards got it. Silly fool was walking alone behind because Bates said he didn't want anyone to see a policeman with him, and someone half strangled him in mistake for Obadiah. The old boy turned, saw what was happening and hopped it quick, he's all right. He wouldn't have been, though. It's only because Edwards is young and tough that he'll pull through. No, it's another of the girls.'

Auguste went pale.

'No, not Miss Maisie,' said Rose quickly. 'I don't know who she is. No identification, no purse.'

'Then how did – ah!'

'Same thing, crossed arms. I want you to try to identify her before I tell Archibald. Not a pretty sight, though.'

They walked in silence across the Strand, crowded with omnibuses, hansoms and carriages of all descriptions.

Office life was beginning for the day, theatres and restaurants taking a back seat till they should come into their own again that night. The Royal Strand Theatre blazoned forth its banners advertising a Willie Edouin farce. The two men turned into the narrow Strand Lane.

'Uncaring old city,' murmured Rose. 'Tucking its dirt out of sight. Farce here – tragedy round the corner. Remember the old Strand Bridge landing stage down there?' he went on. 'I met a fine villain there one day. Triple murderer. No complications. Not like our puzzle. He just did it for money. Case that made my name.'

'Apricot boats,' murmured Auguste in reply.

'I beg your pardon, Mr Didier?'

'So your *Spectator* says. Addison landed there with ten sail of apricot boats.'

'Trust you to think of food,' grunted Rose.

'It helps,' said Auguste simply, as they turned into Surrey Lane.

He stared down at the body lying now by the side of the bath, police doctor in attendance, flanked by stalwart constables. It was not a pretty sight. He turned pale, despite the fact that he had seen death by strangling before. Madame Marchand had died so, victim of a thief that broke into her Café de Commerce. He knew the protruding tongue, the blue lips, the staring eyes . . . but all the same he gulped hard.

'This is the reality of murder, Mr Didier,' said Rose, watching him. 'Not so nice as sitting down thinking.'

'You reproach me, *monsieur l'inspecteur?*' said Auguste quietly. 'You think I treat it as a game, because I liken detection to my profession?'

'No, I never thought that. But it does help bring it home to you. We must be quick. You recognise her, Mr Didier?'

'She is Mademoiselle Gabrielle Lepin, *pauvre fille*, a show girl. And as you supposed a show girl at the Galaxy Theatre.'

146

Chapter Nine

Robert Archibald's face blanched. The stuffy crowded office was suddenly quiet, still, the photographs of laughing ladies on the walls looking out of place.

'Another?' he whispered. He looked at Auguste in despair and lifted his hands hopelessly. 'What's happening?' he said pathetically. 'The Galaxy, that poor girl. All those girls – I ought to have given them protection, given them all escorts home.'

'But who would you ask to escort them, monsieur?' Auguste pointed out practically. 'You can trust no one.'

'They could escort each other,' Archibald replied weakly. 'No after-theatre engagements; they must go straight home.'

'Monsieur, you cannot bridle youth. If these girls wish to go out to dine, they will – death cannot happen to them, they will tell themselves. They will take precautions and, in any case, so and so cannot possibly be a murderer.'

Archibald sighed. 'When will the news be out?' he said resignedly to Rose. 'We can't keep it quiet, I suppose? Stop the panic.'

Rose shook his head. 'I'd like to. I've no wish to have another Ripper scare.'

Archibald paled even more. 'Ripper? You don't think –?' He turned his back on them swiftly, and stood by the window, fighting to control his emotions.

'It'll be on the placards this afternoon,' said Rose abruptly.

'Then this evening we will see what effect it has on the theatre. It may be time –' he stopped before he voiced the unthinkable: to close the Galaxy. 'Do you have no clues yet, Inspector? No hope of stopping it?'

'We've got ideas, sir. Plenty of ideas. It's a question of fitting them together. Finding out, for example, why our murderer's so keen to rid himself of your Mr Bates.'

'You're keeping a watch on him, I trust, Inspector?'

'He's scared now. It wasn't that difficult to persuade him it was no disgrace to be seen being escorted by a policeman.'

'Three girls,' said Archibald slowly. 'Three of my lovely girls.'

'No doubt about it, I'm afraid, sir. We've a mass murderer on our hands.'

'Then I should close the theatre,' said Archibald decisively. It was his ultimate sacrifice.

'Close the Galaxy?' Auguste was appalled. 'But, monsieur –'

Rose and Archibald exchanged looks. 'It may come to that, sir, but not tonight. I'm keeping the news out of the press till the late editions – I want everyone here at the theatre tonight. If you close – and I don't say you're wrong to do so – the company disbands, the girls go their separate ways and our murderer – well, he may lie quiet. He may not. But I want to see the company all together when you make the announcement.' He took out his Albert watch. He must get back soon. He knew that there would be a stew boiling up at the Yard the like of which Auguste would never approve. Simmer, not boil, he remembered the maître telling him once. Let the pot smile, not laugh. In this case, the time for simmering was over.

'A cup of camomile tea, monsieur?' said Auguste quietly to Archibald, seeing his face.

'Tea?' Archibald hardly seemed to hear what he said.

No, thought Auguste, something more sustaining. A

chocolate. Brillat-Savarin was right on the powers of chocolate to calm the stomach.

'Monsieur, it will break your heart to close the Galaxy. And will the girls be safe even if you do close the theatre?'

'I'm a businessman, Didier,' said Archibald with a wry smile. 'Keep the restaurant open by all means, but the theatre must be closed. Temporarily, of course. For one thing, it's a mark of respect to those poor lassies. For another – one, two murders even, have perhaps a curiosity value. Three, and the public will stay away forever.

'I created the Galaxy for entertainment; for gaiety; to make people forget their everyday cares for an hour or two; to forget the real world. If we stay open after tonight – and I'm not even happy about tonight – it will forever become associated in the public mind with death, unhappiness. The real world intrudes – and stays forever in its corridors. Better lost revenue for a week or two than a bad atmosphere for the rest of its life.

'Look what happened to the old Exeter Change next door when they lost Chunee the elephant. It only takes a little thing to turn the audience away, and popular though the Galaxy is, three murders is rather more than a little thing.'

'You're sure he's here amongst us, known to us, Inspector?' asked Archibald unhappily. 'It doesn't seem possible. We're all just the same as we've always been.'

'You've heard the term psychopath?' asked Rose. The others shook their heads. 'German fellow thought it up a year or two back. Makes the task more difficult really. Man's not insane in the usual sense. A psychopath, according to this German, acts and talks most reasonably – it's just that he don't *behave* the way he ought.'

'And you think that's what we have here?' said Archibald, his mind running horror-stricken through all the possibilities.

'Like the recipes – all the ingredients are there, but they do not make one of Didier's cakes because the balance is wrong.'

'Or an ingredient missing,' murmured Auguste.

'You're right, Mr Didier. A madman don't know what he's doing is wrong, or that's what the McNaghten Rules say. But I don't think that's what we've got here.'

It was a different McNaghten that awaited Rose back at the Yard. He had expected the summons to the presence of Chief Constable Sir Melville McNaughten. The news might not have reached the newspaper placards, but it had most certainly reached the higher purlieus of Scotland Yard. He counted himself lucky it was McNaughten, and not yet the Assistant Commissioner.

'We can't afford another Ripper – find him, Rose,' adjured the Presence.

It was all very well to say find him, but how?

'Can't you haul your chief suspect in, just to satisfy the blood lust?' said McNaughten. 'Question him. Let him go. Be seen to be doing something. Reassure the public. Do you have any kind of a case against anyone yet?'

'Yes, sir,' said Rose woodenly.

'Well, why not pull him in?'

'It's Lord Summerfield, sir.'

McNaughten was silenced. 'Summerfield,' he said with resignation. 'I know his mother. I might have known it wasn't going to be simple. It's the Ripper all over again. The newspapers will be suspecting everyone from the Prince of Wales to Kaiser Willie. Not to mention Gladstone. West End whores last time, chorus girls this time. And with the Prince of Wales' love for ladies in the acting profession –' He did not finish the sentence. He did not need to. The awful prospect of the coming public chimera ahead was in both their minds. Above all, there was the dreaded thought of a Queen and Empress identifying herself with the fears of her subjects, and interesting herself in every move of her police force.

Obadiah Bates slowly shook his head. 'It's a bad business,

Mr Didier. Very bad. Poor girls. I warned 'em, you know. And now another one.'

'And you, too, if you do not take more care, Obadiah. Twice now he's tried to attack you.'

'Mr Rose has given me this policeman.' Obadiah's voice trembled. 'But why me, Mr Didier? I ain't a show girl.'

'It must be something you know. You must think, Obadiah, think,' Auguste urged. 'It might not seem very important to you, just as the addition of the parsley does not seem so very important in a receipt. But it can be vital. Now, last night, did you leave before or after Miss Lepin?'

Obadiah thought hard. 'Before,' he pronounced.

'He followed you, then returned thinking he had dealt with you and attacked her. So what happened about Miss Lepin last night, that only you and the murderer know?'

Obadiah's eyes were anxious in his effort to remember. Perhaps he really was scared now. 'There was a message for her,' he said at last. 'Sent the call-boy up.'

'Then she probably told people what was in it. What *did* it say?'

'I don't know,' he said obstinately. 'I didn't open it. All this gallivanting. That Lord Summerfield again.'

Auguste sighed. 'Nothing else?'

Obadiah thought. 'Yes, there was Mr Sykes. Mr Sykes was asking for her. Most particular he was. Most particular.'

Her Majesty was not in a good mood. The Flemish-style partridge the evening before had been too rich, and the chestnut purée soup definitely a mistake. The parlour was small by the standards of Windsor Castle, which meant it was large enough to be draughty despite the heavy velvet curtains and the enormous log fire. She glanced at the oil painting hanging over the fireplace and sought guidance for her pen.

Albert had never liked that picture, but she could not

bear to put anything away that depicted her beloved consort, however poorly. The old rancour welled up inside her. It was all Teddy's fault! One scandal after another. It had brought about Albert's death. Nellie Cliveden was an actress. Now more so-called actresses were causing trouble, making the streets unsafe for respectable women. The thought of what Albert would have done in the circumstances spurred her on to write her letter.

'. . . the Queen fears that her earlier strictures on the efficiency of the detective department in the matter of the Whitechapel murders were not sufficiently regarded and too swiftly forgotten. Has due thought been given to the possibility that the Ripper might have returned to Her Majesty's capital? The Queen would be glad to be kept informed . . .'

Auguste had determined to make this a spectacular dinner at the restaurant. Archibald had decided it should be closed to the general public, and that the Galaxy cast and staff should foregather there after the performance. If he had to break bad news, they might as well have good food to accompany it.

Auguste anxiously superintended the legs of mutton and chestnut purée garnish, the eels *à la tartare* (to please the stage hands), the red char despatched especially from Wales, the *flanc meringue* of apple, the nougat of apricot (which had meant the sacrifice of some of the special quince marmalade sent up to him by the *bonne* Mrs Hankey, at Stockbery Towers.) He thought back almost nostalgically to the vast kitchens of the Towers. The hot cramped quarters in Wellington Street were no substitute. Yet a good cook can cook anywhere; look at Soyer with his boasts about feats with his Magic Stove on top of the Pyramids. Thank heavens, things had advanced since then. And, thank heaven, he did not need to vaunt his skills like Soyer.

152

Leaving Gladys warily watching the *sauce mousseline*, he went to ask Obadiah's permission to visit the chorus girls' dressing room. Fortunately none had begun their disrobing ceremonies yet; not that they minded Auguste in their midst, as to them he was a benevolent brother. Auguste did not see himself that way at all when surrounded by such a bevy of female beauty, but he did not disillusion them.

The tension was evident. The news must be out. Ten pairs of hands clutched at him. 'Oh, Mr Auguste, isn't it *dreadful*? Poor Gabrielle.' He caught Maisie's eye across the room. She remained quiet as she removed her curling tongs from the open gas flame on which, in strict contradiction to Galaxy rules, they had been heating up.

The room was heaving with ruffled feathers like a henhouse after the fox has left, albeit a very luxurious henhouse. It was clear that Rose had forestalled him, but nevertheless he was determined to get all the facts himself.

'He's mad. He must be. He ought to be locked up. Mr Auguste, you know the inspector. When are they going to arrest him? We're none of us safe.'

'Arrest whom, *chéries*?' he said, not bothering to disengage the clutching arms; the perfume in his nostrils and their bodies close to his were very pleasant.

'Summerfield – he's a madman.'

'Summerfield?'

'He took Gabrielle out, didn't he? She was so excited about it. *And* he took the other two out as well, even if he says he didn't. But he did! He took Gabrielle to dinner the other night, and she must have thought she was safe with him. Then –' the girl drew breath, 'he *struck*!'

'But did she keep her appointment?' said Auguste gravely.

'She set off to meet him. She had a message from him and it wasn't to cancel it.'

'Then what did it say, *ma petite*?' said Auguste, absentmindedly patting a well-rounded bottom.

'Asking her to meet him outside the Royal Strand half an hour after the performance. You know how funny he is about being seen outside the theatre with his coach. He used to wait outside the Lyceum – didn't like to be connected with us Galaxy Girls.'

'So she had to walk from here to the Royal Strand Theatre?'

'What could happen to her from here to the Strand – it's main road all the way,' pointed out a redoubtable young lady with a retroussé nose, blond hair and an eye like Medusa's.

'But the entrance is in Strand Lane,' pointed out another timidly. 'That's narrow. He could – do his worst, there.'

A collective shiver ran round the room.

Seeing Auguste's eye on her, Maisie slipped out of the room. He followed grimly for he was none too pleased with her. Ignoring this obvious fact, she took his arm lovingly. 'You know I went to dine with Mr Manley last night, Auguste.'

'I had heard,' said Auguste stiffly. 'Naturally as your fiancé I am the last to hear . . . but the news did reach me.'

'Fiancé,' said Maisie, diverted. 'But I haven't said yes yet, you know. Don't count your *poule au pot* yet. I don't want you suing me for breach of promise.'

Auguste repressed all thoughts of Tatiana. He was committed. As a man of honour, he could not retract.

'Thomas was late arriving. So I waited –'

'Merely having words with Florence,' said Auguste dismissively, still hurt. 'Inspector Rose still favours Summerfield at the moment,' he added.

'Very well, if you don't want to listen!' said Maisie. 'Anyway, Summerfield couldn't strangle a boiled egg. If the inspector really thinks it's him, he's got no more sense than a magsman's meat.'

Unaware of these in fact unjustified comments on his intellectual powers, but in possession of the Galaxy Girls' interesting disclosures of Miss Lepin's proposed movements the night before, Rose set forth once more in pursuit of His Lordship.

Lord Summerfield was staying in London by the Yard's request. The butler seemed quite resigned now to the lowering of his front entrance requirements. He meekly took Rose's hat, umbrella and coat. Without a look of reproof he placed the Staffordshire puzzle jug upright after its unfortunate displacement by Egbert Rose in struggling to extricate himself from his overcoat, and ushered him into the presence of His Lordship. Summerfield was hunched up over the fire, looking more like a frightened rabbit than a member of Britain's ancient peerage. His mother more than compensated. Bosom swelling, lorgnette swinging to and fro in the hand; even the family pearls looked indignant. Nevertheless, 'I'll see the inspector alone, mother,' Summerfield managed to squeak.

'But –'

'It's better, ma'am.' Rose blandly held the door open for a defeated mama, and turned his attention to her son. 'I hear that you had a meeting with Miss Lepin last night, Your Lordship.'

'I – er – yes – I – she didn't arrive, Inspector.'

'Again? You don't seem to have much luck with the ladies one way and another, do you, sir?'

'Don't you believe me?' A modicum of the patrician crept back into his voice.

'I just wanted to hear your story, sir.'

'I waited in my carriage in my usual place – outside the Lyceum theatre.'

'The Royal Strand theatre, was it not?'

Summerfield blinked. 'The Lyceum.'

'But you sent a message to the young lady to say you'd meet her outside the Royal Strand.

'I sent no such message.'

'But –'

'Lord Summerfield's ancestry triumphed. 'Inspector, I sent no message. A forgery, no doubt.'

155

'Then what did you do, sir?' said Rose resignedly.

Summerfield went pink. 'I – I cannot say, Inspector.'

'Can't, sir?' Rose replied mildly enough, but Summerfield caught the underlying message.

'A lady's honour.'

'But the lady did not turn up.'

'No, another lady.'

'Sort of lady you'd found in the street, sir?'

'I –' Summerfield stopped to consider. He gulped, shut his eyes, then opened them again and said firmly: 'Yes.'

'Not much honour up the Haymarket, sir, if that's where you met this lady. I should have another think about things, sir. See if this lady's honour is as important as all that.'

Summerfield was going to have a hard job explaining away three broken engagements, thought Rose to himself as he left. Just as he would have a hard job explaining to the Assistant Commissioner – or worse, the Commissioner himself – the bad news that a peer of the realm might have to be arrested. Fortunately the Honourable Johnny, interviewed earlier that day, had had an unassailable alibi – in his view.

'I was at my club, don't you know,' he had declared winningly. His sister-in-law and brother had nodded complacently. Clubs were approved of, since the temptations provided there did not include loose women.

'Your club, sir? Indeed,' murmured Rose, wondering if the Honourable Johnny could possibly be as silly as he seemed trotting out the old club alibi for the third time. 'We'll be having a word with them, of course. Have to make it clear to them this is a murder investigation. We often find that sort of thing makes a difference. They're not so sure after all which night it was. And it's important we're sure, sir, ain't it?'

For all the certainty amongst the girls that the culprit was Summerfield, there was a general panic and unease that night that went ill with this conviction.

One of the chorus girls, walking through the wings,

screamed when a stage hand inadvertently touched her forearm. She apologised quickly and walked on. Another hung back in the doorway of the dressing room until a companion joined her. Thereafter they walked down in pairs. Had the newspapers shouted their headlines earlier, the chorus line might have been seriously depleted that evening. Did the murderer know the difference between a chorus girl and a show girl? Would he pick on them next?

There was equal tension in the gentlemen's dressing rooms on the other side of the theatre. They looked at each other askance. After all, Obadiah Bates had been attacked. Perhaps the murderer had a preference for girls, but was prepared to make do with a man? In any case, no one wanted to share a dressing room with a murderer.

Herbert sat in front of his mirror, wrestling with his nightmare. That awful feeling that people were avoiding him. Perhaps they thought *he* was the murderer. These past few days had been so terrible, he was almost ready to be convinced that he was. He looked at his pudgy hands. Could they strangle someone? Had he the strength? The thought of Florence came unbidden to his mind, and with a great effort of will he pushed it away again.

Florence Lytton was perhaps the least frightened now. After all, she reasoned, two girls might have been murdered in mistake for her, but it was hardly likely that three could have been. She was safe. Perhaps the dolls were the end of it so far as she was concerned. Now Props had left she felt better. But then there was the mystery of Thomas. Her stomach lurched again. He acted so strangely. He hadn't come home till two o'clock, and had declared his intention of going out with a chorus girl. With Maisie, it was true, not Gabrielle. But suppose it had been Gabrielle all along? This alarming thought brought back her fears with a rush. She would ask Maisie . . .

The unease spread into the performance. A hammer fell off

the flies and narrowly missed a girl's head. Edward Hargreaves mislaid his favourite baton, a mouse was seen in the wings and chased across the stage by the theatre cat before disappearing in the set. Herbert fell over a coil of rope and banged his head, and Auguste burned the cream of crayfish soup. More ominous than all these incidents, as Robert Archibald walked round on what had been intended as a calming tour, was a report from the box office manager of the number of people asking for their money back and the curious lack of the usual queues for gallery and pit.

When the curtain finally went up, ten minutes late, owing to a need to rearrange the show girls, now lacking three of their number, the brightness of the opening chorus, 'Everything's all right, it's a sunny day in Piccadilly' struck a false note. There was not the usual enthusiastic response from the audience. Herbert, with his normal sang-froid (assumed), succeeded in raising a few laughs when he entered, but it was noted by the stage manager that one of them was at the expense of Miss Lytton, a fact which did not go unnoted by her and which threw her for the rest of the scene. It was a sign of the times, thought Robert Archibald, for Herbert to act so unprofessionally.

The performance lurched along unsatisfactorily to nearly the end of Act 2, newcomers to the Galaxy wondering why so much enthusiasm was generated amongst their friends for this mediocre show. When the curtain rose on Act 3, the audience settled down for the final act, once again in the toyshop setting. They were in reasonably good mood. Not only had the drinks been excellent – hurried instructions from Mr Archibald to the barmen had so ensured – but the closing songs of Act 2 had been a success. In particular, Florence's marionette song had gone better than ever before, its melody still lingering in the memories of its listeners.

Herbert's toyshop was full of shoppers. Several show girls draped themselves fashionably around the walls, backs to the rows of miniature Bengal Lancers and clock-work geese. Chorus girls, swinging baskets elegantly on their arms, sung of the pleasures of childhood. Herbert capered amusingly behind his counter.

Into the midst of this jolly scene tripped Miss Penelope, looking winsome in pale blue chiffon, with silk shoes to match and a darling little white silk hat with real flowers. Ideal costuming for a shop assistant.

'Get over there,' barked Herbert. 'Where have you been, Miss Pearl? We have customers, can't you see?' To the audience: 'How lovely she looks. How I wish she'd look at me as she looks at that doll –'

This touching soliloquy was cut short by a scream. Florence's by now familiar scream. Piercing, long drawn out and very loud. It was not in the least musical. Robert Archibald shot up from his seat at the spectacle on stage. Not another damned doll? Not now.

It was not another damned doll. It was the mouse, who was exposed to public view as Florence removed the doll on which it had been comfortably perched. Alarmed by the noise it leapt to the stage floor, resulting in as great a display of shaking petticoats and agitated legs as ever the Folies Bergères had boasted.

Two new arrivals precipitated themselves simultaneously on to the stage to join the screaming mêlée. One was the cat, in hot pursuit of its prey. And falling over the cat in his haste to succour his lady love was Props, in street cap and ragged coat, blinking in the glare of the stage lights and gazing in bewilderment at the screaming Florence.

Bemused, not having seen the cause of the uproar, the audience waited for this up-to-date burlesque on *Dick Whittington* to develop into something more musical. Archibald, unable to bear the sight of his disgrace, staggered outside to communicate his feelings to a brick wall. Thus he missed the sight of the Galaxy's saviour.

Thomas Manley rushed on to the stage and once more

burst into song with no accompaniment. Unfortunately it was a song from the previous act, but no great matter. Seizing a weeping and hiccuping Florence in his arms, he nobly sang:

> 'Ah, your smiling eyes
> Do my heart beguile . . .'

Edwards Hargreaves picked up his second-best baton, and signalled to Percy. Like courtiers in the castle of Sleeping Beauty, the orchestra came slowly to life.

Somewhat puzzled by the way the story appeared to be regressing, the audience stirred uncomfortably as Thomas reached the end of his song and without ado broke into the finishing chorus of Act 2 once more. Hargreaves by this time was but a beat behind him, and the chorus valiantly joined in, as the verse went on. Thus the curtain fell on Act 2 to a fetching tableau of hero and heroine, fifteen chorus girls, five show girls, one theatre cat and an ex-props man cowering behind a toyshop counter. The mouse had prudently disappeared.

Robert Archibald spoke between the leg of mutton and the dessert, a careful timing suggested by Auguste. 'I have,' he said abruptly, 'decided to take no more chances with the lives of our girls. The theatre –' he gulped, 'the theatre is closed from tonight for an indefinite period. At least for two weeks in respect for our three young ladies, may be longer, depending on police advice. Until this murderer is caught. The police,' he continued unhappily, glancing at Egbert Rose sitting discreetly with Didier in the far corner, 'have asked for all your names and addresses, ladies and gentlemen. I have supplied them. Just a formality,' he added wretchedly. That such a scene could be taking place in his theatre was still not quite real to him. 'If there is

160

anything you have not already told them, please will you do so.' He had no great hope that the murderer was going to surrender himself for the good of the Galaxy, but it was worth mentioning.

'Your salaries will be paid at least for the two weeks to come.' A murmur followed this. It was generous. But the Galaxy closed! Each contemplated his own position. Florence thought of a week alone with Thomas. Herbert of himself abandoned in an unfriendly world. Chorus girls of having to buy their own suppers, stage hands of needy wives and children. Suppose the Galaxy remained closed . . .

It was a prospect Robert Archibald dared not contemplate. For well over twenty years the Galaxy had been his life. From those exciting heady moments as they rushed to complete his building in time for the opening performance, finishing it with ten minutes to spare. The first performance, the coming of Daisie Wilton, of Thomas Manley, his founding of the Galaxy Girls – all precious memories. And now this! Three dead and the theatre closed. Pray heaven it would be open again in time for Christmas.

He regarded his nougat of apricot as he would cold tapioca pudding – with little cheer. Far from raising his spirits it appeared to taste of cotton wool, such was his depression.

Belongings were gathered together in the dressing rooms, huddled groups discussed the situation, rumours of who had been seen with whom, who had been seen at this and that time. And more and more ripples of blame seemed to be settling on Lord Summerfield.

Egbert Rose faced an obdurate Props, who glanced fearfully from Rose to Archibald.

'How did you get into the theatre, Props?' asked Archibald bewildered. 'And what on earth possessed you to rush on to the stage?'

'Came in stage door,' muttered Props. 'Mr Bates weren't looking.'

This Mr Bates strongly denied when asked.

'Props?' asked Archibald again.

'Been here every night,' muttered Props.

'Past Obadiah?'

'Yes,' said Props firmly.

'No you never,' said Bates indignantly. 'You never did.'

But Props could not be budged.

'I shall look forward to a rest,' said Edward Hargreaves. 'I shall compose instead. For the next show.'

'If there is a next,' said Percy.

'What do you mean?'

'I think the Galaxy's finished,' said Percy with a light laugh. 'I've been thinking it for some time.' He glanced sideways at Edward. 'I might look for another position.'

Edward stared at him disbelievingly. 'Another theatre?'

'No,' said Percy slowly. 'In a hotel perhaps. One of the big ones on the Riviera. The Majestic in Cannes, for example.' He flicked a cuff back into place.

'Leave *London*? Leave me?' Edward stared at him in horror.

'Just for a while. You could come with me. If you really think you'll miss me that much.'

'But why leave London?' Edward was bewildered.

'Just for a change, dear Edward, just for a change.'

'I've been thinking,' said Maisie, toasting her toes in front of Rose's small fire in his office, whither they had been summoned this Saturday morning. 'This – what do you call it? – psychopath of yours, suppose he'd got a bee in his bonnet about theatres?'

'Theatres?' asked Rose.

'We don't know about Christine Walters, of course, but

162

Edna Purvis was killed round the back of the Olympic, Gabrielle near the Royal Strand –'

'Coincidence,' said Auguste, somewhat annoyed that he had not had this idea.

'But why then girls just from the Galaxy,' asked Rose practically. 'Why not girls from any theatre?'

'I don't know. Galaxy Girls having a certain reputation with some people, perhaps.'

'But did you not say that the psychopath has normal reasoning? Perhaps we should not be looking for a psychopath, after all,' said Auguste,' but a madman.'

'No, these crossed hands, they must mean *something*,' said Rose. 'It's not the act of a madman. What does it suggest to you, Didier?'

'Your hot cross buns,' said Auguste, then looked apologetic for this flippant comparison.

'And they mean?'

'The cross. Holiness.'

'Suggests a kind of reverence, doesn't it?' said Rose. 'Towards women. He never interferes with them. Who does that suggest?'

It was a rhetorical question for he and Auguste were now fairly certain whom it suggested. And last night Props had supplied the missing ingredient: the way into the theatre without passing the stage door.

'Props or Herbert,' said Maisie slowly.

'Yet the dolls, monsieur,' said Auguste quietly. 'The daggers, strangled necks, these are not signs of reverence.'

'Reverence betrayed, is my way of thinking,' said Rose. 'Something happened to trigger our man off. Miss Lytton upsets him somehow and sends him crazy. Idiosyncrasies, that's what we need to look for.' He paused. 'Like your theatre idea, miss. Now, Lord Summerfield has a little idiosyncrasy about theatres, hasn't he? Always waiting outside the Lyceum, for example.'

Maisie stared at the inspector. Then she retorted

vigorously, 'You aren't still thinking of that poor gommy, are you?'

'It fits, miss. It fits.'

'I know he couldn't have murdered Miss Lepin, and that's for sure.'

'Why's that, miss?'

Maisie shot a cautious look at Auguste. 'He was dining with me, that's why.'

It took a moment for this to register with Auguste. Then: '*Last* night?' he enquired in awful tones. 'As *well*?'

'Yes, and there's no need to sound like Irving in *The Bells*,' said Maisie crossly. 'I was dining with him. That's all.'

'You told me you were dining with Mr Thomas Manley. You lied to me. You have betrayed me.'

'I said I was *going* to dine with him. But he never arrived. And as I was walking to the cab rank I saw Lord Summerfield – all alone. So there we are.'

'Mr Manley told me he dined with you,' said Rose, 'after being delayed by his wife. And His Lordship never mentioned anything about you.' He was not pleased. The case against Summerfield was not good, but it was at least a theory to talk about with the Commissioner.

'He wouldn't, would he? He's a gentleman, that's why. I was' – she studiously avoided Auguste's eye – 'dining at his home.'

'With Her Ladyship that would be?' asked Rose politely.

'Not likely,' replied Maisie forthrightly. 'Can you see old Queen Boadicea passing me the cabbage without raising every single tile on the ancestral roof? But if it's witnesses you're thinking of, I imagine the butler, a few liveried waiters and the coachman will back His Lordship up.'

Rose looked at her. So did Auguste – much as he would a customer who had the temerity to leave a *soufflé d'écrevisse* unfinished.

'I take it,' said Auguste stiffly, 'that you no longer consider yourself my betrothed.'

164

'Oh, Auguste.' Maisie was irritated. 'Are you telling me that you don't believe me when I say I was only dining?'

'Naturally I believe you, but I have my honour –'

'That's all right then,' said Maisie more cheerfully. 'Your honour will be happier after a good luncheon. Isn't that right, Inspector Rose?'

'Indeed, Miss Maisie, I believe Brillat-Savarin remarked that a good meal induces contentment both of body and soul,' replied Egbert Rose gravely.

This display of erudition was rewarded by a glare from Auguste who for once could think of nothing to say. And having nothing to say, found himself forced to smile. But perhaps that was at the thought of the roast ortolans that awaited them.

Chapter Ten

Chapter Ten

The mounted men at Wolferton railway station were of course unaware of the contents of the missive with the Royal Seal, but when their employer, a portly gentleman, read it in his morning room at Sandringham House he was cast into gloom. Mama was displeased *again*. It was so unfair. Why should Mama think that he was in any way to blame for the deterioration of morals in London? Surely even she could not have believed those unfortunate rumours about the Ripper and Eddie. Even after the poor boy's death the rumours continued that his son, the Duke of Clarence, had been the Ripper himself. *Another* Ripper? What did these heavy hints mean? Surely even Mama could not think that he, the Prince of Wales, would creep about the streets of London strangling chorus girls. Chorus girls indeed.

Here he was, but newly returned from an important diplomatic mission – double mission indeed – to Russia, and already Mama was treating him like a little boy again. The funeral of an autocratic crowned head was never an easy event to attend, but everyone agreed that had it not been for his tactful handling of that uncouth King of Serbia things could have got out of hand. All the crowned heads of Europe could have been at each other's throats, acting like a pack of schoolboys. But he'd calmed them down. Why did Serbia *always* have to cause trouble though? Just a tiny little Balkan state and always stirring things up. Sometimes he had an uneasy feeling about Serbia. If he were Franz

Josef, sitting there in his Imperial Palace in Vienna, he would see the Serbs were kept in their place.

His thoughts turned to happier events. The new Czar's marriage to dear little Alix. Nothing could go wrong there. And Mama was delighted with the success of her matchmaking. So why was she in such a bad mood now? One-thirty. It was time for luncheon. And Alexandra was late again. It was clearly not going to be a good day at Sandringham House.

It was not a good day at the Yard either. The painfully written, tart words of the latest edict from Windsor lying across the Commissioner's desk from Rose did not bode well.

'We're looking for a madman, sir.'

'Should be simple enough. It must be someone at that theatre.'

'Or connected with it. The theatre's closing, which will give us a chance to investigate every single man concerned with the theatre. We've several lines to follow up.'

Rose spoke more confidently than he felt.

The case they had built up against Summerfield had been a strong one, though based on circumstantial evidence only. Still, most murders were. Very few villains stayed around to be witnessed in the act. But something had been wrong. Rose tried to be grateful that Maisie had blown their case to smithereens.

It was not a good day in the Galaxy restaurant either. Othello's occupation gone, thought Auguste, gazing idly from his window across the road to the Lyceum. What was the use of a theatre restaurant without a theatre? It was deprived of soul. He thought of the time he had seen Mr Irving, his noble features blackened for the Moor. *Quelle majesté, comme un grand filet de boeuf*. What dignity. Of course his Othello did not compare with his Macbeth. Or, in

168

Auguste's opinion, with his Lear. Though there few would agree with him. It had generally been reckoned a failure and after that short run two years ago he had never attempted it again. He would never forget Mr Irving full in the limelight at the rear of the stage: 'How sharper than a serpent's tooth it is to have a thankless child'. He had been moved to tears at the end of the play when he carried on the dead Cordelia in his arms. Ah, that was tragedy. Now, *la belle Sarah* – a tragedienne, too, but of what different type. As Phèdre – *magnifique, superbe*.

Tiens! he had almost forgotten the *matelote* sauce for the eels. For himself, he was not sufficiently enamoured of this fish, but it was popular with Londoners. It was like the conclusion that he was gradually coming to – it must be the answer, there was no escape from it. There was no other explanation. And what would happen when it was revealed – what would that do to the Galaxy?

'It's Scotland Yard, Mr Didier.' Gladys broke into his thoughts.

Fresh from the Commissioner's office, Rose had arrived at the restaurant in search of reassurance and food. After one glance at his face Auguste went so far as to sit with him, leaving the kitchen in the nervous hands of Annie.

'What's this, Didier?'

'That, monsieur, is an aspic of chicken *à la reine*.'

'Rain?'

'Queen, monsieur.'

Rose did not wish to talk of queens, and glared morosely at the unfortunate dish in front of him. He seemed to have lost his appetite for it somehow.

'All right, so it's not Summerfield – or probably not,' he added darkly. 'But I still wager it's rejection. Disappointment in love. Does strange things to people. Even quite normal people. Ever noticed that?'

'Indeed, monsieur. Why, I –'

'Ophelia,' interrupted Rose, warming to his theme,

'went and drowned herself. Constance Kent murdered her little brother. Thought she'd been rejected by the family.'

'Indeed, monsieur. I –'

'Now, now, Didier, let me speak. You Froggies do love the sound of your own voices. So our Florence rejects our fellow quite properly –'

'Unless –'

'Didier! He shows his displeasure, by giving a fright with the dolls, but because he worships her he won't touch or harm her. Instead he kills her attendants. What do you think of that?'

'But why, monsieur,' asked Auguste meekly, 'the crossed hands?'

'Why not?' said Rose. 'If he is mad?'

'He is but mad nor-nor-west,' said Auguste, 'to quote your *Hamlet*. There is purpose in his madness. It may be, monsieur, that he is not mad as your Ripper was mad but like our friend Mr Robert Louis Stevenson's hero, Dr Jekyll – and Mr Hyde. That one side of him does not know what the other side does. In order to produce the stock you have the scum which must be removed. It is necessary to distil, to purify, like Dr Jekyll, and then one is left with the scum, Mr Hyde. Dr Jekyll did not know of the actions of Mr Hyde.'

'That's as may be, Mr Didier,' said Rose, 'but to the poor lass lying there strangled with her tongue bulging out, it doesn't matter too much for what reason she was killed. Dead is dead, and it's my job to find out who did it. And I still think our Florence is at the heart of it. Yet I admit, Mr Didier, it's odd that there have been no further attacks on her.'

'Love gone putrid, monsieur. He does not wish to kill Miss Lytton. He does not have the courage. But the dolls were a threat, a message that she should not regard his love lightly.'

'Our Props, you're thinking of.'

'Florence just never noticed him.'

'She notices him now,' said Rose. 'Screams every time she

170

sees him. Natural enough since she's convinced he's responsible for those dolls. Said he told her so. Yes, it fits all right.' he went on. 'The dolls are like the violets. A message. Bobbing up like a jack in a box on the stage. He's got some special way in, that's for sure, for all he denies it. Bates insists he didn't come past him last night. And the rope came from his room. He's just the type we're after. Quiet, inoffensive. That's what I find down Brick Street – it's not the big loud-mouthed villains, it's the quiet softly-spoken ones that stay in the background.'

'But I think, Inspector, we should see whether Lord Summerfield had made improper advances to Miss Lytton,' put in Auguste innocently. He liked Props. 'There was something strange, did you not think so, when he spoke of her?'

'Your Miss Maisie's cleared him,' pointed out Rose unkindly.

Auguste glared at him. 'Or Monsieur Beauville, or Mr Sykes.' He was not to be deterred. 'Perhaps we do not yet know quite enough about Miss Lytton. We think of her as the glorious centre of the Galaxy around whom things happen. But suppose, monsieur, instead, she is the cause – like the pole in the carousel. No maypole, whose strings are pulled hither and thither by others, but the centre of power that controls. She makes these players dance to her command.'

'The lady can't help being popular,' pointed out Rose. 'And after all, she's married. She might be thinking: if they want to be foolish enough to fall in love with me, I'm not to blame. No harm in being admired, is there, Monsieur Didier?'

'Devotion is pleasing until it curdles. Then, like mayonnaise, it is difficult to put back together again.'

'Humpty Dumpty,' said Rose diverted.

'*Pardon, monsieur*?' Auguste looked blank.

'Just an old nursery rhyme,' said Rose hastily.

'And Monsieur Beauville,' went on Auguste, ignoring

171

him, 'is well known for his admiration of many ladies, of whom Florence was one. And of course there is Mr Manley. It is not always improper advances that one rejects. Perhaps proper ones also. And Miss Lytton has been observed not to be on good terms with her husband recently.'

'Of them all,' said Rose consideringly, 'Beauville's most likely – or Props, to my mind. Because Bates would have been in the best position to observe their movements, and for them to think he was a threat to them. I think perhaps,' he added, 'our friend Bates had better have another think.'

Obadiah Bates was slumped in front of his fire and a stalwart police constable guarded the front door, to the great indignation of his highly respectable landlady.

He looked up hopefully as they entered. 'Theatre opening again, is it?' he asked. His face looked thin and drawn. He was an old man, a fact brought home to them by the photograph of a younger Bates in a photographic studio, stiffly posed in uniform. It was a very old photograph.

'Not yet, Mr Bates, we've still got to find our murderer,' said Rose soberly. 'And we need help. You don't want another bang on the head, do you?'

Bates clearly took this to be a rhetorical question for he did not answer, merely touched his bandage in puzzled fashion.

'No one attacked you after the death of Miss Walters, so I think we can assume that whoever hit you thought you saw something dangerous to him on the evening of Miss Purvis's death.'

'Mr Beauville came in in a cake,' said Bates firmly.

'No, Obadiah, that was the evening before. This was the next night when all the girls' beaux came to collect them as usual.'

'Yes,' said Obadiah considering. 'That's right. Young Captain Starkey – him as is going to marry Miss Birdie, was round. Miss Purvis, she liked him. Yes, I remember.

Mr Beauville was there too. Ah, it were *that* evening.'

'What evening, Obadiah,' said Auguste eagerly. 'What was special?'

'She were late down,' he said slowly, 'on account of her prettying herself up. Paint and all,' he explained disgustedly. 'They nearly always comes down together, but that evening she were nearly last. I was watching for her, 'cos I knew she was going out with Lord Summerfield, yet Mr Sykes had been enquiring for her and Mr Manley came hurrying down earlier to send up a note. 'Allo, I says. Hallo. Very popular, Miss Purvis. Nice young lady. Sad,' he added. 'Very sad.'

'Was Props there when she came down?'

'Props? I expect so. I can't rightly remember.' His brow furrowed. 'He allus came out of the door when he heard the ladies descending. He likes Miss Lytton best, of course. Likes to see her before he goes home. Or did, I should say. Liked to watch the girls coming down, too. 'Course, he's only young really. But strange. You think he's the one then?'

'He wasn't at the theatre the evening Miss Lepin was killed.'

'Hanging around outside though, weren't he?' said Obadiah. 'I heard that afterwards. Like last night.'

'Are you positive he didn't come in the stage door last night?'

Obadiah looked mulish. 'When I says no one gets past me, I mean he never came in. Pathans, Fuzzie Wuzzies. They don't get past Tommy, oh no.'

'And that's all you have to say?'

Obadiah glared at Rose, folded his arms. Enough had been said. No reason these police fellows had to know everything.

'I'm getting too old for this game,' said Rose, doubling up to clamber across a lowered grave trap, every other available space in the cellar seemingly taken up with machinery or mess.

'There *must* be an entrance down here somewhere,' said Auguste, gazing hopefully upward. 'The entrance to the Royal Box and the gallery and so on are all locked at night, and he could not rely on finding one of them accidentally open. The only other entrance is to the restaurant, to which only Archibald, myself and Watch have a key. Even Bates has no key. And then he would have to know about the secret entrance to the theatre. No, it is not possible. Yet it must be.'

'Does it matter?' grunted Rose, falling over a gaspipe and regarding it severely.

'It cannot be up,' said Auguste thoughtfully.

Rose shut his eyes and prayed that Auguste would not invent an entrance through the roof. He didn't think he could face the grid again. If there was another world up there aloft, he preferred not to know about it.

'So it must be down,' Auguste went on. 'It cannot be right under the stage here in the cellar – it – where does that lead to?' he demanded of one of the cellarmen who had been working industriously away greasing machinery and traps, attending to floats, sinks and rises. From above came the sound of pounding feet. A rare understudy rehearsal was in progress, taking advantage of the theatre's closure to the public, and the sound of girlish voices rose and fell, with the occasional shout interspersed by Edward Hargreaves. Auguste pointed to a smaller corner door.

'Gas room, meter room – and an odd props room,' answered the cellarman indifferently.

They looked at one another in sudden hope.

The narrow stone cold passage was dimly lit by a solitary gas jet, with two doors leading off it. The first proved to be the odd props room. Junk room was more like it. Dusty, cold, forlorn paraphernalia of revels past. Moth-eaten animal heads regarded them sorrowfully from a pile of grinning demon masks. A sad-looking fairy coach waited disconsolately for another hour of glory. Paper flowers strewed the floor haphazardly. A cardboard cloud patiently awaited a summons to Mount Olympus.

The next room was the gas room – occupied by the gasman, that all important gentleman who glared at them for interrupting his serfs' work. Bunches and tee lights stood in one corner, an electric carbon arc fan producing sunrise, Bunsen cells littered tables, gas piping crazed the floor like a maze.

'Way out?' grunted the gas man. 'No way out of here. Only to meter room.'

'Meter room?' asked Rose.

'Where the oxygen and hydrogen tanks are kept for the limelight,' said the gas-man pityingly. 'See it if you like. If you can crawl, that is.' He opened the half size door in the far wall. A short tunnel led to a small brickbuilt room.

'But it has an outside door?'

'Well, someone's got to fill the tanks,' the gas-man pointed out reasonably. 'Not like the old days when they came round with bags on their shoulders, straight up to the flies, press the bag, and hey presto, limelight. We're too fond of our skins for that now.'

'But that door –'

'Leads on to the basement court and up to old Exeter Arcade as well. 'Course, no one ever uses it.'

Herbert Sykes savoured his soggy toast with a slow, suffusing sense of triumph. He had scored over Florence. He did not care any more. Oh, the power he had felt when he sided with Hargreaves over that song! True, the theatre was now closed, but it would open again. Now he felt he could face her again. He felt in command for the first time since he had met her, as though he, Herbert Sykes, held her destiny in his hands. Accordingly, when his landlady showed Inspector Rose and Auguste Didier in, he was, for Herbert, expansive. He bustled importantly, seats were brought forward, coffee was ordered, an air of smugness pervaded him. He had not even bothered to remove the photograph of Florence, smiling incessantly from her flower-decorated mount.

'Miss Lytton, sir,' said Rose, making himself comfortable.

'What about Miss Lytton?' said Herbert. A certain belligerence entered his voice.

'Friend of yours?'

'Everyone likes Miss Lytton,' replied Herbert expressionlessly.

'I understand you quarrelled with her though.'

Herbert went white. 'It was a misunderstanding,' he said, his composure faltering. 'A misunderstanding. She actually thought,' he managed a little laugh, 'that I was threatening her.' He swallowed. 'As though I'd do that.'

'And why should she think that?'

'I – well – I heard someone in the ladies' dressing rooms late. Thinking it might be an intruder, I naturally went to investigate, and found it was Miss Lytton. I suppose being alone in the theatre she might have wondered what I was doing there.'

'But you told her –'

'I was going to,' he said quickly. 'But she was very nervous. Those dolls – it was the dolls,' he said eagerly, grasping at the lifeline. 'She was upset.'

'You didn't touch her at all?'

'*Touch* her, Inspector?' He drew himself up theatrically. The gesture failed in its effect. 'Are you implying – good heavens! Is that what she told you? Poor darling Florence. She *must* have been upset.'

'Yes, indeed, sir. Now the other young ladies. Miss Lepin, Miss Walters, Miss Purvis. I understand you were by way of being a particular friend of all of them.'

'An escort, an occasional escort.' His composure, haltingly recovered, now faltered again. 'I am a principal, Inspector. I do my part in looking after the newer young

176

ladies. Take them out to dine. Introduce them to London.'

'Very good of you, Mr Sykes,' answered Rose woodenly. 'A fatherly interest, you might say.'

'Precisely, Inspector,' said Herbert unhappily, looking at the floor.

'And were you with any of these young ladies the evenings they got killed?'

'No – Good heavens, no!' He gave a high-pitched laugh.

'Then who were you with, may I ask?'

'I don't remember,' Herbert said, eyes blinking rapidly. 'No, really I don't. I don't remember at all.' He gave a slight gesture which this time did not puzzle Auguste. He had seen it before; once from Herbert a few days ago, and before that from Dan Leno. Grimaldi lived on, the eternal mischievous lovable thieving clown.

'Miss Lytton, we are still gravely worried for your safety.'

'But the theatre's closed.' Lying on a chaise longue in an elegant rose chiffon tea gown, Florence looked fragile, petite and entirely bewitching. Edward Hargreaves would not have recognised her.

'That won't stop our villain if he's determined to get you,' said Rose grimly. 'I'm going to post a police constable outside your home till we've caught out man.'

'But *I'm* not at risk.' Nevertheless her eyes widened in alarm.

'With a madman around you are. Those dolls –'

'But it's show girls he kills, not me.'

'It may be you next time. Now he's got up courage. That's what we fear.'

'Oh . . .' Her hands fluttered feebly, but her brain was clearly not affected. Auguste recognised this gesture too. She had used it in *Lady Bertha's Betrothal*, to great effect. 'Then you know who it is?'

'We can't prove it,' said Rose guardedly. 'Of course I

know you're worried by Mr William Ferndale – Props. But there's no proof. He's never touched you.'

'He played that trick with the dolls,' said Florence indignantly.

'Maybe, maybe not, but we've got to be sure. Now, is there any reason that Herbert Sykes should suddenly have turned against you?'

Florence suddenly ceased to mind if she looked a fool. It was as well to be sure where her own neck was concerned. 'Indeed there is, Inspector,' she said eagerly. 'He *is* mad, you're right, I've known all along. It was one evening – the evening Edna Purvis was murdered . . .' And she proceeded to give them a lurid account of how Herbert Sykes had burst into her dressing room with a maniacal expression on his face, babbling about how she, Florence, was his, his alone, how he'd make her his, and proceeded to lay hands on her. He'd torn her clothes, and when she had fought him off, lay slobbering on the floor kissing her feet, and then, as she had gently repulsed him again, sworn eternal vengeance against her. This was an exaggeration as befitted a leading actress, but the basic story was true enough. He was out of his mind. She had been terrified.

She did not mention that a flourish of a button-hook had been all it had taken to quell him.

'And you're sure this happened the evening Miss Purvis was murdered?'

'Yes, Inspector,' she sighed.

'Then why didn't you tell us before, miss?'

'Because' – she flushed – 'I was frightened.' It was true enough. He was a strange fish, Herbert.

'Ah, Miss Lytton, but there is another reason, is there not? A sensible lady who thinks a man is so deranged that he could rush straight from her to murder someone else in revenge, is sensible enough to suppose he might return to murder her. Now why therefore did you not rush to tell me? I take it' – as she said nothing –'it is because you thought you knew someone else was to blame for these murders. Am I right?'

She stared at Rose open-mouthed and burst into tears.

'Come, come, *ma chérie*,' said Auguste, patting her in a way that won Rose's full approval. Though what Mrs Rose would say if he set about patting all lovely young women witnesses on the back . . .

'You must tell us, *chère madame*,' said Auguste, 'you cannot continue. It is too much for you. After all, if he is not the man, then he will not be arrested. He is not Inspector Lestrade, our good Inspector Rose.'

'No, no,' murmured Rose, 'Mr Holmes.'

'It's – it's –' she hiccuped, 'it's my *husband*!' A fresh wail followed.

'But why, *chérie*, should you think that the good Mr Marley should wish to murder you?' Auguste was amazed. A wife suspect a husband?

'He doesn't,' she wailed. 'But he was out – out each of those evenings.'

'Was he, indeed? But he said he was with you, miss.'

'He wasn't,' she shouted, the mask of fragility slipping. 'He told me he was seeing them. He doesn't like me any more.' And she burst into a storm of entirely unassumed tears.

'Would you care to reconsider your statements of where you were on the evening of Miss Purvis' and Miss Lepin's deaths, sir?' enquired Rose resignedly. Just as he'd got it nicely sorted out in his mind again after the Summerfield débâcle, along come another red herring. For red herring he must be. He could not see this tall good-looking actor as a murderer. Still, you never knew. Perfectly ordinary fellows – that's what these psychopaths looked, apparently. Or like Mr Didier's Dr Jekyll.

Thomas Manley went red, then white, an interesting colour change he had never achieved with the aid of stage make-up.

It took Rose three times as long as Maisie to winkle out the fact that Thomas Manley had been with a prostitute on the night of Edna Purvis' murder.

'Recognise her again, would you, sir?'

Thomas gazed at Rose hopelessly.

Rose sighed. 'And when Miss Lepin died? You had arranged to meet Miss Wilson, but you never arrived, according to her.'

'I –' It was a squawk.

'Beg your pardon, sir?'

Thomas cleared his throat. 'Are you a married man, Inspector?'

'I have that honour, sir.'

'Then you understand – there are times – times when one is not in such perfect accord with one's wife as one might wish.'

Rose had a fleeting vision of a silent self cursing the toughness of last Sunday's roast.

'I understand, sir.'

'In short, Inspector, we had a quarrel. And in consequence I was late leaving the theatre, and then Florence demanded I put her in our carriage, and' – he mopped his face with a white silken handkerchief – 'when the carriage had left – I – Inspector, I had forgotten which restaurant I intended to escort Miss Wilson to.'

He looked hopelessly at them as if in doubt that such a story could ever be believed. Indeed it was totally incomprehensible to Auguste that anyone could forget a matter of such moment, but Rose merely said: 'And?'

'I was under the impression it was Rules. By the time I had arrived there, and found neither Miss Wilson nor reservation, I remembered the true destination. I set off back to the Strand, only to see Miss Wilson being handed into Lord Summerfield's carriage.'

Auguste looked black. This was what came of all this detective work.

'What did you do then, sir?' asked Rose inexorably.

'I – I walked to the Haymarket and –'

'Don't bother to tell me, sir,' said Rose grimly. 'I understand.'

'Madonna.' One hand laid a rose reverently in front of the centre portrait.

A match was struck and the candles lit, throwing a hundred flickering shadows over the mass of portraits and photographs, making that well-known face at once mysterious, provocative, elusive, yet attainable. He spoke his litany for the day. All candles had to be lit in ritual turn; he waited carefully till each caught. If one went out and the next burned, he must return to the beginning again, snuffing them all out first. There were candles for thirty pictures. One face: Florence Lytton's.

Props smiled his slow, secretive smile as he gazed at them. Here in her shrine she was kind. Here she smiled at him, and here was his heaven. He could even kiss her if he wanted. She couldn't stop him. Not here. It gave him a sense of power. He looked at the pictures one by one every day. Here just her face. There in *Lady Bertha* in the gown for Act 2. Here in the burlesque she'd been in at Princess'. There sitting in a garden swing.

When he first saw her she had not been at the Galaxy but a different theatre. He had been at the stage door every night. He had bribed the stage doorkeeper of the Royal to buy the doll she'd clutched to her bosom so amusingly in *Lady Daisy*. It thrilled him to hold it now, hold it to his bosom as she'd held it to hers. He looked twice at the picture of her on the swing today, the picture that showed her pretty figure so entrancingly. He shivered. She was beautiful. She was his madonna. Here in his sanctum he could expunge the thought of her distorted face, screaming at him. He did not understand why she had screamed. But he would forget that, here in this shrine. The candles all lit at last, he sank to his knees in homage: 'Florence, full of grace, hear thy servant . . .'

                    *   *   *

Auguste reluctantly left the absorbing task of the Christmas
mincemeat preparation (barbaric his French *confrères*
deemed it; for himself, there was a certain intellectual
fascination at the combination of ingredients, this relic of
mediaeval feasting) to glance out of the window at the
source of the noise. It was mild for December, but the
carolling voices of the street band, singing of deep snow and
wassailing, seemed determined to ignore this fact. He
tossed them some coins, more in the hope they'd go away
than as tribute to their prowess. He wished to concentrate
on the vital decision yet to be made – whether or not to add
spices to the concoction before him. Some said they were a
vital ingredient – but would they not upset the delicate
overriding flavour of lemon that he had been at such pains
to preserve?

'Go on, Auguste, invite them in,' urged Maisie, sticking
her finger into the bowl and licking it.

'But, *ma mie* –'

'It's nearly Christmas,' she pointed out.

'Is that any reason for me to endure a hurdy-gurdy in my
own restaurant?' he demanded.

'You can spare some of that punch for them,' she said
brightly.

He regarded her with horror. 'That is my best Napoleon.'

'It's Christmas,' she said in a tone that would not be
denied.

Grateful for their punch, the band struck up again as
Auguste cowered in the kitchen doorway, longing for
escape. An elderly warbler, who might once have been a
tenor, launched forth into 'Angels from the Realms of
Glory'.

Auguste groaned.

'Cast your light o'er land and sea.'

Somewhere, deep in Auguste's mind, a train of thought
started.

* * *

In a poky Fleet Street newspaper office a junior sub-editor was racking his brains as to how to combine the twin excitements of the Galaxy murders (now slipping in appeal with no new murder to announce) and the advent of Christmas. He too was listening to carol singers. He picked up his pen and wrote a by-line:

'The Angel Murderer: Still at Large'.

In a room at Windsor Castle Queen Victoria was thinking, as was her custom, of Albert. Christmas made her exceptionally sad, as indeed did most times of the year. She could not look at the huge Christmas tree so bravely decked without thinking of the very first tree that *he* had brought from Germany for their very first Christmas. How quickly the fashion had caught on. Dearest Albert. Beatrice had suggested she should not stay at Windsor for Christmas if the memory of times past intruded so greatly. But she would. It was her duty. As she gazed with determined anguish at the gaudy tree with its angel triumphantly adorning the top, she welcomed as an old friend the pricking sensation of gathering tears.

That brought to mind another matter, much in the news, and tears rapidly dispersing, she reached for her pen with a frown: 'Is there yet word on the Angel Murderer . . . ?'

As Christmas approached, public obsession with the Angel Murderer gave way to equally frantic laudings of Father Christmas. With the Galaxy closed, no more chorus girls were found murdered on the streets of London. The populace of London forgot their concern about the return of the Ripper and settled down to buying mechanical marvels at Swears & Wells, and tiepins for Uncle Claude. Satin, lace and embroidered Christmas cards were lovingly prepared, and Kate Greenaway girls coyly smiled from every mantelpiece. The Christmas card trade flourished as never before.

183

Murder was banished. Except in Scotland Yard where Inspector Rose pored over his files.

Even Auguste was caught in the hubbub, and found himself somewhat to his surprise accompanying Maisie on the number 57 'bus to Messrs Gamages on a shopping expedition. Maisie had a number of nephews and nieces whose parents, being nowhere so fortunate as Maisie in their position in life, sat back and generously permitted her to enrich their Christmas.

Staggering under a particularly heavy toy Merryweather fire engine, Auguste was unable to see at first who was greeting Maisie so enthusiastically.

'I say, Miss Wilson, this is a delightful surprise.'

The Honourable Johnny Beauville's delight at finding a Galaxy Girl – and moreover one who did not laugh at him – in the midst of what had threatened to be a highly tedious shopping expedition with his sister-in-law was now tempered with caution, and drew the sister-in-law's icy disapproval on him.

'Oh, ah, Gertrude, let me present Miss Maisie Wilson.'

The stalagmite inclined its head. Miss Wilson bowed so deeply one might have thought the gesture a touch ironic.

'Oh and – ah – Mr Auguste Didier. He's the – ah – cook at the Galaxy. Quite a famous one,' Johnny added anxiously.

Auguste found more difficulty in bowing owing to the fire engine, but this was no problem since Her Ladyship did not consider cooks came into the category of persons to whom one bowed or whose bows one recognised. Her expression of severe disapprobation was all too familiar to him.

'Miss Wilson is – ah – an actress at the Galaxy,' added Johnny.

'That I know, Jonathan. I have accompanied you to that theatre. And besides, I've seen her likeness in Messrs Elli and Walery's range of postcards.' Her tone indicated that

184

those who wished to flaunt their charms in the photographic studios of these eminent gentlemen were not for her knowing.

'It all goes with being a Galaxy Girl,' said Maisie sweetly. Like coronets and butlers with yours. I expect you get used to it, though.'

Her Ladyship was silenced, and clearly realising this would not bode well for him, Johnny broke in with: 'Talking of the Galaxy, when d'you think it'll open again, Miss Wilson? I miss it.' His eager face was hopeful for good news.

'When they find the murderer, monsieur,' said Auguste. 'Only then will it be safe.'

'But they won't,' said Johnny. Then, seeing them looking at him in surprise, he said hastily. 'I mean, suppose he just stops? Like the old Ripper.'

'Scotland Yard believes the Ripper is dead,' said Auguste. 'That he drowned himself – and that's why he stopped. His crimes got too terrible even for him to contemplate going on.'

'And maybe our chap hasn't done his worst yet,' said Johnny thoughtfully. 'Those dolls were rather spooky. Angel murderer. Who do you think'll be next then? Could be anyone. Could be Miss Maisie here.' And he gave her an ingenuous smile.

In his country home in Hertfordshire, Lord Summerfield could not enter with his usual enthusiasm into the decoration of Mama's tree, and the presents for the estate workers. He began to feel as though a dire fate were following him around. Why was it the women that he invited out were murdered? Captain Carstairs, jolly good chap, had had six different girls in the time he had taken to invite one out and each returned inviolate. Of murder at any rate. Even Mama was beginning to look at him a little strangely.

*   *   *

'Puddings,' said Auguste in glee, stirring vigorously. 'I love these English plum puddings.'

'You should have made it weeks ago,' said Maisie severely. 'It will be no good now. It should mature.'

'My love, it is the cheese or the game that has to hang. We will add some more brandy, and you will see.'

'You're too busy being a detective to be a cook.'

'That is an insult,' replied Auguste with dignity. 'One assists the other, and I say it is ridiculous to cook these plum puddings weeks before the day. We cook it together now *hein*?'

Maisie dropped a kiss on the back of his head where the slightest hint of a bald spot was beginning to appear. Her arms crept round his waist.

'*Ma mie*,' he said reprovingly, 'not while I am cooking.'

'Nonsense,' she said, 'any time.'

'Now look,' he exclaimed, 'you have made me forget the lemon – ah, women are in the way in the kitchen.'

'Tell that to Rosa Lewis,' murmured Maisie, dipping her finger in the mixture and licking it.

'There is something' – he stared at her worriedly – 'there is something missing.'

'Are you detecting or cooking?'

'Cooking – how could I be detecting – now the good Mrs Acton says four ounces of minced apples but myself think a little more, and not a small glass but a large glass of brandy. Perhaps two. But what – there is still something missing. *Ma foi*, what is it?'

'I don't think there's anything missing,' said Maisie. 'I think you've got everything there. You're just looking at it the wrong way. It's a pudding, not a cake. You wait till it's upside down and covered in brandy and sugar. You'll see.'

'I am honoured, *ma mie*.'

Maisie laughed as she pulled Auguste close to her in bed. 'I'm getting lazy with nothing to do.'

'I am indebted to you,' said Auguste, somewhat ~~i~~dignantly.

She giggled. 'You know I don't mean you.'

'*Ma mie*,' he said pleadingly, 'I'm tired. *Very* tired. I ~~wa~~nt your arms round me, but – not after that dinner. We ~~ar~~e full every night all right. They all come to see the Galaxy ~~wh~~ere the murders started. They do not care about the ~~foo~~d, they eat *anything*. It is disheartening, my love, when ~~on~~e takes care. One takes pride in one's work but it must be ~~ap~~preciated.'

'Well, you clearly aren't going to appreciate me, and ~~th~~at's for sure,' she said, turning over drowsily.

'*Ma mie*, in the morning,' he said placatingly. 'It was ~~th~~at last party who came in. They were like – '

'Oh, *that's* what I meant to tell you,' she interrupted, ~~wa~~king up again.

'Please, do not tell me of your nieces and nephews now,' ~~he~~ pleaded.

'You said,' Maisie reminded him, 'that in a recipe the ~~sli~~ghtest variation might be of importance.'

'So I did,' he groaned.

'And you're telling me that detection is like cooking, ~~ar~~en't you?'

'Well, I just remembered what struck me as odd when we ~~me~~t Johnny Beauville in Gamages.' And she told him.

'Thank you,' he said courteously. 'I will store it in ~~th~~e larder with the other ingredients.' It was of no impor-~~tan~~ce, of course, but there had been something odd all the ~~tim~~e . . .

~~A~~uguste slept heavily that night, but his sleep was full ~~of~~ dreams. He seemed to be at a performance of some ~~Sh~~akespeare play in Gamages with the hurdy-gurdy player ~~cry~~ing out 'Flights of angels sing thee to thy rest'. But he ~~ha~~d to get back to the restaurant to prevent an army of dolls ~~bre~~aking into his larder. But when he arrived, it was Lord

187

Summerfield who stole a huge boar's head which turned int
Maisie. Then Irving, looking very disapproving, came
to rescue Maisie, and took her away, leaving him to c
impotently, 'Come back, come back, come back . . .' But a
that he was left with was a huge Christmas puddin,
Someone was saying something - was it Maisie? - 'Turn
upside down.' So he heaved and heaved, and the puddir
emerged from the dish. In the middle of the pudding wa
Tatiana, beautiful, beloved, his own. But he couldn't reac
her. She was trapped by the pudding.

He awoke at seven, sweating, trembling, but his mind wa
crystal clear. He leapt out of bed and capered round th
room. Picking up the jug of water left outside by the lan
lady, he poured it into the bowl and began to shave, finge
slightly trembling.

'Auguste?' Maisie sleepily stretched out a hand.

'Here, my love. And thanks to you, I see the whol
pudding.'

The sergeant on the desk at Scotland Yard was not impresse
by the results of Auguste's shaving. It took some time for th
constable to plod up to Rose's office and then down again t
collect Auguste, by now almost dancing with impatience.

'*Inspecteur* Rose.' He stood dramatically on the threshol
at last. 'We have solved it. We *know*.'

Rose had also been awake all night with a missing ingredi
ent. The missing ingredient in his recipe was Mrs Rose'
ability to cook. Her massacre of the pork last night had bee
enthusiastic but ill-timed. She had been inspired by a recip
in her *Lady's Companion* for pork and pickled walnuts.
dyspeptic Rose arrived at the Yard to find a copy of He
Majesty's latest missive; Her Majesty had a longer memor
than most of her subjects, and was exceptionally determined
Almost without hope Rose listened to Auguste. The la
flicker of hope extinguished itself when he had heard hir
out.

'But you *can't* be right, Didier. Not that.'

'We have made the simplest mistake of all in cookery. The pudding must be turned out before you eat it, but we looked at those crimes the wrong way up! It was this way –' and he talked earnestly for some minutes. At the end, Rose reached for his bowler.

'Where are you going, monsieur. To see Mr Beauville?'

'Somerset House, Auguste, my lad. Have a look at a few bills and marriage certificates, things like that. Go back to the recipes, eh Monsieur Didier?'

...

'Open the theatre again? For Boxing Day?' Robert Archibald stared at them helplessly. 'But how can we manage it in six days. And how can we take the risk?' The shock had been enormous. To take such a decision was now beyond him.

'We'll keep a watch on him. Everyone's got to be there, mind, just as before. The same staff, same cast.'

Robert Archibald turned slowly to look at his wife placidly sewing on the Chesterfield. His eyes besought her to make the decision. 'Do, dear,' urged Mrs Archibald. 'Oh, I would, Robert.'

Chapter Eleven

Boxing Day 1894 dawned bright but cold. All over the country, wherever there was access to a town, families were preparing for one of the major events of the social year. Cabs were booked, carriages appeared promptly, sailor suits were donned, eyes sparkled. The visit to the pantomime! What wonders lay ahead – demon kings, fairies, the harlequinade, and for the lucky ones, Dan Leno.

Behind the scenes all over the country, frenetic workers, eager as their prospective audiences, prepared pans of red and green fire, strapped all too solid fairies on to travelling irons, tested traps while strange monsters with grotesque masks and heads stomped by. Wet blankets were checked in the wings, in case the gauze-clad fairies should prove their humanity all too visibly in contact with the floats. The temperature rose as gas jets were lit and adrenalin flowed.

At the Galaxy similar though more stringent preparations were in hand. Robert Archibald's safety precautions were stricter than those laid down by the Lord Chamberlain. Unfortunately neither he nor the Lord Chamberlain could legislate for murder. But for the moment murder was playing second fiddle in the orchestra.

The Galaxy was open again. The public rejoiced. The theatre had served its penance. And, after all, it was Christmas. Even murderers must surely allow a moratorium for the season of goodwill.

And so trains left suburban stations, underground stations and buses disgorged their passengers, carriages drew up and departed with regimental precision, leaving their charges in the care of the linkman. Over 2,000 privileged persons who had rushed to buy the hastily advertised tickets, made their way towards their Boxing Day Mecca: the Galaxy theatre.

Herbert Sykes left his married sister's house in Holloway without regret. They dutifully asked him for Christmas, and in duty he went. But he preferred his own house, even without the ministrations of Mrs Fawcett, the housekeeper, who had departed to her daughter's house for the festive season. Now the Galaxy was open again, and he could lose himself in work – if it weren't for the thought of seeing Florence Lytton. The thought tempered his pleasure as he climbed into his hansom cab.

For Props it was Christmas indeed. The heavens had miraculously opened and by a *deus ex machina* had restored what had so mysteriously been taken away from him – his job at the Galaxy. He did not understand why it was so, but it was enough that he had the job back. With a last look round his shrine he left. Tonight he would see the real Florence Lytton again. What flowers should he take her?

The Honourable Johnny Beauville thought it all stunning. Not only could he see all his little darlings again, but it gave him a marvellous excuse to leave the family table, a table only made different at Christmastime by the holly decorations and not by any enlivening of the spirits around him. His nieces and nephew, small editions of their parents, had dutifully played with their musical pigs and model soldiers, and he had dutifully assisted, but his mind had been elsewhere: on the lovely ladies of the Galaxy. He'd missed them. By jingo, how he'd missed them!

Obadiah Bates hurried to the Galaxy, rejoicing. The theatre

was open again. Now these girls would be safe. He'd make sure of that. He didn't hold the Pathans at the Khyber Pass that day for nothing.

Edward Hargreaves and Percy walked in the Stage Door with relief, just in time perhaps to save their friendship. It had not been easy these last two weeks, looking at Percy and wondering, wondering whether it were he . . . Now surely the police must know the murderer or the theatre would not be opening? It would soon be over.

'I still don't like it, Didier,' said Archibald mournfully. 'But do what you have to.'

> 'The boar's head, as I understand,
> Is the finest dish in all the land . . .'

Auguste sang in a fine baritone voice while popping two prunes into rings of hardboiled eggs for the boar's eyes. Yesterday he had feasted on Christmas goose with Maisie at her parents' house, for once an honoured guest and not the cook. Today was the day of the boar's head – the dish to end all dishes. So it was in mediaeval times, and was brought in with due ceremony and trumpeting. And so it would be tonight – but he, the chef, would not be there to see it. He had other fish to fry this evening.

'But why not me?' demanded Maisie.
    'Because it is known that you are my fiancée. It would not work.'

In the show girls' dressing room, Birdie Page applied her make-up carefully. She slipped the silken gown over her head and as she emerged remarked casually: 'I'm going to dine with Lord Summerfield tonight. Aren't I lucky?'

The hubbub that greeted this piece of news sent a wave throughout the dressing rooms, and had not died down even by the time they reached the wings.

Obadiah passed on a message that Lord Summerfield would be waiting with his carriage outside the stage door of the Opéra Comique in Wych Street. The call-boy took it to Miss Birdie Page who communicated its contents to the dressing room at large, who discussed it in the wings, where the stagehands picked it up. By the time the curtain raiser had started, practically everyone at the Galaxy knew Miss Page was to dine with Lord Summerfield and where she would meet him.

'No, my pigeon, you stay here. Safely in the restaurant until we return. It will be over quickly now. I have not yet had an opportunity to tell you, but we know who –'

'Oh, that,' said Maisie huffily. 'It's *obvious* who the murderer is. You're so full of French bravado you think only a *man* can be a detective. Well, let me tell you this is the age of the New Woman. We've listened to you for too long. Great detective, fiddlesticks! I reasoned it out as soon as you had gone prancing off to Scotland Yard, so pleased with yourself that morning.'

'Then,' said Auguste in exasperation, 'you have no doubt guessed why it is so important to be careful. Not that there is danger to *you*. But to have you around at the wrong moment might distract him – get in our way.'

From the look in her eye, Auguste deduced that the lid was shortly about to be blown off the saucepan by excess steam, and prudently busied himself with last minute instructions to Robert, the underchef, to whom, perforce, the evening dinner must be entrusted.

The carriages drew up with slightly less than their former precision after their drivers' evenings at the various hostelries of the East Strand. Their owners, ushered by the linkman, swept through the door of the Galaxy, cosseted and pampered by the illusion of theatre. The evening had gone well, the final seal on Christmas. Patrons were satisfied. They smiled benignly on the waifs from the rookery behind the theatre who had gathered to gaze on their own version of theatre, remembered it was Christmas and distributed largesse.

As if conscious that it was on trial, the show had gone without a hitch. Florence Lytton had never looked more beguiling, Thomas Manley more handsome, the songs better trilled, the comics more comical. Murder was a million miles away. Or, to be precise, it was to those whose evening, save for a seven-course dinner, was over. But for a small band of players, the last act was yet to come.

In the show girls' dressing room, the others pretended not to notice while Bridie removed her stage make-up and self-consciously donned a taffeta-lined satin evening dress and her diamond bracelet, which looked almost real. Perhaps one day it would be, she thought. She arranged her evening mantle carefully around her shoulders, secured by a jewelled pin the wide-brimmed hat with its profusion of bows and flowers, and drew on her long kid gloves. She took her time, so that the other girls might depart first. In groups for safety they did so, ignoring her, leaving only Maisie in the chorus girls' dressing room. Bridie descended the stairs towards the stage door.

'Goodnight, Obadiah,' she called as she went through the stage door. The theatre was quiet now, the lamps turned down to minimum for the night. The Galaxy was left to itself.

Her cloaked figure with its distinctive hat turned left into Catherine Street as she set off for the stage door of the Opéra Comique. The observant might then have noticed a curious occurrence. Instead of crossing the road to cut through to Drury Lane she turned swiftly left and into the porch of the Royal Entrance to the Galaxy, whence she stepped one second later to resume her journey.

If there was to be bait in the trap, and she guessed that knowingly or unknowingly Birdie was, why couldn't it be she, Maisie? Men were unreasonable. They refused to see the obvious. It had taken them all that time to deduce what she had known right from the beginning, intuitively. She and Florence. That there was something abnormal about Props' devotion. But no, they had to go to all the trouble of closing the theatre, then opening it up so that they could call him back to work.

She regarded the menu without enthusiasm. There were times when she thought she had only to see another of Auguste's masterpieces to be off food for good. Suddenly she wished passionately for the comforting jellied eels of her youth.

She glanced out of the window into Wellington Street where the Lyceum was disgorging its crowds – and was instantly still with shock. A familiar figure was hurrying by. *Props* – but why? What was he doing there? Why going up Wellington Street? Surely Auguste and Rose would be waiting for him to follow Birdie on the other side of the theatre up Catherine Street. There was only one explanation. Props was going to use his private way in, wherever that was, to break back *into* the theatre. Yet he must have a reason. The reason must be Birdie Page, she thought with a sickening lurch. He must have realised that it was a trap, and that the decoy he was following was not Birdie Page, who must have doubled back to the theatre. It had been obvious to her, Maisie, so why not to him? Props must know Birdie was back in the theatre, and now was breaking in to get her. She leapt up. She must go through Archibald's secret entrance and rush across to warn Birdie. Bring her back here.

Thus to the amazement of Auguste's kitchen staff, Mr Didier's pretty lady friend from the theatre suddenly rushed through the kitchen where they were in the middle of serving the *entrées*, and disappeared into a larder.

Any moment now, thought Rose, crouched by a window of the public house, he'll come round that corner. Any second.

Auguste Didier similarly positioned halfway along the narrow road, was more nervous than ever before. Even at the banquet for Maître Escoffier's birthday party, he had not felt like this. As if something might go wrong . . .

A slow fear took hold of Egbert Rose. Bridie Page was almost level with Didier now – and no one in sight. Had he gone by the Strand route by mistake? Was he planning to catch her *there* and not on the way they had assumed he would take?

A nightmare thought occurred to Auguste, as if the dish of his dreams were ruined because he had forgotten the salt. The obvious ingredient. 'Bridie Page' was in sight – but no one followed. It came to him, so blindingly obvious. The obvious that had been overlooked.

Not Bridie, *Maisie*. Maisie, whom he would think alone in the theatre. *Dieu merci* she knew who it was, she would be on her guard, and *dieu merci* he had taken her into the restaurant by his private door. But nevertheless a terrible fear lurked. He rushed out, past 'Bridie', yelling for Rose.

'Maisie, *Inspecteur*! *Maisie*! It is *she* he wants.'

'Strewth!' said Rose simply, blowing his whistle. Six uniformed policemen leapt obediently from doorways, and a wide-brimmed hat and wig went flying from the person of Police Constable Drewman as he picked up his skirts and ran, to the intense interest of the dwellers in the tenements of that narrow street.

Maisie ran down the steps and through the dimly lit corridor linking the restaurant to the entrance the other side of the theatre, past Props' room and the stage door corridor and up the stairs towards the dressing room. 'Bridie,' she risked shouting as she got there.

'Bridie, where are you?' Her voice fell into emptiness and she knew before she even reached the dressing room that it was empty of life.

She paused on the threshold, steadying her nerves, afraid of what she might find: Bridie, strangled, with staring eyes and purple face. She gulped in anticipation as she pushed open the door. It was in darkness and she turned up the gas jet: with trembling fingers she turned on the stopcock, the pilot light bringing the jets flickering to full light. She let out a sigh of relief. There was no one. No body. It had been her imagination working overtime. Bridie wasn't here. She must get back. Back to the warmth and security of the restaurant. She was not fanciful, but it was creepy here. She turned out the gas lights and turned to go. It was then she heard the footsteps. Measured, they were. Slow and heavy. Whoever it was was in no hurry.

'Watch?' she cried hopefully.

There was no reply. The footsteps paused and briefly continued. Up the stairs towards her. He'd been quick. He must have run – heard her. Now she was here. Alone with him. Maisie Wilson, the Angel Murderer's fourth victim.

'Props,' she shouted, trying to sound reassuring. 'It's only Maisie Wilson. Not Miss Page. She's waiting outside for you. Just as you wanted.'

The footsteps halted. She waited, breathless.

'It's you, miss. You I wanted.'

'Who's that?' she said falteringly. It wasn't Props. But the voice, she knew.

'Bates, miss. Only Bates,' came the reply. Flat, normal, conversational.

Not Props, *Bates*! That's whom Auguste had been after. He'd never intended to kill Bridie. It was her, *her*, he had been waiting for all along. He hadn't seen her leave the theatre for the restaurant and had assumed she was still there. And she had walked right back into his hands. His hands. She shivered. Though old, he was a tough man. There was no way she could defend herself. If she tried to reach the window he would get her first. She forced her voice to sound as natural as possible. 'Just coming, Obadiah, sorry to keep you waiting. Just coming out now.'

Fool that she'd been! The recollection of how she had insisted Summerfield meet her before Obadiah's lodge flashed through her mind. She had been signing her death warrant. Her crime in his eyes was all the worse because he thought she was betrothed to Auguste. Auguste! She forced the thought of him away. If she was to see him again, she needed to think calmly.

'I'll come in, miss, if I may.' Still the calm flat voice. Perhaps she was wrong – perhaps, it was imagination . . .

'No, really, I'm just coming. Here –'

She stepped out of the door, turned swiftly and threw several of the chorus girls' frou-frou skirts over his head. Taken by surprise he fought off the layers of gauze for several precious seconds while she frenziedly pushed her way past him and down the stairs. She glanced back to see a Bates she did not know freeing himself from the last of the folds. Then he was at the steps – and she was in pitch dark. He had turned off all the corridor lights. And then the steps came again. Measured. Towards her. She hesitated for one fatal second and turned in panic, not towards the corridor and safety, but the front door.

He heard the sound of the rattling door. He heard her scream. 'It's locked, miss. You won't get through.' His voice came out of the blackness, so eminently reasonable, as though he were explaining the non-appearance of a bouquet of flowers.

'Watch,' she croaked.

'He's not here, miss. I told him I'd stay tonight.' He was standing still, by the sound of his voice. Her searching hands found the side wall and she crept along it towards him. She had to pass him.

'But you like me, Obadiah. You wouldn't want to harm me.' She forced herself to sound calm. 'They'll find out if you kill me. The police are outside. Then you won't be able to work at the Galaxy again.' Stop talking and hurry forward.

'I must still do my duty, miss. I always do. You know that. I always do that.'

She was level with the voice, soon to be past. But he sensed her presence. She felt a movement. She ran into the dark, then stopped as she felt his breath, his presence barring her path. As he lunged at her she pushed, knocking him off balance and half fell through the door to the stage area and wings. And light, blessed light. Low, but sure. She was younger than he, and despite the impediment of her skirts, nimbler. She slammed the door shut, running through the cluttered backstage area towards the wings. The door was opening and she leapt quickly into the stage manager's corner. Implacably Obadiah Bates moved on like an automaton, his movements dictated by some other power.

'It's God's mission, miss. He wants you there, you see. It's for your own good.'

He stood by the wings blinking, looking round slowly, taking his time.

Her very heart beat so loudly she thought it would betray her. But his eyes stopped lower. A fold of her dress must have been showing for his eyes riveted on the ground at her feet and a smile crossed his face. His eyes were blank as he strode towards her corner.

With a cry she ran in the only direction she could – across the stage lit with dim gas-tees. Then darkness swept over her as Bates found the gas plate and plunged the stage and wings into pitch dark.

'Don't you worry, miss, I can see. Comes of being an old soldier. You have to with them Pathans around, you see,' he said reassuringly, spookily, his voice coming from nowhere, as if it were in one of Maskelyne's magic tricks.

The dark disorientated her. She turned round, then was still. Which way was she facing? The floats? The back of the stage? Or the far side with its wings. If she ran, would it be to freedom – or to *him*? The world swam around her; impotently, she heard the footsteps of Obadiah Bates coming towards her through the blackness, and could do nothing.

'The restaurant. I left her in the restaurant,' Auguste hurled back over his shoulder at Rose and his squad pounding along behind him.

Through Exeter Street, into Wellington Street, and first Auguste, then Rose, plus six uniformed constables and an apparent transvestite fell through the doors of the Galaxy Restaurant.

The diners paused, *foie gras* on forks, fascinated at the scene.

Auguste looked wildly round then rushed to the door of the kitchen, colliding with a *veau farci* borne by the youngest of his waiters.

'Maisie,' he said, clutching the unfortunate youth by the lapels of his jacket. 'Where is Miss Wilson?'

The youth gazed back in terror. It was left to Gladys to answer: 'Miss Wilson went into the larder, Mr Didier. That one.'

The kitchen staff looked on in bewilderment as their lord and master rushed into his own private larder, followed by the might of Scotland Yard, like a scene out of a Gilbert & Sullivan opera.

Sixty diners watching through the open door wondered why. Opium den? Or was the chef the murderer? They looked with less enthusiasm at the food in front of them.

* * *

'But you like me, Obadiah.' I must stay calm, keep him talking.

'Oh yes, I'm very fond of you, Miss Maisie. I always was. That's why I've got to do it. I can't let you go to the bad – that's what I told them all, if only they'd stuck to their own class they'd have been all right. Now if you'd been content with Mr Auguste, you'd have been happy. But now I've got to save your soul. God has ordered me to. It's a penance, see. For not saving her.' He kept on coming towards her.

'Her?' said Maisie in a voice she did not recognise as her own. 'Who is she?'

' "You lost her for me, Obadiah," He says, "so you save all the others." And I do. You know how fond of all you girls I am. I'd do anything for you. It's a pity you saw me, of course. It's more painful this way. The others didn't.'

She should run. Try to escape. But where? In the dark he'd catch her. As if divining her thought, he reached out of the blackness and caught hold of her. She screamed.

'It won't take long, miss, you'll see.'

'But you must give me time to say a prayer, Obadiah,' said Maisie quickly. 'If I am to meet my God.' How can my voice sound so steady, she thought crazily, when inside I feel like this?

Obadiah considered. 'Very well, but don't go thinking I'll not do my duty. You'll like it up there with the angels.'

With his arm still grasping hers, she knelt down on the stage.

'Dear Lord, who made me –' Please, please Lord, let me have wit enough to think of something, she was thinking to herself, forcing her voice to go on talking.

'I've got a knife too,' said Obadiah chattily, 'when you're done. If you think you'd prefer that. Here, you feel. It'll slide into you as easy as anything.'

'I haven't finished my prayer, Obadiah,' said Maisie through stiff lips. 'And I pray for –'

* * *

It was at the moment that Maisie screamed that Auguste and Rose arrived, with the help of electric torches, at the door of the wings.

Listening, aghast, Auguste was about to rush through but Rose restrained him. 'He's mad, Didier, one sound from us and he'll kill her before we can get there. Remember, he doesn't care about himself.'

'But –'

'Think. Isn't there any way we can get to him without crossing that stage. Swing down on him, maybe?'

'Dear Lord who made me . . .'

Memories of the Galaxy, of burlesque, of the infinite possibilities of theatre, crossed Auguste's mind.

'Not up. Down,' he said suddenly. 'Down.'

'And I pray for . . .'

Maisie's voice echoed down through the floorboards of the Galaxy stage.

'That's enough now, Miss Maisie,' said Obadiah. 'Time to go now.'

Flight was impossible. There was nowhere to go. Desperation took hold of her.

Perhaps it was her subconscious, perhaps it was her training from Auguste never to overlook anything out of order, however trivial, in the perfect dish. Whichever, she cried out the first thing that entered her head.

'The dolls, Obadiah. Why the dolls?'

'I killed them,' he replied. As he spoke several things happened. A scream from above their heads in the darkness, a long drawn out 'Dolls', the darkness itself transformed by an overpowering shaft of light from the flies, fixing, mesmerising Obadiah Bates as he held Maisie with knife poised at her throat. Simultaneously, behind him, Auguste Didier shot up through the star trap like the demon king, propelled from below by six sturdy policeman.

Grabbed by Auguste, caught in the brilliant limelight, Obadiah dropped the knife. Sobbing, Maisie crawled away. But Auguste was no match for Obadiah, who with one blow of his fist knocked him senseless into the unlit floats.

With a polite smile Obadiah, a manic figure in the wavering limelight, picked up the knife again and dragged Maisie to her feet. But into the limelight danced another figure, maddened, manic and determined. Props was going to get his revenge at last. With no one to control it, the light wandered on and off the fighting men. In the shadows Rose's men stood impotently by, waiting to see their target. Props too was no match for Obadiah. Hands were round the younger man's neck, choking him, strangling him.

From the stage manager's corner, Maisie screamed. Taken by surprise Obadiah relaxed his grip and Props broke free. She took a desperate gamble. She pulled the lever on the only down trap to be controlled from stage level, and Obadiah Bates disappeared. There was no blanket underneath to catch him.

'It was like your pudding, *mon coeur*,' said Auguste, palely theatrical, holding court in Rose's office next day, a bandage around his head, elegantly adjusted over his thick dark hair. 'Upside down. We thought Miss Lytton was *le rôti*, the girls the forcemeat, *les légumes*. But she was not the top of the pyramid. She, like the girls, was attacked for what she represented. And when one perceived that, the sauce clarified. Is that not so, *monsieur l'inspecteur*?'

'Naturally, Mr Dupin – er, Didier,' said Rose gravely.

Auguste managed a weak smile. 'It is true that the greatest detectives, as the greatest cooks, are called Auguste, and I am honoured to count myself a successor of Mr Poe's hero. *Je vous remercie.*'

Maisie laughed, a little shakily. She had not yet recovered from the events of the day before and was unusually silent.

'And if,' continued Auguste, 'the girls were not attacked

204

for sexual reasons, then why, *hein*? This is what we ask ourselves, me and the good Inspector Rose here. What do they have in common? They were to be escorted by Lord Summerfield. *Alors*, Inspector Rose, with your help, *ma mie*' – Auguste could not resist adding – 'has discovered it is not Lord Summerfield who is our murderer. Then perhaps it was because of *what* he was? A peer. An English milord. Yet why should anyone want to stop these girls being courted by a lord? It does not make sense. It is a brilliant future for them. Jealousy? An extreme form to lead to murder.'

'Florence wasn't going to marry a peer though,' Maisie pointed out.

'True,' said Auguste. 'So we seek another reason. When did these dolls appear? At the dress rehearsal of a play. A new kind of play. A play with the theme of a lady disguised as a simple country girl, with whom a lord falls in love not knowing she is the *Lady* Penelope. But this is not the same theme as the girls and Lord Summerfield. Then I remembered that Obadiah had only seen part of *Miss Penelope's Proposal*. He did not know that our simple country maid is really a peeress in disguise, and Obadiah believed very firmly that girls should marry within their own class. But why should he feel so strongly about it as to *murder*? It did not make sense. He was devoted to the Galaxy, to the girls. He had worked there for fifteen years. Then I remembered what Inspector Rose said about the psychopath – that he has a blind spot, that where it is concerned moral judgement is suspended, twisted. But why a blind spot? Perhaps someone close to him had been betrayed by a milord. Deserted, seduced. Perhaps even his wife? She had been dead many years. His daughter also dead. Yet his favourite play was *King Lear*. Henry Irving was his hero, coming on stage with Cordelia in his arms – dead. Gone to heaven.

'It was easy enough for him to kill the girls. They trusted

him. He was just old Bates, who looked after them, was devoted to them. It was simple for him to send a message up by the call-boy, or just to tell them that Lord Summerfield had changed the place of the assignation. Easy to approach them in the street, to say there had been another change of plan, offer to accompany them –'

Maisie shivered, involuntarily feeling her own neck.

'But why the crossed arms?' she said.

'He *was* devoted to you all,' said Auguste sombrely, 'but he was mad. He thought he was doing his best for you, saving your souls, ready for heaven. Even you, whom he liked especially. Then you met Lord Summerfield in front of him. He had no chance to kill you then, and afterwards he was himself away from the theatre. Only on Boxing Day could he strike. And strike he had to for not only had you dined with Summerfield, but you were betrothed to me,' he added a trifle grimly.

'But who was it then,' said Maisie, determinedly overlooking this remark, 'who attacked Obadiah? We thought it was the murderer –'

'Props attacked him, of course,' said Rose. 'Not quite sane, is Props. Harmless on every front – except Miss Lytton. And Miss Lytton had been upset by those dolls. We've talked to him and he seems never to have realised that Miss Lytton thought he was responsible for strangling the dolls – we won't tell him. But he guessed who was and attacked Bates. He's not a robust man, and Bates is an old soldier, so he did no great harm. But he wouldn't give up. So when he heard Bates tell Watch he wouldn't be needed, that he would be staying in the Galaxy that evening, it never occurred to him to wonder why: he just knew his chance had come. So he left as normal and entered by his own secret entrance through the meter room – which fortunately we hadn't yet cut off. Otherwise it might be a different kettle of *sole au gratin*, eh, Monsieur Didier?'

'*Non*, not in a kettle, monsieur. The *gratin* is cooked –'

'I still don't see,' said Maisie hastily, seeing Auguste was about to pontificate, 'why he suddenly started to murder us? We've been dining and marrying into the peerage for years. Why begin now?'

'You yourself gave me the clue,' replied Auguste graciously, 'when you told me of something that struck you as odd when we met the Honourable Johnny Beauville. The first murder, we assume, was the evening after the first night of *Lady Bertha's Betrothal* . . . Suppose Obadiah's daughter was not dead, suppose she had not been seduced and betrayed by a peer and left to die, but had legitimately married him? Dead to Obadiah perhaps. Suppose she had not seen her father since? "How sharper than a serpent's tooth it is to have a thankless child." Irving in *Lear*. Suppose that on the night of *Lady Bertha's Betrothal* he saw her again, that she did not even speak to him, ignored him. Would that not be enough to turn the mind of a man with an obsession? Against a woman who revealed her origins by speaking of a "likeness" not a "photograph" and who accompanied, out of duty, her brother-in-law to the stage door of the Galaxy: Lady Gertrude Charing.'

Lady Gertrude sat stiffly in her chair, clad in imperial purple satin, as if interviewing a recalcitrant servant. Her face was impassive, but out of it stared Bates' eyes, cold where his had been puzzled; the face that both Rose and Auguste had half recognised and failed to place.

'Have you anything else to say, Inspector?'

'You didn't think you might have visited him once in a while? Written to him, if you didn't want to see him?'

Her face remained unmoved. 'I left that life behind me when I married, Inspector. I explained that to my father. He had instructed me always to do my duty. I did it. I have an example to set. I see no reason –'

From somewhere upstairs a scream of fury could be heard from one of Obadiah's grandchildren.

'So you don't hold yourself responsible in any way?'

Lord Charing, hitherto a silent observer, rose in protest. She stopped him with a gesture.

'No, Inspector, I do not.' She folded her hands in her lap. The interview was at an end.

'I think we'll start rehearsing a new show, Hargreaves,' said Robert Archibald thoughtfully. 'Something a bit different. Cheer everybody up. Got any tunes in mind? Let's call it, *A Kiss for Lady Katie.*'

Hargreaves smiled. A tune was already adrift in his mind, even the words, if he could persuade the lyricist of their merit:

> 'You've returned
> And it is spring . . .'

Darling Percy. A new year. A new start. A new play.

Henry Irving walked to the front door of the Lyceum. He sniffed the bracing, cold air. New year, new play. Something different. Something to lift people's spirits. *King Arthur.* Yes, it had been a good idea. Nothing like blank verse to get them cheering with patriotic fervour.

The Prince of Wales relaxed after reading the long missive from Mama. Thank God the murderer was found. A tramp so it appeared – Lord Charing had worked hard on his wife's behalf. Mama seemed to be implying that she personally had achieved it. She was in a good mood. Now he could return to the Galaxy again – after a decent interval, of course. Perhaps the next first night. Now whom should he escort?

The gallery and pit queues shivered, part with cold, part with anticipation, keeping an eye on the stage door behind them lest Miss Lytton and Mr Manley arrive without their noticing.

1895 and the coldest winter for ninety years, but it would be worth the long wait to see *Miss Penelope's Proposal*. What a relief that tramp had been caught and there would be no more murders. The Galaxy was itself once more.

Florence sailed through the stage door, bestowing her bewitching smile on Fred Timpkins. Obadiah would never have approved of his replacement, a mere stage-hand. But it saved trouble and he knew the ways of the Galaxy, Archibald reasoned.

A hand thrust a posy of flowers into her hand. She looked up and smiled even more bewitchingly.

'Thank you, Props dear. Thank you.' She had spoken for him. After all, no great harm had come to Obadiah from the blow – and he was a murderer. Conscience-stricken at her treatment of Props, Florence had exerted all her charm at Scotland Yard – everybody loved Florence . . .

Especially Props. Miss Lytton had passed. God was in his heaven, and so was William Ferndale. All was right with his world.

Much later that evening the temperature in the kitchen was high and rising further, despite the cold outside. The revellers had gone. Only Auguste and Maisie remained to see that all was in order before retiring to their rest.

'I tell you, *ma fleur*, that grilled cod is not a dish that I wish to serve to you. It has no part in a respectable kitchen. It may have been the Duke of Wellington's favourite dish, but one must recall he it was who did not appreciate the cuisine of the Maître Monsieur Ude, even dismissed him. He cannot have been a great general for he had no respect for his stomach. And neither,' he added rudely, 'if you desire grilled cod, have you.'

'I only said that it would be a change.'

'Ah yes, a change. But a change from what? From the

greatest wonders of Escoffier and Didier? From the choicest *poulets gras* set on a delicate bed of *cresson*? From a *homard* with sauce rémoulade. You have no finesse, no palate,' he railed unreasonably.

'It's only that I still don't feel quite right here yet, after what happened. To sit and eat food – poor Obadiah.' Her voice trailed off.

'Yes,' said Auguste, softening. 'Poor Obadiah. But you must remember he was mad. And I cannot forget that he attacked you.' The thought brought back all his terror on that nightmare evening. 'But if you had not disobeyed me and left the restaurant, it would not have happened,' he said severely, so as not to betray these emotions. 'That will not happen when we are married, my heart.'

'Ah, that's what I've been meaning to tell you,' Maisie said more cheerfully. 'I won't be obeying you after all.'

'*Comment*?' he enquired blankly. 'What do you mean?'

'I won't be marrying you.'

He stared at her, speechless, and she went on quickly, 'I'm very fond of you, Auguste, very fond indeed, but it wouldn't be right. I know it wouldn't. You think about it. You're a master chef used to ordering people about and all that, you want a little wife who'll obey your every word.'

'But –'

'Not someone like me.'

'But –' Auguste broke off and stared at the remains of his *filets de perdrix*, for once with unseeing eyes. Not marry him? But he loved her. She loved him. She was his Maisie.

'There, Auguste,' she said anxiously, 'don't take it amiss. You'll find someone *much* better than me. Tatiana –'

But Auguste was not to be mollified. He suspected the real truth. 'Does this have anything to do with –?'

'Yes, I'm going to marry Summerfield. He doesn't know

yet, but he'll see it my way. Someone has to protect him from his mother. I can't wait to see her face.'

'*Summerfield*,' said Auguste in tones of disgust. 'And will he hold you as I have held you, make you laugh as I have done, love you as I have loved you? Have you not enjoyed my arms about you?'

'Oh *yes*, that was ever so much fun,' she said robustly. 'But Summerfield *needs* me. You don't. And *I'll* be able to rule the aristocratic roost. You'd never let me do that.'

'I am just a cook, *hein*?'

'Oh, Auguste, no.' She was hurt. 'Now I never said that. You're the maître. Didn't Monsieur Escoffier say that only *you* could cook his birthday dinner?'

'That is true,' said Auguste, brightening just a little.

She patted his head in a motherly fashion. 'I'll go now. He's waiting, bless his heart, further up the road. No more, though.' She donned her mantle, drew on her gloves, walked up to the door and looked up Wellington Street. A patrician opera-hatted figure was standing by the Summerfield carriage, saw her, but did not move. It waited. Then, as she vigorously beckoned and waved, slowly, reluctantly, it climbed into the carriage to approach her. She turned for one last look at Auguste, smiled and was gone.

He watched the carriage drive off down the Strand into the January night, amid a path of twinkling yellow lights. With a slight sigh he turned back into the empty restaurant. He was cold, he was alone and something seemed to be blurring his eyes. He rubbed them impatiently. When they could see again, they fell on the rejected cod. Grilled cod! Who could make a dish out of grilled cod? It was not even at its best in January. What could one do with grilled cod? Nothing. Maisie, his Maisie. Gone. Never again her arms round him in bed. Never again hear her happy laughter . . .

One could add French wine sauce – not sherry, too heavy – and oyster – cream of oyster perhaps and – and – he felt excitement rise within him – a Chablis. Had not

Tatiana herself always declared the superiority of Chablis over Muscadet in a sauce? Tatiana, with her black hair and dark eyes. Yes – and not oyster sauce but *shrimps* – puréed. *Mon dieu*, that was it! That was what one could do with grilled cod. He would serve it tomorrow. He would call it: *Cod au crème d'écrevisses Maisie*.

America's Reigning
Whodunit Queen

Charlotte MacLeod

WRITING AS

Alisa Craig

Join the club in Lobelia Falls—

THE GRUB-AND-STAKERS MOVE A MOUNTAIN
70331-9/$3.50 US/$4.25 Can
THE GRUB-AND-STAKERS QUILT A BEE
70337-8/$3.50 US/$4.25 Can
THE GRUB-AND-STAKERS PINCH A POKE
75538-6/$3.50 US/$4.25 Can
THE GRUB-AND-STAKERS SPIN A YARN
75540-8/$3.50 US/$4.25 Can

And for more disarmingly charming mysteries—

THE TERRIBLE TIDE	70336-X/$3.50 US/$4.50 Can
A DISMAL THING TO DO	70338-6/$3.99 US/$4.99 Can
A PINT OF MURDER	70334-3/$3.50 US/$4.25 Can
TROUBLE IN THE BRASSES	75539-4/$3.50 US/$4.25 Can
MURDER GOES MUMMING	70335-1/$3.99 US/$4.99 Can